FIGHTING *with* FAITH

NIKKI ASH

Never lose Faith.

Fighting with Faith
Copyright © 2017 Nikki Ash
All rights reserved

Cover and interior formatting by Juliana Cabrera, *Jersey Girl Design*

This book is a work of fiction. Names, characters, places, and incidents are the product of the author's imagination or are used fictitiously. Any resemblance to actual events, locales, or persons, living or dead, is coincidental.

In accordance with the U.S. Copyright Act of 1976, the scanning, uploading, and electronic sharing of any part of this book without the permission of the publisher constitute unlawful piracy and theft of the author's intellectual property. If you would like to use material from the book (other than for review purposes), prior written permission must be obtained by contacting the publisher at AuthorNikkiAsh@gmail.com. Thank you for your support of the author's rights.

To Cindi,

who told me in life all one needs to have is faith.

Prologue

KAYLA

Nine Years Ago

"I THINK I SHOULD BE ALLOWED TO DATE. I'M FOURTEEN years old and will be fifteen in May, which is only three months away. I'm a freshman in high school and plenty of girls are dating. I get good grades and I wouldn't let dating affect my schoolwork in any way. May I please go to the movies?"

Both of my parents are sitting on the couch—backs straight, chins up in the air, in the same stuck up way they always sit, like they're better than everyone else. Nancy and David Peterson are big time divorce attorneys in South Florida and treat everything and everyone like it's a business deal, including parenting. I learned a long time ago that when I want something it's best to approach it like one would in business. I called their secretary and scheduled a time to meet, and after them only rescheduling three times—which I don't think is good business practice—here we are in our living room where I'm attempting to state my case as to why I should be allowed to date.

If I had to bet, I would say my parents never even dated. They probably sat down and negotiated their entire relationship. I've never even seen them hug or kiss my entire life.

"Who is this boy you would like to go on a date with?" my mom asks, keeping a straight face.

"His name is Jake. His dad works at the accounting firm you guys do your taxes at."

"Is Jake your boyfriend?" my mom questions me further, and I can already see the trial beginning. We might be in our living room, but my mom is no stranger to bringing her work home. She lives and breathes law. There's a reason why my brother, Zach, and I practically live at Liz's house. We can't get away with anything here unless we're extremely careful.

I think about this for a second, trying to figure out which answer will allow me to win the argument. I'd imagine a parent would want their daughter to be in a relationship if she's going to go on a date, and while Jake isn't technically my boyfriend, I'm hoping that will change after we get to go out.

"Yes, he's my boyfriend." I dart my eyes back and forth between my parents, gaging their reaction.

They quickly glance at each other but give nothing away. This is why they're such good attorneys. They can keep a straight face better than the poker players my dad occasionally watches on television. Zach and I could get in the worst trouble ever at school and my parents would approach the situation calmer than anybody I've ever seen. They stick to the facts and never let their emotions show—I'm not even sure if they have any.

"Do you love him?" My mom's question throws me off, and before I answer, I need to get myself together. Does she even know what love is? I didn't think those words were even part of her vocabulary. She sure as hell has never said those words to anybody in this home that I know of.

"Not yet, but I think I could over time," I say honestly, hoping this will work in my favor, showing my parents I'm taking this whole thing seriously. She may not say the words, but I can't imagine her daughter loving someone would hurt the situation. It's not like I'm trying to go on random dates. I'm interested in one person specifically. That must get me some points.

"Sweetie, I think it's time we have a talk." My mom smiles, but it almost looks like she's in pain, as if having to spread her lips up to form the smile is actually painful for her. She looks at my dad and he nods, then excuses himself. Oh, great, she's about to give me the birds and the bees talk. Fabulous! Do my parents even have sex? I mean I know they must've done something because they had my brother and me, but still...Unlike the noises we hear at my best friend Liz's house coming through the walls of her parents' room at night when I sleep over, I've never heard noises coming through the walls of my parents' room—thank God!

"Kayla, I know at fourteen you want to believe in love, but the truth is love doesn't exist. Love was created by Hallmark to get people to spend money on each other for all sorts of holidays like Valentine's Day and Anniversaries. If you go back hundreds, if not thousands, of years ago, marriages were arranged. The original contracts were made to preserve power, forge alliances, acquire land, and to produce legitimate heirs. The churches eventually got involved ,which again helped to preserve the power in the churches."

What the hell! This is definitely not the type of talk I was expecting…

"The truth of the matter is, up until the nineteenth century, marriage and love didn't even go hand in hand. Don't get me wrong, I'm not against love, because without the loss of it, your father and I wouldn't make a living, and you and your brother wouldn't be living as comfortably as you are. But as your mother, I'm going to tell you what all my clients should've been told before they made the decision to get married for all the wrong reasons. You do not fall in love. It's a fake emotion that people are lead to believe is real. It's okay to have fun: Date, go to the movies, and enjoy being a teenager. Get good grades and go to college to make something of yourself. Of course, I would love for you to go to law school, but to be honest, I'm not sure you'd be up for the challenge. My point is, make sure you pick a career where you can bring something to the table in a marriage one day. Make sure you're completely independent, and more importantly, make sure the man you pick is financially stable."

Oh. My. God!

She continues her speech…

"What I'm trying to say is that when the time comes for you to be in a relationship, you don't do it based on love. Love isn't concrete. You do it based on mutual respect and on what you both can bring to the table. Every day in court I hear the same excuse, 'I fell out of love', but what people don't understand is that love is in your head. Money, education, goals, values, religion, political affiliates are all concrete reasons to base a relationship on. Love, on the other hand, is abstract. It changes constantly. Do you understand what I'm saying?"

I open my mouth and then close it. I don't even know how to respond to this. I decide to go with the first question that pops into my head. "Do you and Dad love each other?"

"I care about your father and he cares about me. We have mutual respect for each other. We met in law school and knew we would be compatible. We both had the same goals, came from the same upbringing, and vote for the same political party. We work well together. That's why, after over twenty years, we're still married. At fourteen years old, you can't possibly know where this boy is going in life. Anything you know about him is simply based on abstract thoughts and feelings that can and will change over time, and I can assure you, Kayla, those feelings will be your downfall."

I always suspected my mom felt this way, but it didn't feel real until she verbally confirmed it. Now I can no longer pretend because she put it all out there. My mother doesn't believe in love.

"I just don't understand. I know you see people divorce a lot, but what about all the people who are still married? The couples who kiss and hug and love each other. Why wouldn't you at least try to feel that way?"

I probably shouldn't push it, but I just don't understand why she'd keep herself from love. I see it on the television and I see Liz's parents, and it seems like something everybody would want in their life.

"Kayla, building a relationship based on emotions doesn't create a solid foundation. Like I said, emotions change. Would you build a home on the ocean? No, because the waves change. They get bigger and smaller. The tide can be high or low. You never know what you're getting. It's what you enjoy about surfing. You build a home on a concrete slab on the ground because you know it will be stable.

"You're too young to understand, but seventy percent of marriages end in divorce. It's why people have to hire your father and me, and why they end up having to split up the house and kids and assets. They base their foundation on an emotion that changes instead of thinking logically about the issues that matter like if he's able to balance his checkbook. Does he plan to have a 401K? What type of investments will he consider? What kind of family does he come from? None of those things have anything to do with love."

I want to tell her that none of that makes sense, but I know she'll just argue with facts like she always does. It's pointless to argue with either of my parents. I know how I feel about Jake. He's sweet and popular, and to be honest, I don't care who he's going to vote for in the next election or whether he can balance a checkbook. I think my mom is wrong, and I'll prove her wrong. When she sees that love is real, she'll understand not everybody is like her clients or herself for that matter.

So instead of arguing, I nod. "I understand. So, can I go out on a date with Jake?"

She releases a heavy sigh. "Yes, Kayla. Just please remember this conversation. I don't ever want to have to say, 'I told you so.' I would rather you be smart and not make stupid, reckless decisions in the first place so that I won't have to clean up whatever mess you make, just like

I have to do with my clients."

Three Months Later

"I'M GOING TO DO IT."

"Are you sure?"

"Yes, I'm totally sure. I love Jake, and I know he loves me too."

I've been dating Jake for three months now and things are going good. Clearly my mother had no idea what she was talking about because I'm falling in love with him and I don't see it changing any time soon.

"Okay, Kayla. If that's what you want to do, I'll support you. Not that there's much I can really do to support you in this."

I'm sitting on the beach with my best friend, Liz. I just finished surfing while she sat on the edge of the water on her blanket, reading her latest romance novel. We both recently turned fifteen and are about to be sophomores. Liz is the ultimate best friend. We met in Kindergarten and have been inseparable ever since. Most people who don't know us question our friendship because we're the definition of opposites attracting. While Liz is the shy, quiet, book-obsessed type, I, on the other hand, am more outgoing. I love life. I love to have fun, and if it wasn't for my book-loving best friend, I probably wouldn't even pass my classes. This year I was made cheer captain and I got Liz to join. I know it really isn't her thing, but I love that we get to see each other after school and at games. What I love most about Liz is that she accepts me for who I am and allows me to make my own choices without ever judging. Which is exactly what she's doing right now.

"Just make sure you're safe, okay?" she says softly, clearly embarrassed to even be talking about this subject.

"I will. I promise."

"And make sure you use protection." Her cheeks turn pink.

"I know." I try not to laugh.

"You don't want to get an STD."

"I know."

"And you're sure you're ready? I heard it really hurts."

"I'll be okay. I'm sure Jake knows what he's doing."

The summer is about to begin, and my boyfriend of three months, Jake, is about to go away for the summer. He's been begging me to have sex with him, and I'm going to do it. I love him and I believe he loves me. No, we haven't said the words to each other, but tonight I'm going to tell him. We'll have something to remember each other by and when he comes back from vacation we'll pick back up where we left off.

"This is going to be great. I'll call you as soon as he leaves. My parents are working late tonight on a case and my brother is spending the night at your house with your brother."

We get up and head back to our neighborhood, which is right across from the beach. Liz's house is before mine, so when we approach her house, we hug goodbye and then I walk a little farther down the street to my house. I throw my surfboard onto the sidewall and use the outside shower to rinse the sand and salt off my body before I go inside. Today was a great surfing day.

Once inside, I call Jake to let him know he can come over in an hour. I jump in the shower, shave my legs, and throw on a cute navy blue halter-top and white shorts. I blow dry my naturally blonde hair quickly. It's naturally straight so I don't have to do anything else with it.

At exactly five o'clock, Jake knocks on the door and I let him in. I'm not going to lie. I'm nervous about tonight. While we've made out like a million times and he's felt me up plenty of times, we haven't gone any further. I'm a virgin, and I'm okay with this, because unlike my parent's beliefs, I believe in love. And Jake is the one.

"Hey, babe. You look hot." Jake reaches for my waist and pulls me into a kiss. Once the kiss is over, we walk over to the couch and sit.

"So, I've been thinking and I'm ready." He looks confused at first about what I'm referring to, but then his eyes go wide when he realizes what I mean. He doesn't say anything. He just nods and takes me by my hand, leading me up to my bedroom, clearly not wanting to waste any time. Unlike me, Jake isn't a virgin. We haven't really talked about it, but I know he's been with a couple girls at school. I do know I'm the longest relationship he's had, which should say something about us.

After he closes the door behind us, he pulls out a condom from his wallet and places it on the bed, giving me a huge smile. He takes his shirt off and then his pants and boxers, while I just stand where I am, staring at him. I'm suddenly completely freaking out on the inside, but I mimic his moves and remove my clothes as well. He takes me by the hand and moves us to the bed.

"DAMN, BABE. THAT WAS GOOD." I'M LYING ON THE BED, naked and in pain, next to Jake. I'm not sure why people are so big on sex because *Ouch!* That shit hurt. Jake clearly enjoyed it based off his noises and grunts and calling out my name at the end, but as for me, no, that was not enjoyable. It felt like it lasted hours, but in reality, it couldn't have been more than a couple minutes. In my head, I imagined kissing and holding and words of love being whispered, but none of that happened.

I roll over to face Jake, pulling the covers up my body. He smiles at me like he just won the jackpot. It might've not been the best sexual experience, but the look on his face is worth it. It must be love. I'm sure over time it will get better.

"Kayla…"

"Jake…"

We both say each other's names at the same time and laugh.

He tells me to go first, so I do.

"I love you, Jake."

"Kayla." He says my name, and I'm waiting for *I love you, too* to follow but it doesn't, so I wait for him to say something. He stares at me for a few seconds and then his lips curve down into a frown.

"Kayla, babe. It's been fun these last few months, but it's about to be summer. I'm about to go away and you'll be here."

"I know, but you'll be back." I get this tightening feeling in my stomach, and it feels like I'm going to throw up.

"Look, Kayla, I like you, but we're young. I'm sorry, but I don't love you. To be honest, I don't even want to date anybody this summer. I just want to be single and have fun. You get that, right?"

I can feel the tears welling up, threatening to spill over. If I didn't know it's scientifically impossible for the human heart to physically break from somebody's words, I'd be scared my heart is literally shattering into pieces.

Jake gets up from the bed and puts back on his clothes. He goes to the bathroom to throw the condom away and then comes back into the room. I'm still lying in bed, frozen, unsure of what to do. I just gave this guy my virginity, but more than that, I gave him my heart. I told him I love him and was so sure he felt the same way. when all along he never felt any love toward me at all. Suddenly, my mom's words come back to slap me right in the face.

He gives me a chaste kiss on my cheek and, before walking away, says, "No hard feelings, Kayla. Seriously, it's been fun." And before I can even respond, he's out the door. I don't see him out. I don't lock up the house. I curl up in the fetal position and cry myself to sleep.

I hear my phone going off, and when I look at the clock, I see it's morning. My body is sore from last night and it reminds me of Jake using me for sex before dumping me. When I glance at the caller ID, I see it's Liz.

"Hello."

"Are you okay?"

"Yeah, why wouldn't I be?" I'm not ready to share how bad Jake hurt me, even with my best friend. I know I will eventually, but right now I'm too embarrassed.

"Have you been on Myspace? Jake is telling everybody he had sex with you and dumped you."

"What?" I get out of bed and then remember I fell asleep after crying and never got dressed. I quickly throw on some clothes and then run over to my computer and log into my account. I click on Jake's name and scroll down his wall, where all the comments are, and sure enough, he's bragging to his friends that he got in my pants and won a bet.

She finally gave it up.

About time! Took longer than I thought it would.

Was she any good?

Damn, I knew you would get it in before the summer.

"I'll call you back!" I say before I hang up.

I continue to scroll down the comments and read every nasty thing he wrote about me for everybody on social media to see. I think about everything I thought I felt and everything I thought he felt. It was all a lie. My heart hurts so damn bad. I don't ever want to feel this way again. If this is love, then I don't want it. My parents might not hug and kiss all the time, and they're not exactly what one would call nurturing, but I've never seen them cry or get upset. I've never seen them in pain or hurt each other the way I'm hurting right now.

While I'm looking over the comments, there's a quick knock on the door and then my mom walks in.

"Kayla, your dad and I are going to head out..."

I look up at her, and she stops speaking.

"Kayla, what's the matter?" She comes to my side and kneels next to me, so we're at eye level. I don't want to tell her what happened, but

I need my mom right now, so I decide to tell her a shortened version of what happened.

"Jake and I broke up and he's talking crap about me to his friends. Everybody is going to be talking about me at school."

My mom's face turns into what looks like a sympathetic frown and I think maybe she'll comfort me and give me some mom wisdom, but instead she says what I knew all along she would say.

"Kayla, I told you this would happen. I hope you take this as a lesson learned. When you open your heart, you're going to get heartbroken. Instead, open your mind and be smart about your decisions. At least it happened now instead of years from now when you would've had the opportunity to make even worse decisions."

She looks at my computer screen before I can hide it and she stands straight up, glaring down at me.

"Did you sleep with him, Kayla?"

"Yes, and he's telling the whole school."

Of course my mom doesn't even attempt to sympathize with me in any way.

"That's great. So, not only did you not listen to me, but you also allowed your ridiculous emotions to tarnish your reputation, as well as your father's and mine. You know we do business with Jake's father. Hopefully in the future you'll think about what happened when you make decisions based on emotions. I swear, Kayla, sometimes you can be so obtuse. It's why you'll never go to law school. You have to think with your brain and not your fickle emotions."

"I'm sorry. I thought he loved me," I say as tears prick my eyes. I have no idea why I'm even trying to defend myself. I hate that I've let my mom down and disappointed her once again. I hate that I'm an embarrassment to our family. But what's even worse is that I hate she was right about love. I wanted so badly to prove her wrong.

"Well now you know the truth. There's no point in crying over this. Learn from it." As she turns to walk out of my room, she says, "Your father and I are heading out to get lunch. Would you like anything?"

I shake my head and then she closes the door behind her.

And in this moment, I make a promise to myself to never disappoint my parents again. I'll never give my mom another reason to say, "I told you so." The fact is, my mother was right. Love only causes heartbreak and it hurts like a bitch. It's not concrete. You can't use it as a stepping stone. I did and look where it got me, tumbling down the stairs headfirst with no one at the bottom to catch me. Fuck that! And fuck love.

I vow to never fall in love again.

One

KAYLA

Present Day

LIVING IN FLORIDA HAS ITS PERKS. FOR ONE, THE SUNSHINE is amazing. It's February, and in many other states the snow is still coming down, while here in sunny South Florida it's a beautiful eighty-five degrees. I'm lying on the lounge chair in my bikini, soaking in the sun by the pool. I can smell the ocean breeze in the air, and it's such a tease. I'm only a few yards away from the beach and that beautiful ocean water, yet I can't even do what I love, which is surf. I mean I guess I could, but I'm not sure how well that will go over. Surfing requires balance, and now that my belly is beginning to swell, my balance is definitely not what it was before. I look down at my stomach and smile to myself. At only sixteen weeks pregnant, if you didn't know my condition you'd think I had a few too many beers and fries, but that's not the case. I rub my belly and take a sip of my orange juice that's sitting on the deck table next to me.

I'm excited to become a mom. When my best friend, Liz, got

pregnant right before our freshman year of college, she couldn't find the father, and so we worked as a team to raise her daughter, Bella. Because of that, I'm not ignorant to the fact that having a baby isn't going to be easy, especially since I'll most likely be raising the baby on my own most of the time. However, unlike the situation Liz was in all those years ago, I've since graduated from college and have a degree in physical therapy.

"Kayla, I'm leaving for work. Have you thought more about what you plan to do?"

I look over and see my mom standing just outside the back door.

"I haven't made any decisions yet."

"Well, I hope you've thought about what we've talked about. You can live here as long as you need to, but do you really want to once again raise a baby without a father? There's nothing wrong with giving the baby up for adoption. Successful men don't want to be with a woman who has an illegitimate kid in tow."

"Mom, I want this baby, and I'm not looking for a man anyway, so it doesn't matter. Plus, Bella does have a father, and Liz and I did just fine before he came back into the picture."

"You're never going to learn, Kayla" She sighs. "How many times will you make horrible decisions which require your father and me to help clean up the mess while embarrassing this family?"

"What are you cleaning up? I'm staying here temporarily. You don't have to do anything."

"Not yet! Wait until you have to deal with custody and child support. A child is forever, Kayla. Once again you made poor choices out of lust and supposed love, and look where it got you! When will it stop? How many times must we have this conversation? I swear sometimes I don't even think you are my kid."

Without waiting for a response, she huffs and walks back inside, closing the sliding glass door behind her, clearly ending the conversation.

I've only been living back in Florida for about six weeks, but I know I need to focus on getting a job. I'm fortunate that as a physical therapist there's quite a few options and I have some amazing references, but I'm not sure what I want to do yet. I liked my old job, but moving was something I had to do. If I'm honest with myself, I haven't put forth the effort into finding a job because somewhere in the back of my mind I know this isn't really where I want to live. It's simply the only option I could think of at the time.

I'm what you would call a runner. Life is good, too good to be true...I run. Life turns to shit, I feel like I can't handle it...I run. Life gets confusing, I have to make a decision...I run. I'm way better at handling other people's lives than my own. For the last five years, I've focused on Liz and Bella. We both went to school and both took turns caring for her daughter. I used the two of them as an excuse to never date. Don't get me wrong, I've had my fair share of one-night stands, but I never allowed it to turn into more. I'm not interested in love and it's not interested in me either.

I'm currently living in my parents' pool house and it's okay. I could have gone back to my old room but decided the pool house would give me space from my parents, especially my mom. If I hear her say *I told you* so one more time I just might kill her. Yes, she was right about Jake all those years ago. Yes, she was right about my current situation. I get it. Everything I do is wrong. I'm a continuing disappointment in my mother's eyes. Luckily, my parents work a lot and are rarely home, but I still need to get my own place soon. Time is running out and unfortunately, I have nowhere else to run to, so I'm going to have to make a decision. I look out at the crystal-clear pool water and think to myself *tomorrow*. Tomorrow I'll attempt to get a job. Tomorrow I'll figure out my living situation. Tomorrow I'll deal with the reality that I'm pregnant and haven't told anybody other than my parents. Today, I'll swim a few laps in the pool. It may not be the ocean or surfing, but at least it's in the water.

After spending the next thirty minutes swimming laps, I realize it's lunchtime and decide to go inside the main house and make myself a sandwich. I grab my towel and dry myself off, throw it back on the lounge chair, and then walk inside. I'm thinking a peanut butter and jelly sandwich is sounding really yummy right about now. Ooh! Maybe a peanut butter and jelly with banana...Pregnancy cravings are the weirdest. I watched Liz go through it, but experiencing it firsthand is something else.

I pull all the ingredients out of the cabinets, when I hear the doorbell ring. It's only noon here, and with my parents at work and my brother at school, I can't imagine who'd be at the door. As I walk over to answer it, I don't bother covering myself up. I left my towel outside and whoever is at the door will just have to deal with seeing me in my bikini. Without checking the peephole, I swing the door open and come face-to-face with none other than my best friend, Liz. I don't know why I didn't think about this. She told me she was going to be in Miami and begged me to join. I should've known she would make a stop to see me. Damn pregnancy brain!

"Holy shit, Kayla! Are you pregnant?" She looks down, and I attempt to cover my protruding belly, but it's too late. My bikini is as tiny as it gets. Only then do I realize she isn't alone. The whole damn gang is with her, standing in my parents' doorway and staring right at my stomach. Liz's fiancé, Cooper, who owns the gym I used to work at, their daughter, Bella, our friend Hayley, who is the medic at Cooper's Fight Club, Kaden, the guys' trainer and friend, and Caleb, who fights for the UFC and is my ex-roommate. But more importantly, who is also standing on my doorstep is Bentley, and on his arm is the bitch he's dating, Sophia.

For a beat, nobody says anything, and then I remember she asked me a question. Apparently, they're all waiting for my answer. Although, I'm pretty sure it's meant as a rhetorical question because anybody who knows me knows my stomach pre-pregnancy was as flat as a board. Not that I do so much to work out other than surfing, but I'm naturally a tiny woman with amazing genetics and a fast metabolism, standard-sized breasts, small stomach with toned legs and arms from my years of surfing. The only feature of me that contradicts my many years of surfing is my naturally pale skin that never tans. I look at Liz and notice her golden brown tan I've always been envious of. The girl doesn't even like the beach and has beautiful caramel skin. Oh! Did I mention Liz is pregnant too? She looks so adorable with her little belly, and she's so happy...

The sound of a deep throat clearing causes me to snap out of my internal thoughts, and when I see the look on his face, my skin goose bumps, and not in a good way—more like in a *Oh damn, shit is about to get real* way.

Bentley steps forward, clearly done with waiting for my verbal confirmation that I am indeed pregnant, and asks the question he wants to know. "Am I the father?"

Don't worry, it's not about to get Jerry Springer up in here—hopefully.

Two

KAYLA

Six Years Ago

ONE WEEK IN MIAMI. NEED I SAY MORE? LIZ AND I GET ONE week in the hottest, sexiest city in the world to party it up before we're thrown back into jail, and by jail, I mean school. We have finally graduated high school and do we get a break? Of course not. After our week in Miami, we'll be moving to Las Vegas, Nevada to attend college at the University of Las Vegas. I know what you're thinking. How can I complain when I'll be spending the next four years in Sin City? I get it, I do. But how can I fully experience what Las Vegas has to offer when in two short months I'll be stuck sitting in college classes, writing essays, and studying for test after test?

On the bright side, I have two months before school begins. Unlike my bookworm best friend who is insisting on taking summer classes, I won't be starting until the fall, which means parties, guys, and more parties with guys. I'm not sure how many I'll convince her to go to with me, but the fact that we're sitting in a resort in Miami, she's wearing the cute little black dress I bought her without her knowledge, and has agreed to go to a club with me tonight, gives me hope that once we're in Las Vegas she'll continue to submit to my best friend charm.

We get to the club and walk to the back of the line. Liz is completely self-conscious about her dress, even though she looks beyond beautiful. She has the most amazing body that goes to waste because she dedicates her entire life to school. She's thick and curvy in all the right places and her little black dress accentuates all those curves. Her gorgeous curly brown hair is flowing down her back and she doesn't even need to have an ounce of makeup on her face because her skin is naturally flawless.

On the other hand, I'm in a super cute silver dress that helps push up my breasts, giving me a little more cleavage. I'm not a member of the itty-bitty-titty-committee, but they definitely aren't naturally voluptuous like Liz's breasts are. I have on light makeup, just some smoky eye shadow and lipstick. I'm in matching silver fuck-me heels, and I'm ready to show my fake ID to the bouncer and do some serious partying.

Just as Liz is getting restless and I'm afraid I might have to tie her up and drag her inside, the oversized bouncer comes over and tells us a VIP guest has invited us in. VIP? You sure as hell don't have to tell me twice! We show our IDs and head into the club.

The music is pumping, the lights are pulsating throughout the club, and I'm in heaven right now. I've been to more than my fair share of high school parties, but this is nothing like those. I look over at Liz and she's just as mesmerized by the scene in front of us as I am. This is our first time in a club, and if I can make a prediction, it won't be our last.

We head to the dance floor immediately and begin dancing our asses off, grinding on each other, on other people. The music has me in a trance, and when I look over to check on Liz, I see some hot guy all over her After a couple songs I notice he's leading her away. We lock eyes and she confirms all is good. That's all I need to know. Liz is probably the smartest damn person I know. I continue to watch her and see she's heading up to VIP. That definitely makes me feel better knowing she's just going to be a few feet away from me. I decide I'll dance some more with these hot guys down here and join her in a few.

After quite a few songs, my body is covered in a light sheen of sweat, so I head upstairs to find Liz and rehydrate. The bodyguard stops me, and I explain I'm with people who're in the VIP area. In order to be up here, I have to confirm who I'm with, so, with him trailing behind, I go in search of Liz. After walking past a few booths, I find Liz sitting on the same guy's lap from earlier.

But my eyes don't stop on them, because just past them is the sexiest guy I've ever laid eyes on. He has blond hair, shaved short but still long enough to grab ahold of in bed and navy blue eyes like the color of the water when you paddle out to a deep area of the ocean. His intense eyes lock with mine for a second and it feels like the wind has been knocked out of me. I can't stop looking at him. His arms look strong and he's built but not too built. He's perfect. He must sense me ogling the shit out of him because he looks at me again, but this time he gives me a knowing smirk, then begins to trail his eyes down my body. *That's right, baby. Eat your heart out.* Liz's guy confirms I'm with them, and the bodyguard makes a grunting noise and then walks away.

I approach Liz and her new man friend, and he gives introductions. His name is Cooper, and his friends are Kaden, Caleb, and Bentley. The only name I'm concerned with is Bentley. He's my target, and judging by the way his eyes are intently stuck on me, I would say I got this shit in the bag. One thing I learned from Jake is, if I use the guy, I can't be used, and I'll be damned if I'm ever used again. I also learned Jake sucks in bed (as well as the other high school guys I've been with) and I'm glad to be done with high school, so I can hopefully find a guy who actually knows what he's doing. After my one shitty time with Jake I hoped it was him and not me that was the problem, but the truth is most guys I've slept with have no idea what they're doing, so I'm beginning to wonder if maybe it's me.

I've learned a few things the last couple of years.

One: Guys are nothing like the characters in the movies and books. They're selfish as hell and are only out to pleasure themselves.

Two: Guys have no idea if a girl orgasms during sex. Trust me, I've faked it enough to know this.

Three: It's easier to give myself an orgasm than to rely on a guy to do it for me.

Don't get me wrong, I've had orgasms with the guys I've been with, but I've had to walk them through it and it hasn't been anything worth applauding over. The foreplay has been decent, at least good enough that if the guy can't handle finishing the job, I'm primed and ready to get myself off. But looking at Bentley, I wonder if maybe I've been with all the wrong guys—the man drips sex.

Once the introductions are done, Bentley comes over and asks me to dance. I follow behind him to the small dance floor in the VIP section. The music is pumping to the fast rhythm of The Black Eyed Peas *Boom Boom Pow*. I turn away from Bentley and back my ass up against him at the same time he brings his hands to my waist and rubs his dick against by ass in a pulsating motion to the music. This guy definitely has some moves. I once read a man that can dance is good in bed. Let's hope it's true.

The mix morphs into Mariah Carey's *Obsessed* and I twirl around to face Bentley, whose eyes are glossed over with lust. We dance so close it's as if we're fucking with our clothes on. His knee comes up the middle of my thighs to separate my legs, causing my dress to rise. He rubs back and forth against my pussy through my panties, creating a friction that has me salivating with want. It has never felt like this before and we haven't even done anything. I wrap my arms around his neck and he nuzzles his face into my hair while he slowly continues to grind that sensitive area between my legs.

The song ends and I need a breather. I'm so hot and if I don't back up I might end up making him take me in the bathroom and that would be an absolute travesty because a quickie against a sink would not do this man justice at all. I'm pretty sure I'm going to need hours with him before I'm ready to move on. And I'll move on, because I always do. You can think what you want about me, but the fact is while you are getting your heart broken time and again, my heart is perfectly intact, and it's going to damn well stay that way.

The rest of the night is spent with Liz and me doing shots of top shelf vodka and dancing on top of the table while Bentley and Cooper watch us from below. Eventually everybody is ready to go and I'm seriously praying Bentley is having the same thoughts as me. While I'm definitely feeling good, we have danced more than we have drank so I know I won't have a hangover in the morning.

My prayers are answered when Bentley comes over and whispers into my ear, "I want you in my bed tonight—naked, legs spread, and wet just for me." Chills run down my spine and he chuckles knowingly at what he's doing to me. He doesn't ask, he demands. I need to be careful with this guy. I always keep the ball in my court. The minute the guy is in control, he will use you and leave you high and dry. I've learned my lesson and won't ever let that happen again. I make sure to remain calm, cool, and collected at all times.

"I have to make sure it's okay with my friend first. You know how it is...sisters before misters." I give him a saucy wink and walk away from him to speak to Liz, swaying my hips just a little more knowing he's watching me walk away.

When I get over to her, she's cuddling up with Cooper and I'm genuinely happy for her. She never lets loose like this. "Hey sexy," I say to get her attention. She laughs at my flirting.

"Would it be okay if I went back to Bentley's hotel with him? I'll completely understand if you don't want me to. I don't want to leave you hanging."

She sighs and says, "No, it's okay. You can go..."

"But?" The thing about being best friends for more than half our lives is that we know what each other is thinking.

"No, buts...I just don't want you to do anything you might regret."

"Like what? Fall in love?" I snort out the last part.

"No, I know you won't fall in love, Kayla. It's just that it's one thing to sleep with the guys from high school, but this guy is older and way more experienced. I just want you to be safe." And that's why she's my best friend. No judgment at all. She just cares.

"I promise I'll be careful." She nods and we all head down to the awaiting SUV.

Bentley and I both get into the third row and I whisper to him that I'm down to go back with him. His face lights up with a bright smile that makes my stomach get butterflies. *What the hell? I don't do butterflies.* I need to get my shit in check, and fast. This is a one-night stand. I've done this several times. This is no different.

After dropping off Liz—and Cooper, because he ended up staying with her, which is a conversation we'll definitely be having tomorrow—we head to the hotel the guys are staying at. It's down the street from our resort but even nicer. We get to the top floor, which is the penthouse, and Kaden and Caleb go to their rooms leaving us alone.

"Would you like a drink?" Bentley points to the mini fridge full of bottles of liquor.

"No, thank you."

He closes the gap between us, and twisting his fingers into my hair, brings my face up to his. He leans in close, and in a soft voice says, "I've never done this before. What are you doing to me?"

Before I can even process what he means, his mouth connects with mine and my mind goes blank. His tongue hits my lips and they automatically part for him. At the same time, his other hand comes down around me to grab my ass, pulling my body into his. I let out a small groan and it spurs him on.

Never taking his mouth off mine, he moves his hand from my hair, and with both hands now on my ass, lifts me up, continuing to lay soft kisses to my collarbone. My thighs close around his waist and my ankles lock around his back. I feel a bit dizzy, but I'm nowhere near drunk, at least not from the alcohol—maybe off this man and his touch. I've never felt like this before, and I'm not quite sure if this is a good thing. As he walks us to his room, Kaden comes back out of his, and gives us a smile of approval. I lock eyes with Bentley and my heartbeat quickens. I need to stop these feelings. I don't do feelings.

I'm suddenly nervous. The lust brewing between Bentley and me is stifling and I don't know if my heart can handle spending the night with him. As a last ditch effort to protect myself, I turn my head to Kaden and ask, "Wanna join us?"

Bentley's whole body goes rigid and he growls out a "I don't fucking think so!"

Before Kaden can even respond, the door is slammed closed and all I can hear is loud laughter coming from the main room.

Bentley drops me onto the bed on my back and looks at me like I just committed a murder. I try to hide my smile by biting down on my lower lip, but I don't think I do a good enough job because he raises his eyebrows and says, "Woman, you think that shit is funny? You think

I won't be enough that you need two men to please you? Fuck that! When I'm done with you, you won't even be able to walk straight for a week."

Without giving me a chance to answer his question, he lowers his body down to mine and kisses me with what seems like every ounce of built up passion in him. My tongue enters his mouth and he sucks on it, tasting me. His hand moves to my breast and he attempts to tweak my nipple through my clothes. When he sees how thick my dress and bra are, he puts our kiss on hold, gets up on his knees, and slides my dress over my shoulders and down my body. I lift to help him out and he slides the dress, as well as my panties, the rest of the way down.

My strapless bra opens from the front and with two fingers he expertly pops the clasp open. The two cups separate, falling on each side, leaving my breasts open for him. I'm completely naked under him. His eyes rake down my body slowly. He swallows hard and then his eyes lock with mine.

"You're fucking gorgeous." It isn't the words but the way he says them that sends chills down my spine. It suddenly feels extremely hot in here to the point I feel like I can't even breathe. Nobody has ever looked at me like he's doing in this moment. It is almost as if I'm everything to him. But that can't be possible because we just met.

"It seems like there's a bit of an imbalance," I say, trying to play it cool. I haven't felt this vulnerable in front of a guy since Jake, and we all know how that turned out.

He chuckles and then with one hand pulls his shirt over his head. And hot damn, he's a sight to see. While he looked sexy as hell dressed in his blue and yellow plaid collared shirt and jeans that hugged the curves of his ass just right, Bentley without a shirt on is a whole different ball game. His pecks look like they are carved from stone, and as I lower my eyes to his abs, I begin to count: two, four, six, eight. Eight goddamn pack of abs. I quickly do a recount to make sure I'm not seeing things, and I'm not. This man is definitely sporting an eight freaking pack of abs. I look over him again and notice his body is clean. Not a single tattoo on him. His skin is a beautiful golden brown and I get this overwhelming need to lick down his body starting from his neck all the way to that gorgeous V that meets the top of his white boxers which are partially hidden by his jeans.

"Take off the rest," I say and nod towards the rest of the clothes I want him to remove. He sits back and unbuttons his jeans and then maneuvers them and his boxers off him, throwing them to the side of the bed.

He gets back up to a kneeling position and his dick springs up with him. I can't take it any longer. I need to touch him. I sit up and grab hold of his cock, forcing him to move closer to me. He realizes what I'm about to do and tries to stop me.

"Wait, baby. Let me please you first."

He doesn't realize what his words do to me. They chisel away at the ice chunks covering my heart, scaring the shit out of me. Nobody has ever put me first, and this guy can't be the one to do it now. This is a fucking one-night stand.

With my legs straight out in front of me, I pull him toward me, not giving him a choice. He looks confused but moves over me like

I want, setting one knee on either side of me. I grab his hard length and begin to stroke it. I lick my lips readying myself to take him, and then place my mouth right around his hardness taking him all the way down my throat.

"Oh, fuck. Kayla." He moans my name over and over again as I rotate between licking and sucking his hard length. Please don't judge what I'm about to admit. Well...actually...fuck it, judge all you want. What the hell do I care? There is nothing better tasting than a cock. I love it in my mouth, on my tongue, down my throat. The taste of the precum alone gets me wet. I love the feel of figuratively holding a guy by his balls. I hold all the power and it feels damn good.

While I continue to fuck him with my mouth, he takes my nipples between his fingers and pulls and tugs and pinches them so hard it's almost painful, but damn, it feels so good. I moan around his cock and he must feel the vibration because the precum on my tongue multiplies, telling me he's getting close.

"You like that?" He continues to pinch and pull my nipples, causing my core to drip wet. I squeeze my thighs together, hoping to find some relief, but it's not doing anything. I have a feeling the only relief I'll find is from this man's cock inside me.

I'm torn, though. I want it in me, yet I really want him to come in my mouth. *Decisions. Decisions.*

Bentley looks into my eyes and says, "Fuck, Kayla, your mouth feels so good." And the decision has been made.

I work him harder and faster. The saliva that his dick and my mouth has created allows me to slide him in and out smoothly. I take one hand and cup his balls with enough force that it massages him but not too much that it would hurt him. This is his undoing. He twists my hair into his fingers and begins relentlessly fucking my mouth.

"Kayla, baby, I'm going to come in your mouth," Bentley warns. I don't stop, though. "Holy shit, I'm..." He finishes his sentence incoherently as he shakes and groans out his release. His seed shoots straight down my throat and I swallow it all. When it stops, so does Bentley. He attempts to back up and remove his dick from my mouth, but I grab ahold of his ass to keep him in me. I lock eyes with him while I gently suck him clean until I feel him going soft, and then I release him from my mouth.

He doesn't wait before he lies down on his stomach and sticks his tongue right between my legs. It happens so quickly, I startle. I can feel the vibration from him laughing at my reaction, but he doesn't say a word. His tongue never moves from my clit.

Out of habit I go to tell him what to do to get me off, but before I can say a word he takes a finger and puts it into me, hitting a spot I never knew existed—this must be the infamous G-spot I've heard of but never experienced firsthand—causing my body to almost convulse on the spot.

Remember when Liz warned me he's not like the high school guys? Well, she was right about that. This guy is not at all like the high school boys at home that I've wasted my time on. He actually knows what he's doing, and at this rate I won't have to lock myself in the bathroom to finish my orgasm off myself like I've had to do half the time with the other guys I've been with.

He continues to finger me while his tongue massages my clit. He adds another digit and within a few seconds an overload of sensations hits me all at once, and the next thing I know I'm going dizzy, experiencing the biggest orgasm I've ever felt to date. I swear I almost black out. Bentley doesn't let up until I come down, and with one last lick, he moves his lips to the top of my pussy and gives it a wet kiss.

He looks up at me and gives me the most adorable boyish grin, and in this moment, if I believed in love, I could see myself easily falling for him. It almost be too easy. But I don't believe in love, so it doesn't matter. This was just sex, technically oral sex but just sex, nonetheless. And that's how it will stay. Just sex.

He licks my wetness off his lips and says, "Woman, you taste unbelievable. I'm going to need another taste of that later. But for now, let's shower, and by the time we're done I should be ready to go another round."

He doesn't have to tell me twice. I jump up from the bed and follow his tight sexy ass to the shower.

He turns it on and once it's warm enough we both get in. I reach for the soap as he grabs my hand and brings it up to his lips to give it a soft kiss.

"You're beautiful, Kayla."

"You already got me in bed. No need for the compliments." I laugh it off, but his expression looks serious and it's making me nervous. I don't do feelings.

"You. Are. Beautiful." He takes my face in his hands and bends slightly to kiss me softly. The water is spraying on us, but because of his height, it's mostly just hitting his back.

I wrap my arms around his neck and he grabs me by my ass and pushes me against the wall of the shower. He continues to kiss me with such vigor I feels as though he's devouring my mouth with his. My body ignites from his touch, making me want more. I've never wanted more before. I try to reach down with one hand to find his dick, but he stops kissing me.

"Woman, you're going to be the death of me. I've never wanted someone like I want you. I don't ever do one-night stands. What are you doing to me?"

I don't answer him. I ignore what he's insinuating. This conversation has the prospect of getting deep and I'm not about to let that happen. Instead, I tap his hands to let me down. I grab the soap and begin to wash his body, starting from his neck and moving my way down. While I'm washing him, he grabs my nipples and pinches.

"Hey!" I shriek.

"Sorry, I thought I was losing my balance. I grabbed hold of the first thing I could to keep me upright."

I laugh at his comment, thankful he's letting the serious shit go. Once I'm done washing him I take the soap to wash myself. He takes the bottle from my hands and then turns me around to face the wall. He massages my neck, and after a few minutes moves down to my arms. It feels so relaxing I let out a soft moan.

When he gets to my ass, he rubs circles on my ass cheeks and then steps closer, so he can wash between my legs. He brushes his fingers over my clit, causing me to tense up. With his dick poking my back, I know he's ready. I rub my ass against it to tease him and he groans into my ear, sending shivers down my spine.

Finding his dick with my hand, I stroke it while he keeps one hand on my clit and the other holds me tight against him.

"I want you right now," I whisper.

He tenses up. "I can't use a condom in here. Let's move this to the bed."

What the fuck was I thinking? Was I seriously about to let this guy fuck me in the shower without a condom on? Yeah, I'm on birth control, but still. He's making me crazy. I need to get my emotions in check. This is not like me at all.

We wash off our bodies, step out of the shower, and before I can even grab a towel, I'm over Bentley's shoulder being carried to the bed. He drops me on the soft mattress and I get a good look at his wet, sexy-as-fuck body. He sees me checking him out, but instead of calling me out, he climbs up my body and hovers over me.

He stares at me for a beat and then says, "I don't know if I'll ever get enough of you. I might just need to keep you a while longer."

"Uh-uh, handsome. Tonight is all we have," I say, pulling him to him.

His jaw clenches for a second. "We'll see about that."

Before I can say another word, his lips are on mine. I can feel his hard cock pressing against me and I lose the fight inside me to argue.

WHEN BENTLEY SAID, I WOULDN'T BE ABLE TO WALK

straight for a week, he wasn't kidding. I wake up to the sound of huffing and puffing causing me to sit straight up, wondering what the heck is going on. My body is stiff and sore like I worked out for hours. Well, technically I did. After the first time Bentley and I made lo—had *sex*, we both fell asleep, and then he woke me up in the early morning to go another round. The man is insatiable. I've never met anybody who can keep up with my sexual appetite, yet he's given me a run for my money.

This is the first time I've ever spent the night with a guy and I'm hoping he doesn't regret it. After what happened with Jake, I've made sure to never put myself in a vulnerable position again. I choose when and where to have sex and I always make sure I'm the first one to leave. I'll never be made a fool of again.

I scan the room to find none other than Mr. Insatiable himself doing pushups in front of the bed. He's dripping in sweat with his muscles bulging out from the workout.

"Morning, he huffs out through his pushup.

"Morning," I say, stretching my arms and legs. I can't believe how sore my body is, meanwhile it's like he wasn't even affected.

"Are you feeling okay?" he asks with a small laugh, jumping onto his feet like it's nothing. Damn him. He must have seen me wince when I stretched.

"I'm just fine. Thank you very much." I glare at him and it just causes him to laugh harder.

He bridges the gap between us and kisses me softly on my lips. This kiss is simple and sweet and it makes my heart thaw a little bit more. I lean in, wanting the kiss to continue, but he pulls away. I give him a small pout, making it clear what I want, but it only causes him to smile brightly.

"Woman, didn't you get enough last night and this morning? I don't want to break you. So, what are we doing today?" His question makes my heart soar and that scares the ever-loving shit out of me. I haven't even known Bentley for twenty-four hours and he's already tearing down every wall I've worked so hard to build up. The wall that keeps my heart safe. That keeps guys from getting in and hurting me. The same wall that needs to remain erect to keep me safe.

"Whoa there, buddy. Who said anything about us continuing this today?" I give him a smirk and wrap the sheet around me to use the bathroom. He might have seen all of me last night, but it's a bit different once everyone is sober and the sun has come up.

He follows me to the bathroom, but I close the door before he can make it in. I don't care how close we got last night, we're never going to be close enough that I'm comfortable going pee in front of him—or any man for that matter.

Through the door, I hear him say, "I heard you and your friend say you're here for the next week. My boys and I are only here until tomorrow, but I was thinking we could chill until then. My boy Coop is staying with your friend anyway." Hmm...speaking of my friend, I need to text her and make sure all is well. I definitely don't want to rain on her hopefully no longer virginal parade, so I decide it won't hurt to chill with Bentley until he leaves. It's not my usual M.O., but I can take one for the team—or in this case for Liz's vagina. I just need to make sure to keep him at a distance.

I flush the toilet, wash my hands, and open the door to see Bentley standing right in my face. I already know I'm going to hang out with him, but I decide to mess with him a little. I love getting him all riled up.

"Um, well, I'm going to first go and see what your friend Kaden is up to, and if he isn't available, I might consider chilling with you." I shoot him a playful wink as I walk past him to get dressed. It's then I remember I only have my dress from the club. I find his shirt still on the floor, so I throw it on with my underwear and head out the bedroom door.

Before I know it, I'm in the air over his shoulder. "Woman, don't test me," he says as he playfully smacks my ass. I yelp and tell him to put me down, but he ignores me as he carries me like a sack of potatoes out to the main room.

Kaden is in the kitchen making some coffee. When he sees me he starts laughing. Luckily Bentley's shirt is so big on me my ass isn't showing. He puts me down when we reach the coffee pot and Kaden offers me a cup of coffee. I take it with a smile and pour some cream and sugar into it. I imagined the morning after would be awkward, but with Bentley it's not awkward at all. It's like we just click.

"So, what are we doing today?" Kaden asks nobody in particular.

"Have you talked to Cooper?" Bentley asks as he takes a bottle of water from the fridge and downs it all in one long gulp.

"Yeah," he says, smiling at me. "He said he's staying with Liz until we have to go. I've never seen him like this before. You would almost think the guy wants something other than—"

Bentley quickly cuts him off before he can finish his sentence. "Yeah, well, let him enjoy it because in twenty-four hours he'll be on lock down."

Lock down?

"What kind of lock down are we talking here? Is my best friend his last screw before he gets married? Is he about to go to prison?"

Yeah, yeah, I know we should have thought about this before leaving with guys we don't know, but c'mon...we're young and dumb.

They both laugh and Bentley says, "No, is that how you view marriage? Being on lock down? He's going to be working for his dad when we're done here. His dad is a dick. He might as well be going to prison."

I nod, but don't ask any more questions. As long as Liz is safe then it's not my business, and the fact is in six days Liz and I will be on our way across the country to the kickass apartment my parents are paying for in exchange of me going to college like a good little girl. I have no idea what I plan to major in other than partying, but if my parents are going to foot the bill and it means four more years of no responsibilities, I'll take it.

"So, fellas, who here is going to go downstairs to the gift shop and get me some shorts and a shirt so we can go get some grub?"

Kaden puts his hands up in protest and laughs. "I'm not the one getting laid, so I sure as hell am not playing errand boy."

Bentley smacks him on his chest and says, "I'll go down and get you an outfit while you jump in the shower. I was thinking of going surfing today. If you want, I can grab you a suit and you can chill on a blanket under an umbrella and watch."

Chill on a blanket and watch? Oh, boy, does he have another thing coming to him. He's got this girl here all wrong. I'll let him think what he wants, though, and when I tear him apart in the water later it'll be that much more satisfying.

"Sure," I say in a sweet voice, knowing he's going to be shocked to learn there's more to me than a blond chick in a tight silver dress. "I'll jump in the shower and then we can go grab something to eat and then head to the beach, but would it be okay if I joined you in the water?"

He looks over at Kaden and furrows his eyebrows unsure of how to respond. Clearly, he's used to girls like Liz who would rather watch with a book in her hand then get in the water and have fun.

Kaden gives him a shrug and says, "We can get you a board so you can paddle around. If it gets to be too much you can always go back to the shore." It's taking everything in me not to laugh at these guys. It'll just be that much funnier when they realize I'm not that girl.

After we finish eating breakfast, we walk down to the beach and head to the hut that rents and sells surf gear. I send a quick text to Liz to make sure she's okay, and when she says she is, I let her know I'm going to chill with Kaden and Bentley until tomorrow. She texts back a happy face. *Yeah, I bet she's happy.*

Bentley picked me out a blue and white bikini, which is cute but totally not doable if I'm going to be surfing, so I grab a wetsuit to throw over my bikini and rent a board. Bentley offers to pay for my stuff, but I'm not having it. I don't like to owe anybody anything. That goes right along with my feelings on love. The guys are looking kind of confused and it just makes me laugh even harder to myself.

We grab our boards and walk down to the area where people are allowed to surf. Because of the crazy weather lately off the coast, the waves are rolling in, not as high as I'd like, but anybody who surfs knows even the small waves can be amazing. Kaden and Bentley stick their boards in the sand and I can tell they're gaging the surf, trying to decide what the sets look like in front of us.

While they're doing that, I stretch to loosen up my muscles. Surfing can be hard on the body. Paddling out really works the upper body, so I make it a point to focus on my arms, shoulders, and back. I look a little over to the left and see some of the guys I've surfed with several times. I don't want them to see me yet because they'll give away my secret.

"C'mon, boys! There's no time like the present. Let's get out there and surf."

They both look at me and laugh, but I don't wait for their response. I grab my board and head to the water.

"Kayla, wait up. Why don't you watch us first and then we can walk you through the basics?" Bentley suggests, looking a little worried. I can tell he isn't at all trying to be condescending because the fact is he has no idea of my surfing capabilities. However, there is no way I'm going to sit on the sidelines and watch them surf.

"I'm just going to paddle out with you guys so I can observe from up close."

I drop my board into the water, lie down on the deck, and begin paddling out. I look over at Kaden and Bentley and they're right behind me. When we get to the back, I sit on the deck, spreading my legs out around the board, and check out the sets.

Being out here feels freeing. If you've never surfed, it's hard to understand. Surfing is an experience. It's about the next wave you're going to catch because you always want more, always crave more. It becomes an addiction, and at the end of the day, you might be tired and sore as hell, but it still feels amazing.

I see the guys from earlier paddling out and know if I don't catch a wave soon they're going to out me. Without saying a word to Kaden and Bentley, I wait for the next set of waves, and when they come, I charge for the wave and begin paddling my ass off, pop up, and take the drop. It's hard to describe what my mind goes through while I'm riding the wave. Beforehand, my mind is all over the place. Once I paddle out, my mind only thinks of a few things, but once I'm riding the wave, my mind is clear, and the only thing I can think of is contentment. Before I experienced love, I would have described it as such, but once I experienced the toxicity of love, I would never again associate surfing with love. Surfing isn't like pathetic ever-changing emotions. It's concrete and it's life.

I get to the shoreline and wait for the guys to meet me back here. Bentley goes first and he's decent. He pops up and rides the wave to the shore without wiping out. Kaden is clearly not as good. He tries to take a larger wave and completely wipes out. Bentley gets to the shore while I'm still laughing at Kaden.

"Well, aren't you just full of secrets?" he says through his laughter.

"You didn't ask."

He saunters up to me, grips my wetsuit in his hands, and he pulls me close to him until our bodies are flush against one another. His mouth attacks mine with such force it's just not painful. I'm learning that Bentley is an extremely passionate individual. He doesn't seem to do anything half-ass. Every time he kisses me he gives me all of him. His tongue slips between my lips without asking for permission. He just takes what he wants. My hands go up to his neck and I hold on to the back of it while he continues to assault me in the best way possible.

I don't see Kaden and the guys approach, but when I hear one of the guys yell out, "What's up, *Wahine!*" I push Bentley away. His brows furrow in confusion like he isn't even aware that we were just making out in front of an entire audience. I never do shit like this. This guy is totally getting under my skin.

When Kaden and Bentley realize the guys are referring to me, they both raise their eyebrows. I don't give them an explanation though. I just nod to the guy. "What's up?"

"Nothing much...chilling and surfing. What are you doing with these *Bennies?*"

Before I can answer, Bentley asks, "How do you guys know each other?"

"*Wahine* is a local and a bitchin' surfer in case you haven't noticed. We all see her at different events and competitions. She's a cool ass chick."

Bentley and Kaden look at me in shock and I bite my lip to stifle my laugh.

"All right, well, it looks like the sets are picking up so we're gonna get back out there."

The guys all say their goodbyes and then take off, leaving Bentley, Kaden, and me alone.

Kaden asks first. "What the hell is a *Wahine*? And why did he just call us *Bennies*?"

I smile big. "A *Wahine* is a female surfer. I've been surfing most of my life. I live across from the beach. Liz and I have been friends since we were five years old, and she's spent her life watching me surf while reading a book from the shoreline. A *Benny* is someone who's not from around here. When you live on the beach you know who's local and who's not. I'm not from Miami, but I surf all over."

"Will you marry me?" Kaden asks with a straight face, and for a second I feel like I'm going to hyperventilate until Bentley punches him in the arm causing Kaden to bark out his laughter. *Oh, thank God, he was kidding!*

"If she's going to marry anyone, it will be me." And now I really am about to hyperventilate because for a second I can imagine myself spending my life with this man. I haven't known him long but the little I do know of him already has me addicted. This isn't good. Addiction is need and need leads to commitment and commitment leads to marriage, and you don't base a marriage off any of those things because they're all emotional, and emotions change, leaving you heartbroken. I know all of this already, but for some reason when I'm with Bentley, all my sensible thinking goes flying out the window.

Bentley wraps his body around mine. I feel so protected and... I'm not going to use the L word because it's not possible, but I feel something and it scares me. I move out of his arms to get myself together.

"All right, boys. The tides won't stay like this forever. Let's do some more surfing."

And that's what we spend the day doing. We surf and talk and surf some more. We paddle out together, talking about nothing of consequence, but it's nice. We agree to keep it light. Well, I request to keep it light, but Bentley and Kaden go along with it. Bentley tells me about his friends and how he loves to work out and fight. I tell him about being a cheerleader in high school and about all the trouble I've gotten Liz and me into over the years. Kaden doesn't really say much. He just laughs and joins in occasionally.

Our competitive sides show as we playfully banter back and forth throughout the day over who can surf better. However, when I hit the last wave just right and ride that bitch like I own it, they both agree I'm the better out of the three of us. In another life, Bentley and I could effortlessly be friends. It's just so easy with him, and if I'm truthful with myself, if given the chance we could probably be more than friends. Last night was about sex, but today has been about so much more than that. I've never just hung out with a guy since Jake—and if we're being honest, his immature ass doesn't compare to Bentley—and it's rather refreshing.

Dusk approaches and Kaden takes off to meet up with a couple of friends including their friend Caleb. Bentley tells him we aren't going to join, and then comes up with the idea for us to sleep under the stars on the beach. Bentley mentioned where they live has no beach nearby and where they're about to move to doesn't either. His love of surfing came from his trips with his parents over the years.

We go to a local store and pick up a large sleeping bag, some blankets, snacks, and a bottle of vodka. We make our way down and find a secluded spot to build a small bonfire.

We spread a blanket out and use another one to wrap ourselves up with me between Bentley's legs. It's spring in Florida, but the ocean breeze adds a bit of a chill so we're snuggling close. We don't say anything, just watch the small fire crackle and the waves crash. It's a comfortable silence, though. I've never felt so at ease with anybody except Liz before. Being in Bentley's arms feels so natural like he was made with the sole purpose to hold me.

He moves my hair off my neck and begins to trail open mouth kisses from my earlobe working his way down to my collarbone. His soft kisses give me goose bumps and cause me to visibly shiver. He moves his hands underneath the blanket to my tank top and pulls my top down, releasing my breasts. His mouth goes from kissing to sucking and nipping. Using his thumbs and middle fingers he pinches my nipples making them peak, and using his forefingers he rubs them over the top of my nipples causing them to get hard. The sensation hits my core instantly and I can't help but moan as he continues his sexual assault on me.

I take my hand and move it to the back of his head, pushing his mouth into my neck to show him I need more. He sucks harder, then bites the side of my neck, moving back up to my earlobe to bite it as well. He removes one hand from my breast and taps my legs for me to spread them open. I like him behind me, but I want to see him.

I turn around on my knees—keeping the blanket around us in case anybody wanders by—and go up high enough so his face is right in front of my breasts. I grab him by the back of his head and pull his face to me. He knows exactly what I want because his lips wrap right around my nipple and he sucks hard, tugging on it until it pops out, and then he moves to the other one to give it the same attention.

His hand goes into my shorts and under my bikini bottoms, straight toward my clit. He rubs it for a few seconds and then moves his hand lower to gather up the juices that are already flowing down there.

"Jesus woman, you're dripping wet." I push his head back to my breasts and he chuckles, but immediately goes back to sucking and licking each one. I need to be in control tonight. I feel like I'm losing all control and that doesn't sit well with me at all.

His fingers, full of my wetness, move back to my clit and he starts rubbing it up and down and in circles causing me to squirm a little. It's insane how he knows exactly how to get me off. He should give classes on how to give a woman an orgasm. I know quite a few guys who would benefit from this.

"C'mon baby, let go for me," he murmurs. I want to, but I want him in me when I do. Taking his swim shorts in my hands, I pull them down and then push him onto his back.

"Do you have a condom?" I ask.

He nods and takes it out of his pocket. He must have grabbed it when we stopped by the hotel earlier to grab our stuff. Knowing we would be sleeping here and he would be leaving early, we took our stuff from the room so we wouldn't have to go back there in the morning.

I take it from him, rip it open, and roll it onto his hard length. I lift and then sink down onto him in one fluid motion, both of us moaning as he fills me. He looks into my eyes as he takes my hands in his, holding me steady, and I begin to ride him up and down. His dick hits the inside of me just right causing an unbelievable amount of pleasure. After a few minutes, he places my hands on his chest and I start to pick up speed. He's in me so deep it feels like we're one. He moves his finger back to my clit and rubs circles against the sensitive nub.

Between his dick hitting the inside of me and the friction of his finger on my clit, I know I'm about to lose it, and he knows it too.

"C'mon, woman. Give it to me. Come for me. I want to feel you come all over my dick."

His words throw me over the edge. My body spasms and my legs shake, and at one point I'm not even sure I'll be able to keep riding him so he can find his own release. But the one thing I've learned about Bentley is even though he's only known me for twenty-four hours he still knows me. Once I've ridden out my orgasm, he grabs my hips, holding me down, and begins to pump up into me from the bottom. His thrusts get faster and deeper and I feel another orgasm coming on.

"Oh, my God, Bentley. Please don't stop," I beg. And this time we find our release together.

WE'RE LYING WRAPPED UP IN THE SLEEPING BAG WITH Bentley spooning me from behind when he quietly says, "I don't want to let you go."

My entire body stills. I don't even know how to respond to that. I would be lying if I said I wasn't thinking the same thing, but at the same time I already know how this type of story ends. Boy meets girl, boy makes girl fall for him, girl falls, and boy doesn't catch her. Girl hits the ground face first. Splat! The End.

"I just want a chance to get to know you more," he continues. "I've never done anything like this before. I know you feel what I'm feeling."

I take a second to get control of my emotions and then I say, "I'm not at a place in my life to give you anything more. I don't do more. I'm sorry."

He grabs my hips and rolls me over to face him. I keep my eyes down, but he lifts my chin so I'm forced to look at him.

"Kayla, do you believe in soulmates?" Oh, boy, here we go. Why did I have to pick the guy who doesn't want a one-night stand?

Figuring it's probably best to put him out of his misery, I tell him the truth. "No, I don't. I don't believe in love, or soulmates, or happily ever after."

He makes a pained expression like I just ran over his puppy, and it makes me want to take it all back just to see him smile again, but I'm doing what I have to do. I don't want to lead him on and I need to protect myself.

"Who hurt you, baby?" he asks, trailing his knuckles down the side of my cheek softly.

"It doesn't matter. The only thing that does matter is that my mom warned me love wasn't real, but like any teenager I had to experience it for myself, and I learned the hard way she was right."

He thinks about what I said for a few seconds then asks, "Are your parents still married?"

"Yeah, they have a business relationship. They are both divorce attorneys who watch people destroy their lives as well as their children's lives every day. They have been married for over twenty years, though. When my mom gave me advice on relationships, at first I thought she was a cynic. She told me love is an emotion and emotions aren't concrete so they don't last. It took me having my heart broken to realize she was right. And on top of that, I disappointed her and embarrassed myself."

I don't ask him to give me his opinions because I don't want to know how he feels. Feelings only hurt. He waits a beat and when he sees I'm not going to say anything else he decides to give me his opinion anyway.

"Well, my parents married for love, and they have been married for over twenty years as well. They spent so much time all over each other while I was growing up I thought that's how all parents were, until I got old enough to go to other kids houses and saw that not every parental unit is like mine. I believe in love and soulmates"—he pulls me closer to him until he's so close I could kiss him without moving—"and I believe you very well could be my soulmate. I just want a chance, Kayla. One chance to prove to you that love is real."

I hate how determined he looks and I can't stand to hurt him, so I say, "I'll think about it."

He accepts that answer and we fall asleep with my head on his chest as he rubs circles on my back.

I wake up and it's still dark outside. The small fire has gone out and Bentley is still fast asleep. He looks so peaceful with just a hint of a smile on his face. I would like to think I put that smile there. I check my phone and see it's only three in the morning. I gather up my stuff and carefully slip out of the sleeping bag leaving Bentley sleeping by himself. It's just easier this way.

Three

BENTLEY

Present Day

SOMETIMES THERE ARE PEOPLE AND SITUATIONS IN LIFE that we just can't control. No matter how much we try, it's out of our hands and we have to learn to accept that it's out of our hands. Kayla is the person in my life and her refusing to allow me to show her what love is, is the situation that is completely out of my control. I've loved this girl from the day I met her six years ago at the club in Miami. I know what you're thinking, so for argument's sake, let's just agree to disagree. I know what I felt and I know how I feel. Unfortunately, the woman I fell in love with is incapable of letting somebody in, so none of it really matters at this point.

However, what does matter is that at this moment I'm standing in front of said girl staring at her adorable pregnant belly while she's rocking a tiny string bikini that makes me want to devour her while I'm currently holding hands with my girlfriend, and the only thing I can think of is, *is the baby mine?*

Everybody around us goes silent and I realize I just asked the question out loud. Kayla opens her mouth to respond, but Sophia, my girlfriend of three months, cuts in. "Are you fucking kidding me?" Jesus, when did her voice get so damn whiny?

"Isn't this the bitch from your apartment?" she asks. "Why the fuck would she be carrying your baby? We have been together for months, Bentley." She draws out my name and it sounds like nails to a chalkboard.

I go to respond, but Kayla beats me to it. "Bitch? Who are you calling a bitch? Just because I'm pregnant doesn't mean I can't kick your ass back to wherever you came from. You don't know shit about what Bentley and I have done."

Sophia turns to me, glaring. "Bentley, what the hell is she talking about? Is it possible this baby is yours?"

Ah, hell. Shit just got real.

Six Months Ago

THE CROWD IS CHANTING "RAGE. RAGE. RAGE. RAGE." I'M standing in the corner, watching the announcer declare Cooper the winner of the fight, which means that in February he'll be going head-to-head for the title at the MGM Grand arena. I'm so fucking proud of him. He busts his ass every day at the gym and has been putting up with his dad for the last several years just to get to where he is. I honestly don't know how the hell he does it. Yeah, I work out at the same training facility as him, but I don't have his piece-of-shit father breathing down my neck like he does. If I did, I would have quit years ago.

Before Cooper leaves the octagon to head back to the changing area, he nods for me to come over to him. "Look straight out, four rows back."

I do what he tells me to do and then I spot them. More importantly, I spot her, the girl who left me on the beach all those years ago. The girl I knew was my soulmate but wouldn't let her guard down long enough to give me a real chance. *Well I'll be damned.*

"I need you to make sure Liz is at the after-party."

I give them a smirk when I see they're both looking my way, and nod. I know Cooper feels the same way about Liz that I do about Kayla.

Once Cooper and everyone with him make their way out of the octagon, I approach the girls.

"Well, God damn. If it isn't the girl who got away...And her best friend." I direct my statement at Liz so Kayla doesn't know how much that shit hurt to wake up on the beach by myself in Miami five years ago after she told me she would think about giving us a chance. When I get done looking at Liz, I turn to Kayla and fuck if she doesn't look even more beautiful than she did all those years ago. She still has the same long blonde hair with captivating blue eyes. Her body is still thin and toned, but she's matured. "Never thought we would see you two again."

I wait for Kayla to respond. Most girls would look remorseful when approached after dipping out on a guy after spending the weekend with him, but not Kayla. She puts her hands on her hips, lifts her chin and makes it clear where she stands. Well, we'll just have to see about that.

"Looks like you were wrong because here we are."

"So, I take it you two are UFC fans?"

She laughs at my question. "Ummm...No. I'm a fan of hot guys in no shirts fighting and getting all sweaty, and Liz is along for the ride. Our best friend Hayley got us tickets to the fight and invited us to the party that is going on afterward."

I'll have to thank Hayley when I see her. She's our on-site medic at the gym. I lean in close to Kayla, just enough to invade her personal space but without touching her. "Well, you're in luck because I'm one of those fighters and I'll gladly take my shirt off and get sweaty with you any day."

Kayla's laugh deepens, like she isn't affected at all by me, but I can see her thighs rubbing together—she's putting on a front. I'm going to let it go...for now.

"So, that means we'll see you at Kaden's for the after-party?"

"I didn't know it's at Kaden's. Hayley just sent me an address, but yes, we'll be there. Whether you see us is up in the air."

If it's possible, I swear that woman has gotten even sassier since the last time I saw her, and if I'm honest, I love it. What I would give to kiss the fuck out of that girl just to shut her up, but I need to formulate a plan. I never imagined seeing her again, but now that I have another chance, I need to do this right. I nod to both of them and head to the back to meet up with the guys.

Cooper, Caleb, and I arrive to Kaden's house and the party is already in full swing. I take a look at Kaden's home and the land he's sitting on and I can't help but feel a little nostalgic. I miss the days when we were all roommates. Don't get me wrong, I'm happy for Kaden and Cooper each getting his own place. Kaden has worked his ass off as a trainer to purchase this home on his own. It's a decent-sized house on probably a half-acre of land. Nothing huge, but he's put his heart and soul into making it a home. Back in Boulder we were all roommates minus Caleb. I can afford my own place, but I hate living on my own. It gets lonely. Growing up, my parents and I were very close and when I moved out of their home I moved right in with Cooper and Kaden. I like having my own space but I enjoy the company of others as well.

It's a little different living with Caleb. He's more of a loner. He's an amazing friend and will have your back without question, but something fucked up happened to him. I can see it in his eyes. The problem is, he doesn't talk about it. He has a passion for fighting like the rest of us, but for him it's more like he's fighting something within him. He also works a lot of hours as a bouncer at a club on the strip. I might as well be living on my own, to be honest.

As soon as I see the overflow of people everywhere I immediately start looking for my little firecracker. I don't see her, but I do see a couple friends from the gym, so I bullshit with them for a few minutes before continuing my search. When I finally find her she's making herself a drink in the kitchen. Her phone is on the counter and before she sees me coming I snatch it up. Luckily, it's not locked.

"Hey! What the hell do you think you're doing?" she screams, thinking her phone is being stolen. When she sees me, she simmers down, but then her face morphs into the cutest glare I've ever seen. Before I answer her, I type in my number and call myself. She realizes what I'm doing and tries to snatch her phone back.

I turn around so my back is facing her and she jumps onto my back to try to get to it. I hear my phone ring and know I got her number. Her ass isn't getting away a second time.

I grab her body off my back and put her onto the counter, spreading her legs and positioning myself between them. I think she's in shock at how easily I could fling her around because for the first time she's speechless.

I hand her back her phone. "Now I have your number. There'll be no getting away from me this time," I say with a wink.

She snatches her phone back and huffs out in annoyance. I must be a sick guy because the more pissed she gets, the more turned on I get. She shoves me back and jumps off the counter, grabbing her drink and walking away without saying a word. I follow her outside to the bonfire, and once we're away from the loud noise, I grab her by her arm and spin her around.

"Woman, please stop walking away from me."

She lifts one brow in defiance, and I tug her over to me. For a brief second, she melts into my touch, lowering that impenetrable wall. But before I can jump across, she realizes what she's done, and it shoots back up, blocking me on my side.

"I'm pretty sure I can walk wherever I want, including away from you, and I'm not particularly fond of guys who take my number without asking."

I try to contain my smile. I learned quickly with Kayla when she doesn't think I'm taking her seriously it only fuels her fire.

"Look, I'm sorry. But can you blame me? We had an amazing couple days together in Miami and when I asked you for your number, you said you would think about it, then I wake up to you gone without so much as a goodbye. I searched the beach that morning hoping to find those surfers who knew you, but none of them were around. I've been back to that beach several times over the years hoping to see you surfing and now you're here. I can't take the chance of you disappearing again. I believed you were my soulmate all those years ago, but now that I've run into you again, I know you are."

"Well, obviously, I did think about it and decided not to give you my number," she sasses. "And I'm pretty sure in order to be soulmates, two people have to agree." She crosses her arms over her chest, pushing her amazing tits up, and before I can stop myself, my eyes dart down to appreciate them. Her eyes follow mine and then she lets go of her arms.

"Are you seriously staring at my chest right now?"

I chuckle and then bite my lip to contain my laughter and smile. She's so fucking adorable.

"I'm sorry. They're just there." I shrug. "The memory of you in that hot bikini, and then naked, wrapped around me on the beach is seared into my mind. I've spent five years thinking about you."

Her face softens and she gives me a small smile. "You just remembered me because I'm probably the only girl to ever out surf your ass."

"Hey, now! I let you out surf me!"

She playfully slaps my chest and we both laugh. Finally, I feel like I'm getting somewhere with her, but then her friend Liz walks toward us looking really upset, and I have a sinking suspicion my time with Kayla is up...at least for now. I nod to Kayla to let her know that her friend is walking over. When she sees Liz, her hand drops from my chest and she runs over to her. I can't hear what's being said, but within seconds both girls are walking away.

I follow them out to their car and see Cooper screaming for Liz. I don't know what just happened, but it can't be good. The next thing I know Cooper is walking away and Kayla is peeling out of the driveway.

A little while later, I find Cooper sitting by the bonfire with a whiskey in his hand. "Bro, what the hell happened?"

"It doesn't even fucking matter. She's gone and it's for the best."

I want to talk to him, but I know when he gets like this he just wants me there without my lectures, so I do what he wants and drink with him. At one point in the night Cooper is so drunk he decides he's going to find Liz.

"I never should have let her leave," he says through slurred words. The problem with being drunk is you're always the last person to realize you are in fact drunk.

"Just chill out. You need to get some sleep, sober up, and then you can talk to her in the morning."

He nods in agreement and then takes another swig of his drink. At this rate, he'll probably be sober next week.

The next morning, we're at the training center and I'm totally fucking with Cooper. His ass is so hung over, I don't even know how he's fighting back, but it makes it that much more fun. At one point, I throw a punch to his stomach and he looks like he's going to upchuck all over the ring. I can't help but laugh at his ass. Serves him right for drinking so damn much last night.

While he's catching his breath, I ask him if he's going to contact Liz and he tells me he can't because he has no way to get ahold of her. This guy gives up way too easily, but as much as I want to let him know that, I decide to give him a break.

"You are aware her best friend works at this gym, right? And even if she didn't, I got Kayla's number last night." I must admit, I'm still damn proud of the way I stole her number. Hopefully her stubborn ass doesn't change it just to spite me. I wouldn't put it past her.

I shake myself out of my inner thoughts to hear Marc, Cooper's dad and owner of this training facility, bitching at him and apparently, me.

"...And you need to stop fucking around and take this shit seriously. Any more losses and you're going to be removed from this team..." He goes on and on about my upcoming fight, but all I can focus on is not decking this asshole in his face. He doesn't know shit about me, and if he did, he'd know I fight for fun and I don't give a fuck if I win or lose. I do it because I love it. Sure, I want to win. I'm a guy. I'm competitive. But I do it more to spend time with my friends and have fun, and this asshole isn't going to suck my love for fighting out of me like he's done to his son. Fuck him and the horse he rode in on.

Four

BENTLEY

IT'S BEEN EIGHT DAYS SINCE THE UFC FIGHT AND PARTY, and I never imagined so much shit could change in that short amount of time. I'm sitting at the hospital with Kayla holding her hand to comfort her as they treat her for smoke inhalation while praying for Liz and Cooper's daughter Bella, who's in the children's wing with the same diagnosis. If you had told me that I would end up here with Kayla, I would have told you you were crazy. If you had told me Cooper has a four-year-old daughter, I would have laughed in your face.

After Cooper and his dad got into it the other day, Liz showed up at the gym shortly after to let Cooper know she got pregnant all those years ago in Miami. Unfortunately, Cooper's ass of a dad stopped her and sent her away. Cooper ended up finding out about his long lost daughter when he ran into them at the grocery store. When he confronted his dad, the asshole made it clear he didn't give a shit about anything but Cooper fighting, so Cooper ended up quitting.

Nobody has seen him in the last several days and since he refused to go back to the gym, so did I. Kaden's ass is stuck there because he's under contract with the gym as a trainer, but Caleb and I aren't. So, until we hear from Cooper about what he wants to do, we're using guest passes at another local gym. I have a fight coming up, so I can't just stop training. Luckily, Caleb is helping me train, so it works out well.

I sent Kayla a few texts, but she only replied with single word responses. I had been working up the courage to ask Hayley for her address so I could confront her in person, but after today it won't matter what her address is since her apartment caught fire with her and Bella in it. Thankfully both of them are okay.

All my life my parents have said we can't control who we love. We're destined to be with one person, and when we meet that person we will know it. It's called fate, and we don't stand a chance against it. I believe that Kayla is my soulmate. The problem is my parents never explained what would happen if you met your soulmate and they don't believe in love. If I didn't already believe in fate, I would be a believer after today.

While I was training with Caleb, I hit my hand the wrong way on the punching bag, something I never do, and decided to go to the ER to have it checked out to make sure there wasn't any huge damage. Imagine my surprise when I saw Kayla and a small little girl being wheeled in by ambulance. Kayla asked me to call Liz to let her know what's going on—that their apartment caught on fire and both Bella and her are at the hospital—and of course she came immediately. I tried to contact Cooper, but he didn't answer.

That leads me to the present time. While Liz is in the children's wing with her and Cooper's daughter, I'm currently sitting in the recovery wing with Kayla. Her eyes are closed and she has on an oxygen mask so she can't really talk. I just hold her hand and massage my thumb into her palm to let her know I'm here.

Finding her today in the hospital only strengthens my argument that we're meant to be together. Now if I could just convince Kayla of this, we would be golden. Easier said than done, though.

The door swings open and Liz and Cooper walk in. Liz looks terrified, but as soon as Kayla opens her eyes and lifts her oxygen mask, she calms down and runs right to Kayla. They exchange hugs and Kayla explains that she fell asleep with Bella and woke up to a fire in the apartment. She's so upset and heartbroken that something could have happened to Bella. It's clear she loves that little girl like her own.

Of course, Liz tells her it's not her fault and calms her down by telling her it's okay. Those two are more like sisters than best friends. A few minutes later a police officer and a couple firemen come into the room to explain what happened. I'm trying to pay attention, but all I can think about is that Kayla almost died. Whoever set that fire should be dead, and if I ever come across him or her I'll probably kill 'em myself.

I look over to the officer handing Liz a photo of the guy who set the apartment on fire and Liz begins to freak out and then hands the photo to Cooper.

"The man in this photo is Marc Cooper. This is my father."

What. In. The. Actual. Fuck. I know Marc is a first-rate asshole, but to burn down their home to keep Liz away from Cooper is fucking crazy. That man belongs in the loony bin.

Liz and Cooper are exchanging words and their conversation is getting heated, but then what he says next shocks the shit out of all of us.

"He's dead, Liz. My dad is dead."

I walk over to Cooper to give him a hug and tell him I'm sorry. "I know you two didn't get along, but I never thought he was capable of this."

Cooper doesn't say anything. He looks fucking defeated and I don't blame him. I have no clue how I would react if I found out my dad almost killed his granddaughter and then saved her. I'm pissed as hell that he didn't save Kayla, but Cooper doesn't need my anger on top of what he's already dealing with.

I look around and realize the officer and firemen must have left at some point. Liz tries to comfort Cooper but he ends up spouting out some shit about them being better off without him and then storms out. Once he's gone Liz loses it. Kayla is laying in the hospital bed after almost dying from being caught in a fire and she's comforting Liz. She doesn't cry or even look upset. She's the strongest fucking woman I know.

Finally, Liz calms down and asks the question of the hour. "Now what?"

Kayla sighs and says, "It will be okay, Liz. We'll figure it out. We always do."

The love these two women have for each other is undeniable. I think back to that night on the beach when Kayla told me love isn't real. Doesn't she see how much Liz loves and needs her? No, it's not the same as a relationship, but love is love, and Kayla is surrounded by love.

Kayla looks like she has the world sitting on her shoulders and I vow to do whatever I can to show her that it's okay to love and accept love from a man. She doesn't always have to be so strong.

I clear my throat to get their attention and when they both look at me I tell Liz to go focus on Bella and suggest they move in with me. I don't know what I was thinking except that I want Kayla near me and if she's living with me maybe she'll give us a chance. I also don't want any of them being homeless. Hopefully Cooper will come to his senses and figure his shit out, but until then I figure I can make sure they're all safe.

After getting emotional, Liz goes back to her daughter. I can't even begin to imagine what she's going through. Being a single parent and at such a young age can't be easy. That gets me thinking about Kayla and how she fits into all this.

Once she's gone, Kayla says, "You didn't have to do that but thank you. Apparently, Cooper isn't going to man up right now."

"That's not fair and you know it," I tell her. "He just lost his dad. He has struggled for years dealing with that man. Marc has Cooper so fucked up he can't see straight. Just give him some time."

"I get that, but he has a woman and a daughter who need his support."

"And he will come around. Have you and Liz been close the entire time she's been raising Bella?"

I see the adoration in Kayla's eyes when I say Bella's name. "Yeah, that little girl is amazing. When we got back from Miami, Liz found out she didn't wait long enough to have unprotected sex after starting her birth control pills and was pregnant. We tried to look up your names but got nothing. We lived together and made it work. We went to school, worked part time, and raised Bella the best we could. I love that little girl like she's my own."

"Do you want to have your own kids one day?" I ask, hoping she'll open up to me.

"I do. I want to find a man that wants the same things as me so we can have kids and raise them."

"What things are those?"

She thinks for a second before she answers. "Somebody with a career and his own money who wants to partner up to have a family. Somebody who is looking for an equal and is willing to share the responsibilities, bills, etcetera."

Her response tells me she still feels the same way she did all those years ago. I can give her all that, but I can do it with love if she would just let me.

"Sounds like the perfect business relationship, just like your parents."

She just nods and closes her eyes.

"That's all I can give anyone," she mutters before falling back asleep and ending the conversation.

I use this time to text Cooper, and when he doesn't respond, I send out a text to Kaden and Caleb. I get a text back from Caleb letting me know Cooper is there. I let him know the girls are coming to stay with us in our spare room until they figure shit out, and for him to let Cooper know as well.

A few hours later Kayla is still sleeping, but I can hear her whimpering like she's scared. She must be having a bad dream. I decide to lie in the bed with her to comfort her. She tries to be so strong, but sometimes we just need to let someone else hold us up. Carefully, I kneel onto the bed and gently move her over, and once I'm situated, I wrap my body around hers, pulling her close to me. She instantly calms and continues to sleep. She may not want to admit it but this woman is my forever and I'm hers.

I MUST HAVE FALLEN ASLEEP BECAUSE WHEN I OPEN MY EYES the sun is shining and s staring at me with a smirk on her face.

"Well, good morning, sunshine. First, you take my number without asking, and now you take half my bed without asking? Have you no manners?"

I attempt to stretch, but with the bed being so small and me being so big, it doesn't work out well. I just end up cuddling closer to Kayla, which is absolutely okay with me.

"You haven't seen anything yet, sweetheart. Now that you'll be living at my place I plan to take much more from you. Although, if you would just give it all to me willingly, it would make everything go a whole lot smoother."

She laughs and shakes her head, then attempts to push me off the bed. Good thing the rails are there or my ass would be on the floor right now.

"Let's go, big boy. Out of my bed. You won't be taking anything else from me, and I definitely won't be giving you anything."

The nurse walks in and eyes me in her bed not looking too thrilled, so I get up but not before whispering in Kayla's ear, "Oh, I will, and you will, and the sooner you accept you are mine, the sooner we can get to the fun stuff."

She tries to look like what I said doesn't affect her, but I can see the blush appear on her beautiful alabaster skin. I decide not to point it out though. I don't need her realizing she's giving her true feelings away.

Kayla and Bella finally get discharged from the hospital. Liz came to the hospital in her car, so she takes Kayla to get hers from the apartment complex, and then they meet me at my place.

When the girls walk in, Kayla seems to be impressed at our place, but Liz looks nervous. It must be frightening to suddenly be homeless and have a kid in tow. I had Caleb clean up the night before, but there wasn't much to clean up. We're actually pretty clean guys. I give them a quick tour of the place and they see all the stuff Cooper bought the night before. I knew he was picking up some clothes for them since they lost everything in the fire, but he definitely went above and beyond. There are toys and dolls, and a bunch of girly crap for Bella. He picked up a bed for her as well and a bunch of movies. I don't want to overwhelm them, so after I let Liz know when the funeral will be, I give Kayla a kiss on the cheek and give them their space.

IT'S BEEN A FEW DAYS SINCE THE GIRLS MOVED IN AND everything is going fine. We have had a few meals together and Bella is absolutely adorable. I've watched more Disney movies than I care to admit, but I can't help it. That little girl knows exactly what she's doing with her cute little pouty face and the way she bats her eyelashes. She even got Caleb to watch one with us. Every night Kayla makes sure to go to bed when Liz and Bella do to avoid me, but I think I'm wearing her down. She still won't answer my texts, but I catch her staring at me quite often. I'm not giving up.

It's a little after eleven at night when I hear a banging noise. I know Caleb is working and everybody else should be asleep so I walk out from my room to check it out.

I realize the banging is coming from the front door and I rush to answer it before it wakes anybody up. When I swing the door open, Chelsea, a girl I was dating up until a couple weeks ago, is standing at my door, looking drunk as hell.

"Hey, baby!" She slurs out the words as she wraps her arms around me.

"Chelsea, what are you doing here?"

"I miss you, baby. Can I come in?" Oh lord. This isn't going to be good. After getting to know Chelsea for a few weeks, I learned that she has a drinking problem. I backed away from her after that, but clearly she didn't get the message.

"Chelsea, you can't be here. How did you get here anyway?" I ask, looking out toward the parking lot to see if there is a cab waiting for her. Maybe I can catch it before it leaves.

"My friend dropped me off." I walk her into my room so she doesn't wake up the entire house while I try to figure out how to handle this. She plops down on my bed, so I take her phone and try to call a couple of people I know she's friends with. Of course, nobody answers.

"Chelsea, I'm going to call you a cab so you can go home." When she doesn't answer me, I look up and find her passed the fuck out in my bed. It's late and I'm tired, so I decide to let her sleep it off. I'll just take her home in the morning once she's coherent. I grab a blanket from my bed and lay across the futon I have in my room. I sure as hell am not going to sleep in the bed with her. I don't need to give her any more reason to think she has a chance with me.

I wake up with a kink in my neck and for a second wonder why the hell I'm sleeping on my futon, when I remember what happened last night. I take a second to stretch when I hear screaming coming from the living room. I look at my bed and it's empty. *Oh shit!* I haul ass out to the living room to find Chelsea is in my fucking shirt, going toe-to-toe with Kayla. Then I look around and see Liz, who looks like she's trying to be pissed, but is also attempting to hold in her laughter. And of course the scene wouldn't be complete without Bella mimicking Kayla's stance with her hands on her hips.

"Okay, I can explain." All three and half women look over at me and I put my hands up, metaphorically waving a white flag while praying they don't all team up and kill me.

The first one to speak is Bella. "Bentley, your friend is wearing no shorts, and Mommy says it's rude to not be dressed when you have company over. You should tell your friend to put on some more clothes." She scrunches her nose up, and if I wasn't scared for my life right now, I would laugh at her cuteness.

Liz snorts and Kayla shoots me a death glare. Chelsea looks like the sight of a child revolts her. What was I ever thinking when I decided to go out with her? I don't like to waste my time with women I don't see a future with.

Before I can explain the situation, Chelsea lets out a sound of disgust and retreats to my bedroom.

"Let me explain," I say again to the women left standing in the living room.

Liz speaks up this time. "There's no need to explain. This is your apartment. I'm just thankful for you letting us stay here." Damn, Cooper is one lucky guy. He better get his shit straight before he loses her for good.

"Excuse me? No, Liz! It is not okay..." Kayla begins to yell, but Liz cuts her off.

"Can we please continue this later? I really need to get Bella to school."

Kayla and I both nod, and I get the hell out of there before Kayla finds something to stab me with.

After I drop Chelsea off at her place and make it clear to her we are over, I head over to the gym. Cooper sent everyone a text requesting a meeting.

Once we all gather, he announces that his father left him the training facilities in the will so he's officially the new owner. I'm extremely happy for him. He deserves it.

After telling him congratulations, Caleb and I head to the ring to get a workout in. I'm going to be fighting in less than two months and now that Cooper's shitty dad isn't breathing down my throat, I find myself wanting to win. With Cooper's name on the line, I want to make him proud.

"Holy shit, man! I haven't seen you fight like that in years!" Caleb is bending over panting like a little bitch after I just whooped his ass.

I smile widely and laugh. I have to admit, it feels good to give it my all again.

"So, what's up with you and Kayla?" he asks as we head to the juice bar to get a drink.

"I don't know. She comes from a home where they apparently don't believe in love. I just don't get it. What mom tells her daughter that love isn't real and to never marry because of it?"

"Not every family is perfect like yours, Bent. And to be honest, maybe you're dodging a bullet. In my experience, women are fake as hell and just want one thing from a man. Money."

Caleb looks sad when he says this and it's probably the most he's ever said about relationships.

"From your experience?" I ask, trying to get him to continue, but he shuts down.

"Doesn't even matter. I like Kayla. She's a cool chick, but I don't trust any women. Let's practice."

I spend the rest of the afternoon working out, then shower at the gym, and when I can't put off the inevitable anymore, I head home.

It's almost ten o'clock when I arrive, so I'm hoping everybody will be asleep. I open the door quietly and attempt to tip toe to my room. No such luck.

"Oh, well, look who it is? Sneaking any more whores into your room tonight so Bella can wake up and see them half naked? Maybe this time you can give her your boxers to wear to go along with your shirt."

There is so much shit I could say, but I'm a man and I'm not stupid, so I decide to just beg for forgiveness. "I'm sorry. It's not what you were thinking. You know I've been texting you every day asking you to give me a chance. Do you really think I would bring some woman home and sleep with her while you are here?"

For a second her face softens, but then it hardens into a stoic expression and she no longer shows any emotion. And I know that infamous wall is going up. "I don't give a shit who you bring home. I don't want you. What we had was a one-time thing. I'm not your soulmate or your forever. So just give it a rest. We both know you just wanted in my pants again, and when I wouldn't give it up, you found someone who would. The only problem is you got caught."

"You know what, Kayla? I've tried so damn hard, but you just won't listen. She was drunk and needed somewhere to stay and I let her sleep on my bed while I took the futon. It was late and I forgot about Bella being here. If I would have remembered I would have made sure she was gone before she woke up. I didn't do this to hurt you."

Suddenly the door opens and Cooper comes walking in, assessing the situation.

"What's going on?"

Of course, Kayla is the first to respond. "Oh, you know. Bentley thought it would be okay to bring some whore around here last night and when she went to leave after he was done with her, she walked out half naked and Bella saw!"

Oh my God! This woman is not going to give it a rest. She doesn't listen to a damn word I say. The next words I say rush out—and immediately I wish I could take them back.

"Look, I said I was sorry fifty damn times! Liz is being understanding about this. Why can't you be? I forgot there is a child here. You act like I purposely brought her here and told her to walk out of my room half naked knowing Bella was out here. Damn it, woman! We both know you're just mad because you said you wanted nothing to do with me, so I went out and found someone who does!"

Yep, I just fucking lied and it is going to totally come back to bite me in the dick later. But, fuck! That woman could test the patience of a damn saint.

Kayla lets out a huff in frustration. She honestly looks like her head is about to explode. Luckily, Liz walks down the hall at this moment and joins us, and then Cooper decides to alleviate the situation.

"Kayla, I have a job opening at the training facility..."

Is this guy serious right now? I don't even know what the hell else he's saying because all I can imagine right now is chopping his head off and stringing it on a light pole. If I have to work with this woman every damn day I might kill her or myself.

"...you girls can stay with me. I have three extra rooms and I promise I won't bring any other women home." Well, isn't he the smart one? I'll have to pat him on the back later for using my shitty situation to his advantage.

Then Kayla shocks the shit out of everyone. "Actually, I think all of us would be too much. How about Liz and Bella stay with you, that way you can spend time with Bella, and I can stay here. It's just temporary. I can handle the whorehouse."

Fucking woman. Of course she has to add that in. However, I must give her credit. She's totally taking one for the team right now, and by team, I mean team Cooper and Liz, because she isn't batting for my team. Although, her staying here means I'll have more time to convince her to let down that cement wall and maybe even get her to thaw out her icy heart.

"I agree with Kayla. It's a good idea."

And it's settled, tomorrow Liz and Bella will be moving in with Cooper, and Kayla will be staying here. Now, I just need to formulate a plan to convince her that love is real.

Five

BENTLEY

Me: Dinner tonight...you and me.

Kayla: NO

Me: Please...just one dinner.

Kayla: Still no.

Me: What time will you be home?

Kayla: None of your business

JESUS, THIS CHICK IS CLEARLY NOT GOING TO MAKE THIS easy. It's been a few days since Liz and Bella moved out, and Kayla is still insisting on giving me the silent treatment.

"What's up?" Caleb comes out of his room dressed in jeans and a shirt with the club logo on it that he works for. He must be heading out to work.

"Nothing, man. Just trying to convince Kayla to go to dinner with me, but of course she isn't having it."

He chuckles at my situation...*fucker.* "So, bring dinner to her. Pick up food and wait for her to get home, and then make her sit with you and eat."

Hmm...Not a bad idea.

He pats me on the shoulder as he walks out. Caleb isn't a man of many words but when he does speak he makes it count. I also noticed him and Kayla have been getting closer. He never hangs out with women so maybe whatever they've both been through has helped him to open up and trust her.

I run out to the store to pick up sushi, some flowers, and candles. If I'm going to bring the dinner to Kayla, I'm going to go all out. I may only have one shot to convince her to give us a chance.

I get home and set it all up. Flowers and candles are spread all over the living room, the food is set out, and now I just have to hope she comes home soon.

As luck—or fate—might have it, Kayla comes strolling through the door not even fifteen minutes later. She closes the door and then stops in her tracks, glancing around the room. After assessing the situation, she looks like she's ready to bolt.

"Please, just one dinner. I got your favorite. California rolls, shrimp tempura, and fried rice, and for dessert, I got mango mocha ice cream."

I hold my breath praying she'll give me a little bit. Standing here right now reminds me of Will Smith in the movie *Hitch.*

'One dance, one look, one kiss, that's all we get...Just one shot to make

the difference between happily-ever-after, and oh-he's-just-some-guy-I went-to-something-with.'

This is my one shot. Five years ago, we were younger and she had been recently hurt, but now this is our moment. If I can just get her to see this could be the beginning of our story, we could have that happily-ever-after.

I'm staring at Kayla as she closes her eyes. It's as if she's afraid to see what's right in front of her, but luck is on my side today because when she opens her eyes, she bites down on her bottom lip and nods slightly. She clearly afraid and I need to handle her with care.

I give her a small encouraging smile and pull her chair out for her. She has a seat and I push it in. I pour us both a glass of white wine to go with our sushi.

"How was your day?" I ask, trying to start up conversation without scaring her away.

"It was good. I started at the gym today. I didn't see you there. Cooper was showing me around and I met a bunch of the guys. I think I'm going to like it there. Everybody seems really nice."

"That's good. I was in the weight room and ring for most of the day. I saw you but wanted to give you some space."

"How is your training going? Are you ready for the upcoming fight?"

I roll my neck and shoulders, remembering the weight training I did today. Getting ready for this fight is putting a lot of strain on my muscles.

"Up until now I haven't taken fighting as seriously as I should so my body is in shock. I know I have a natural talent for fighting because when I fight and try, I win, but the issue is my motivation for it. Unlike a lot of these guys I don't have to win so I do it because I love it."

She nods, showing me she's listening.

"When I moved here to support Cooper, I think being away from my parents and being around his dad pushed me away, but lately I've been feeling that motivation again. Problem is, my body isn't exactly feeling the same way."

We continue to talk while we eat and the conversation flows smoothly. It probably helps that she has several glasses of wine, which appears to loosen her up.

"So, you moved here to go to college?" I ask, hoping she'll open up a little.

"Yeah, when we left you guys in Miami, we came here for college. Liz found out she was pregnant and we could've moved back home, but made the decision to stay here instead."

"I'm glad you stayed. I hate that it took this long for us all to cross paths again, but if you would've moved back it probably never would have happened."

She blushes slightly and shakes her head a little before going back to eating.

Once we're done and have eaten dessert I pour us one last glass of wine and move them to the coffee table in the living room.

"Sorry, I'm sore. I need the comfort of my couch."

She laughs and joins me in the living room. I expect her to sit next to me but instead she pushes me forward and sits behind me, pushing me onto the ground.

"I wouldn't exactly call the floor comfortable," I joke.

She ignores me, so I stay seated on the floor. And then a second later he hands begin to massage my neck and shoulder muscles.

"Holy shit woman, are you trying to kill me?" I say, groaning in pain.

"Physical therapists don't massage for pleasure. We massage to help loosen up the trouble areas. No pain, no gain."

She continues to massage my upper areas, and after a few minutes I can feel my muscles loosening, and it feels good. I think I let out a couple small moans because she chuckles behind me.

"What are you laughing at? This shit feels good."

She moves her hands over my shoulders and over my pecks and I shiver. Suddenly this massage feels a little less medical and a little more sexual. She rubs my pecks up and down and then I feel her breath against my ear.

Before I can turn around she's laying kisses on the side of my neck. My dick stands at attention, realizing where this is going. I mentally tell it to stand down. I'm not about to have another one-night stand with this woman. I want it all.

"Kayla, what are you doing?" Probably a dumb question to ask, but I don't know how else to word it.

"I thought it was obvious..."

I swivel around to face her. Her legs are spread from giving me a massage, so I kneel between her thighs. Like this we're almost at eye-level.

"I know what you're doing. What I mean to ask is where is this going?"

"Um, again, I thought that was obvious."

Okay, I'm going to have to explain myself better.

"Kayla, when I'm with a woman my intentions are to get to know her in hope that something more will come about. I don't sleep around just to sleep around. If we get together I don't want it to just be a one-night thing. I want more. I meant what I said to you five years ago. I believe in love, and I believe you are my forever."

She removes her hands from my body and frowns. I know this isn't going to be good. I grab ahold of her tiny hands and hold them in mine, not wanting our connection to be lost.

"Bentley, you know I don't believe in love or forever, but that doesn't mean we can't have some fun. What we had all those years ago was hot and we can have that again."

I know my dick is going to disown me for this, but...

"No, when we hooked up I felt something." I stop to give her a kiss on her lips. They're so soft, especially when she pouts like she's doing right now. "I still feel something and I think you do, too. I think you're too scared to admit it because you were hurt. The next time we're together physically it will be because you're giving us a real chance." I give her another soft kiss on her lips and then stand.

"Are you seriously going to walk away from having sex with me over some bullshit obsession with love?"

"I'm not walking away and I don't think it's bullshit nor is it an obsession. I believe that you and I could have something real. It would be fucking magical. I care about you and respect you too much to just have sex with you for fun. What we did back in Miami shouldn't have happened. We should have gotten to know each other more first."

I walk over to the entertainment center and glance back at her. She looks pissed, but once I turn on the music from my iPod, her anger morphs into confusion.

"Dance with me," I ask, taking her hands in mine.

She doesn't answer, but she doesn't pull away either. I wrap her up in my arms and begin to sway to lyrics that couldn't be more fitting. Having Kayla in my arms feels like home. I could spend the rest of my life dancing with this woman and be completely content.

After a few minutes, I whisper the lyrics to certain parts of Brad Paisley's *Perfect Storm* in her ear. It's about a man loving a woman so much, it hurts. She's his *perfect storm*. Kayla doesn't say anything, but she puts her head on my chest and lets me sing to her. When the song ends, I tilt my head to meet hers, and holding her chin, I slip my tongue into her mouth for just a second, just long enough to taste her. Then I kiss her with a little more force before pulling back.

"Good night, Kayla."

I don't turn back to see her facial expression and she doesn't say a word. I don't know if I'm doing the right thing here, but I would rather give up the for-now if it means I can have the forever.

I'm in bed, flipping through the channels, when there's a light knock on my door.

"Come in."

Kayla walks into the room and closes the door behind her.

"Can I lay with you?" she asks nervously.

I'm not sure where she's going with this, but I can't say no to her. I'm not sure why, but I get the feeling it took a lot for her to come here.

"Sure," I say, pulling my covers up so she can lie down next to me. I continue flipping through the channels until I come across *Titanic*.

"Wanna watch this?"

"Sure, gotta love a movie that at least portrays the truth about love." She laughs at her own joke. I look at her quizzically not understanding, so she explains.

"You know...Rose chose to love Jack... She chose love and what did it get her? Heartbroken."

"Maybe so, but during the short amount of time together she got to experience a powerful, unconditional love. It was worth the heartache in my opinion."

Kayla yawns and lays her head on my shoulder. "No amount of love is worth getting your heartbroken. Plus, she completely disappointed and alienated her family. What she did was selfish."

I put my arm around her and stroke her hair. Within a minute, I can hear her softly snoring. The more I get to know Kayla the more I realize her anti-love feelings go hand-in-hand with her relationship with her parents. I've watched her with Bella and Liz and can see how selfless she is. There is more to this story, and I have a feeling Kayla rejecting love is more about others and less about herself.

Six

BENTLEY

IT'S UFC FIGHT NIGHT, AND I'M FIGHTING. EVERYBODY IS AT the fight and by everybody I'm referring to Cooper, Kaden, Caleb, Hayley, who is my medic for the fight, and Kayla. Several other guys from Cooper's Fight Club are here as well and Kayla is working with a few of them who are still coming back from an injury since she's the physical therapist for the training facility.

The last couple weeks have been calm compared to the week's prior. Kayla and I have settled into a comfortable truce. Since the night she fell asleep in my room, she has slowly come around and we actually spend time together. It's usually just working out at the gym or watching TV and Caleb is almost always with us, but it's progress, so I'll take it. Also, Cooper and Liz are officially a couple and are heading forward full force. Kayla and I even babysit Bella together while they had a romantic night away just the two of them. I'm hoping that with Liz opening her heart and giving love a chance, Kayla will see can as well.

Of course, once we got to Boulder, shit got crazy. Because what's a trip without drama? Cooper was missing Liz and saw a photo of her all over another guy at a club that she and Ashley were at—Ashley's also a mom and is a teach. His caveman ass flew back to Vegas to claim his woman and luckily it was all a misunderstanding. Now he's back and I'm about to fight against Dante Cobalt. He's an up and coming fighter in the circuit and is currently undefeated with a record of seven-and-zero. My record isn't perfect, but I have more fights under my belt with a record of nine-and-four. We're the main event for the evening so people are going nuts. A lot of people are cheering for Cobalt, but I have a decent fan base, and after I beat his ass tonight, I have no doubt it will grow even more. Regardless, it's a fucking rush being here.

Cooper and Caleb are standing in the corner of the octagon and I'm in the middle facing Cobalt. We bump fists, and then the referee goes over the rules, separates us, and say says, "Ready, ready, fight" and moves out of the way.

Cobalt immediately opens with a leg kick. I see it coming and block it. He does another leg kick and this time I'm not fast enough. He gets the meat of my leg and it hurts like a bitch.

While he's good at striking, I've practiced Brazilian-Ju-Jitsu my entire life and know that to win I need to get him on the ground because that's where my strengths are. He has obviously studied me and knows that his only way of keeping up is to keep striking. I back up a bit to give myself some room.

He comes at me with a strike to my face and grazes my temple. I attempt to strike back but he hits me again right below my eye and

I can feel the blood beginning to trickle down. I quickly strike back, rocking and tagging him and he hits the ground. I've got him. It'll be over in the next thirty seconds. I immediately jump on top of him and start throwing blows to his head. He attempts to cover his face, but it's over. The ref jumps between us and calls the fight. The announcer declares me the champion and the crowd goes fucking crazy. Women are screaming my name, but I only have my eyes on one woman—Kayla.

Cooper and Caleb run out to hug me as they raise my fist in the air, and then Hayley is pulling me toward her to clean up my cuts. I've won many times, but for some reason this win feels different. It feels like everything is finally coming together. If I could just get Kayla to give us a chance, everything would be perfect.

"TO BENTLEY!" WE'RE ALL AT A LOCAL CLUB PARTYING IT UP. I don't even know what round we're on at this point and it doesn't even fucking matter. I won my fight and it feels damn good. Kayla has been eyeing me all night and I'm afraid that soon I won't be able to resist her.

Before I can think further on the subject, she's handing me a shot and sprinkling salt on my wrist. She brings my wrist up to her mouth and licks it slowly. My dick goes hard at the sight of her tongue lapping my skin. She takes the shot out of my hand and downs it, and then takes a lime and puts it into her mouth to sucking it. Jesus. She's going to be the death of me.

She closes the space between us and pulls my neck down to her mouth. After sucking briefly on my neck, she whispers into my ear, "Let's get out of here."

I pull back and assess her. Her eyes aren't dilated and she's not sweating, so I don't think she's wasted, but I ask anyway because I know I'm fucked up right now.

"Are you drunk?"

She smiles wide and says, "Not nearly enough. Let's go."

She grabs my hand and pulls me down the hallway into the ladies' room. I should probably stop this, but I want her so badly. I don't think there's anything I wouldn't give this woman. The word no doesn't seem to exist when it comes to her.

She hops onto the sink and spreads her legs. Her short dress rides up, and when I bend down, I have a clear view of her bare pink pussy. The fucking woman isn't wearing anything under her dress. I pull her to the edge of the sink and begin stroking her clit with my tongue tasting her juices. She's already wet. I don't stand a chance against her, and she knows it. I insert a finger into her core and then another. She's riding my fingers while I continue to lick and suck on her clit.

"Damn, baby, you taste like heaven."

She doesn't say anything, but moans and moves her ass, riding my face with her pussy. I insert one more finger deep inside her and hit the spot I know gets her off. It does exactly what I predict, and within seconds she's coming all over my fingers and tongue. I suck her on her clit, drinking her juices while she comes down from her orgasm.

She grabs my shirt collar and pulls me up to her face.

"Fuck me, Bentley. Please, I need you inside of me now." She hops off the sink and begins to undo the button on my jeans and then works the zipper down.

"Are you sure, Kayla?" I've warned her repeatedly that if we make this jump we're both all in.

"Yes, I'm fucking sure!"

She pulls my face toward her and our mouths collide. When she tastes herself on my lips, she moans into my mouth. *My woman likes it dirty.*

"Kayla, if we do this, you're mine."

She tugs my jeans and boxers to my knees. "Just fuck me now."

And I do. I grab her ass and lift her. She wraps her legs around me and simultaneously wraps her arms around my neck. I push her up against the wall and thrust deep inside her.

"Holy shit, woman," I groan as her warmth and tightness grips my dick.

"Move, Bentley! Fuck me."

I start off slow, fucking her up against the wall. She lowers her shirt, exposing her perfect tits, and I latch onto her nipple with my teeth, sucking hard while I continue to pump in and out of her. I can feel her pussy contracting and know that she'll soon be chasing another orgasm.

I move my body closer to hers and nuzzle my face in her neck, getting close enough to go even deeper inside her. I can feel my orgasm building, so I angle my cock to hit her deep.

"Oh, yes. Bentley, right there. Yes!"

Her pussy tightens around my cock. She's close. I thrust deeper into her tight pussy as we both find our release.

Once we've come down from our highs, I move her back to the sink and set her down. I get a paper towel, wet it, and clean her up.

She sits and watches me and when I'm done I go to give her a kiss but she pulls back.

"What's wrong?" I ask nervously

"You're always so damn sweet to me."

"That's because I love you, Kayla." I take her face in my hands and try to make her understand. This woman means so much to me.

"Bentley, I can't do this." She's shaking her head back and forth and I know I'm losing her once again.

Is she fucking kidding me right now?

"Do what?" I hope I'm wrong, but my gut is telling me I already know the answer to my question.

"I know what you said, but it was in the heat of the moment. I wasn't thinking. You can't love me. You can't say shit like that to me. I'm not capable of love. I don't want love. I'm already a fucking disappointment to my mom as it is. The last thing I need to do is give her another reason to remind me how badly I always fuck up."

Fuck, she's freaking out. I never should have used those words with her. What the hell was I thinking? I can't take it back now.

"Are you serious, Kayla? You knew how I felt. You know how I feel about you. I know we've been drinking, but I fucking asked you. You said okay. Forget your mom, please. Listen to your heart, baby." My voice bounces off the walls, getting louder with every word I speak. I'm fucking hurt and desperate and beyond pissed that I can't make her see what we can have. I should have known she would pull this shit.

She looks at me with remorse in her eyes and says, "I'm sorry but I can't give you anything more."

I see red. I'm drunk and angry and so fucking upset that all I can see is red. If she were a guy, I would fucking deck her. I don't even know how to handle this. I punch the closest thing to me—a paper towel holder. It falls to the ground, making a loud clanking noise. Kayla jumps in fear. I need to walk away.

"Fuck this!" I shout in her face. "Fuck this and fuck you. I don't need this bullshit. You're right. You said you didn't want this and I ignored it thinking you would eventually come around to wanting more. I was wrong. Enjoy your lonely fucking life because I'm done." I slam my fist into the mirror behind her, shattering it to pieces and then storm out.

It's time for me to let go. It is clear she's never going to give us a chance.

IT'S BEEN ABOUT TWO MONTHS SINCE KAYLA AND I HOOKED up and a lot has changed, some good and some not so good. It's Christmas morning and we're standing in Cooper and Liz's new home, although it's more like a damn mansion, as he kisses her like nobody else is in the room. He just proposed and she said yes. On top of that, she announced that she's pregnant with their second child. I'm happy for them. I'm happy they found their forever. Their daughter

Bella doesn't even know what's going on as she chases around her new puppy, Elsa, which she named after the movie *Frozen*. Don't look at me like that...I know Frozen. It may be because the adorable almost five-year-old made me watch it and nobody in their right mind says no to her, but the point is, I know the damn movie.

I look across the room and lock eyes with Kayla. She looks so sad. I would do anything to make her smile, but she doesn't want me to be the man for that job. I look to my left at the arm hooked with my own. The owner of that arm is my girlfriend Sophia. We've been dating for about a month now and it's going okay. She's not Kayla, but she's nice and attentive and wants a future with me. Now, I know what you're thinking. Why did I move on so quickly? Don't judge until you know the whole story...

It was a couple days before Thanksgiving and I had gotten off work and decided to meet Caleb at the local pub for a drink. I was walking through the door with my head down, staring at my phone. Kayla sent me a text saying she needed to talk to me so I was texting her back to find out when and where.

Kayla: ASAP

Me: I'm at Mitch's Pub. Do you want to come here?

Kayla: No, I'll just see you at the apartment.

Me: Okay

I wasn't looking where I was going when I ran into a woman walking toward the restrooms. I almost knocked her to the ground, but luckily I grabbed her arm and caught her before she hit the floor.

"I'm so sorry. I wasn't looking where I was going. Are you okay?"

She gave me a shy smile and nodded. She had pretty green eyes unlike Kayla's light blue and red hair that flowed down her back unlike Kayla's blond hair. She wasn't skinny and toned like Kayla, but had a body shaped like an hourglass. I realized I was comparing her to Kayla and that looks-wise they were exact opposites.

"It's okay. I was in a rush to wash my hands. I spilled my martini on me and my hands are all sticky."

She raised her hands up to show me the invisible stickiness while she scrunched up her nose in disgust. I chuckled at her cuteness.

"I'm Sophia."

"I'm Bentley. Nice to meet you."

"My friend and I are just having a drink at the bar. Would you like to join us?

Now, right here is where a smart man who has feelings for another woman would have said no and walked away, but I never claimed to be smart. I've spent weeks being turned down by Kayla and to be honest it was nice to have a woman who actually wanted to spend time with me.

"Sure. I'm meeting my friend though, so let me make sure it's okay with him."

"Okay, cool! And your friend is totally welcome as well.

She showed me where she and her friend were sitting and I told her I would come over either way to let her know if we would be joining them.

I found Caleb sitting at the bar only a few seats down and told him Sophia and her friend invited us over. He reluctantly said okay and we moved down the few seats to join them.

About thirty minutes later the girls were tipsy. Apparently, they had been drinking for quite a while. I heard a throat clear behind me and when I turned around I saw none other than Kayla standing with her hands on her hips. I didn't get her anger until I realized Sophia was practically sitting on my lap at this point.

"So, I take it you've moved on to your *new* happily-ever-after."

I don't get women and I don't think I ever will. If you really think about this logically, I've pursued the woman the entire time I've known her and been around her, and of course after she has pushed me away repeatedly she decides to get mad when I'm around another woman. It just doesn't make sense.

"We were just having a drink. I thought you said you wanted to talk at home."

"Never mind. I changed my mind. We don't need to talk."

I moved Sophia off my lap and went toward Kayla. This girl has me in fucking knots. I would give anything for her to just give me a chance but she just keeps dicking me around. There's only so much a man can take and I'm sick of acting like a fucking pussy.

"Look, I don't understand why you're mad. You have said repeatedly you don't want me. I'm just trying to move forward. Have you changed your mind?"

"No, like I said, never mind."

She turned around and walked out the door. I should have gone after her, but I was just so fucking tired by the back-and-forth bullshit.

Several hours later, Caleb and I headed home. Sophia asked for my number and I gave it to her. She seemed nice enough, and since she's the opposite of Kayla, maybe it would help me get over her.

I got home to find Kayla in her room with the door shut. I knocked but of course she ignored me. I went to bed and decided it was really time to move on. I couldn't keep doing this.

The next day I received a text from Sophia and replied. We started to text throughout the day and it felt good to text with someone who wasn't annoyed by me.

Kayla, Cooper, and Liz all took off to Florida for Thanksgiving and while talking to Sophia I learned she would be alone. I invited her to join me in Boulder to visit my parents, and Caleb ended up tagging along as well.

We had a good weekend. My parents seemed to like Sophia and she seemed to enjoy herself. A few times she complained about me wanting to spend so much time with my parents and not go out, but I let it go. I've learned most kids don't have the relationship with their parents that I have with mine.

We got back Sunday, and on Monday Sophia asked if I wanted to go to dinner. After I picked her up I realized I forgot my wallet, and instead of her offering to pay, she got an attitude, so I turned around to go home and get my wallet.

"I'll be right back." I jumped out of my car and sprinted back to the apartment. We made reservations and if I didn't hurry we would be late.

I got to the apartment, opened the door, and didn't bother to close it behind me since I would only be a minute. When I came out of my room I saw Sophia and Kayla squaring off.

While glaring at Sophia, Kayla said, "Seriously? You couldn't leave the trash outside?" Whoa! I wasn't sure what her deal was, but she clearly had her claws out and ready to fight.

Before I could get between them, Sophia lunged at Kayla. I grabbed Sophia by the waist and spun her around. Then I looked at Kayla with a *what the fuck* expression on my face.

"Whatever," she hissed before retreating back to her room.

After that day, Caleb came to me and told me Kayla was moving out. As much as I wanted to stop her, I figured it was for the best. I sure as fuck couldn't make her happy, so maybe she would find happiness elsewhere.

I also decided not to bring Sophia to my apartment anymore. Since Kayla would be moving out soon there was no point in starting unnecessary drama.

Now it's Christmas and from what I've heard from Caleb, Kayla has decided to move back to Florida. I'm staring at the girl I know deep down my heart wants and it feels like it's shattering into pieces. I know I have Sophia with me and that we're dating, but I can't help feel like when Kayla leaves, she's ripping my heart out and taking it with her. I can't make her believe in love. I can't make her want a future with me. I can't make her want to give us a chance. All I can do is have faith that maybe one day our paths will cross again and she'll feel the same way I do. I know it's not fair to Sophia, so I make the decision that starting today I'm going to give her my all. The only problem is, my all is nothing more than a broken, mangled heart.

Seven

BENTLEY

Present Day

EVERYBODY IS STARING IN SILENCE, SOPHIA LOOKS LIKE she's about to kill someone and is muttering a string of curse words, and Kayla still hasn't answered my question.

I completely ignore Sophia and ask again. "Is the baby mine?"

I can feel Sophia start to shake and know she's about to explode, so I turn to her and put my hand over her mouth. "Shh...I'm asking Kayla a question. Give me a damn minute." I know it's wrong to lose my patience with her, but I'm a little more concerned with the fact that the woman I was with a few months ago with no protection is standing in her doorway pregnant. I'll deal with Sophia's temper tantrum later.

I turn back to Kayla to ask her for a third time, when she answers. "Yes, I'm pregnant, and yes, you are the father." Liz gasps in the background, but nobody says anything.

"Cooper and I have decided to get married June twentieth. That's why we're here. When you wouldn't join us in Miami, we decided to come to you." Leave it to Liz to break the tension.

"Are you serious right now?" Sophia hisses. She's obviously not about to let this go.

"Soph, chill out."

"No! Are we all just going to stand here and act like this skank didn't just tell you she's pregnant with your kid when you've been with me the last three months? Who gives a shit about when those two are getting married?"

"I don't know who you think you're calling a skank, but I'll knock your ass out if you call me a skank again, and Cooper and Liz getting married is a big deal. So don't ever talk negatively about my best friend again. You need to get the hell off my property." Kayla is fuming and I need to speak to her alone. Nothing is going to get accomplished with Kayla and Sophia anywhere near each other.

I give Liz a *please help me* look and thankfully she gets it.

"I understand this is a shock to everyone, so I'm going to ignore your comment about my wedding. Why don't we all go to the car and give Bentley and Kayla a minute?" She puts her hand on Sophia's back, but she moves out of the way.

"It's probably not even your kid, Bentley. You need to get a paternity test. All she wants you for is your money."

Kayla growls, and I quickly attempt to diffuse the situation before Kayla kicks Sophia's ass.

"Soph, please just go with Liz and everyone. I'll be there in a minute."

She huffs and stomps away with everyone except Caleb. He stays staring at Kayla for a second and she walks up to him and gives him a hug. I know they became close while she was living with us, but I hate that he gets to hug her and I can't.

"Congratulations on your contract with the UFC and on your amazing win," Kayla says.

"Thank you. Congratulations on your baby," Caleb says while continuing to hug her. I never see him touch women let alone hug them.

Kayla pulls away and wipes a tear that's falling down her cheek. "Thank you. You know, you better get prepared because you'll be this baby's Godfather."

If I'm not mistaken, I see tears pool in Caleb's eyes as well, but he just nods his head and walks back to the car.

"Wow, after the baby is born it looks like you'll have two children." Kayla smirks, her eyes lighting up with silent laughter as she refers to Sophia as my child. This is her defense mechanism. I've seen it a hundred times and decide to ignore her comment

I move closer to her without even thinking about it. When she's near me, it's like we're two magnets and I can't help but gravitate toward her.

She swallows hard at my closeness as she tries to look away. I put my thumb and forefinger on her chin and turn her face toward mine. I look into her eyes and see a mixture of emotions. Fear and nervousness, mixed with a little bit of sadness, but my strong girl doesn't let those cling to her for long. Her final emotion is anger. It's her go-to emotion. It's what keeps her strong. If I want answers, I'm going to have to handle her with care.

"When are you due?"

"End of July."

"I thought you were on birth control." It doesn't make sense how this happened.

"Yeah, I was. But then Liz decided not to get her shot and she always scheduled the appointments for us to go together, so I forgot to go, and then when I went to go, they said I was pregnant. I'm sorry."

"Were you going to tell me?" I keep my tone neutral, not letting my frustration show.

"The baby isn't due for several months. We can figure out visitation once the baby comes. I plan to breastfeed so it will be awhile until you can take the baby anyway. I wasn't keeping the baby from you. I just figured until she comes I wouldn't bother you."

She's rambling on, so I know she's nervous. Her face is close to mine, but her eyes are darting everywhere but at me. I turn my face a little to catch her eyes and lock them in place.

"Kayla, you could never bother me. Do you really think I would be okay not knowing about the baby until after she's born?"

"No, I just needed time to figure it out. I went to…" And before she can finish, I hear Sophia coming up the walkway talking some more shit.

"Bentley, I hope you aren't believing a word she's saying. She's conning you. Why can't you see that?" She turns to Kayla. "Once you have a paternity test then we can talk about all this."

She grabs my hand to go, and before I can shake her off me, Kayla glares and slams the door in our faces.

"What the fuck?" I stare at Sophia, shocked at the person I'm seeing. I know this must be a shock to her as well, but I don't get why she's acting so nasty toward Kayla.

The plane ride home is long. Sophia is cuddled into my lap, and even though I'm seriously pissed at the way she acted, I don't bother to push her away. Liz keeps shooting glances my way and I keep looking elsewhere. I know she wants answers, but the truth is I have more questions than answers at this point. All I can think about is that Kayla is carrying my baby. I know Sophia thinks I should get a paternity test, but I know deep down this baby is mine. Kayla isn't like that. She wouldn't say a baby is mine if it wasn't.

I just don't understand why she would move to Florida to be with her parents instead of staying in Vegas with Liz. Her parents are not the nurturing kind and, while I'm sure they would support her, Kayla is independent. She doesn't need anyone. Well, actually, she does, but she would never admit that. Why would she think it's okay to hide a pregnancy from me until the baby is here? I get I can't do anything about it while the baby is in her belly, but I still deserved to know. The more I think, the madder I get. I have a feeling Kayla ran from Vegas to get away from me.

One thing is for sure is when I get off this plane, I'll be giving Kayla a call so we can talk.

Eight

KAYLA

HOLY SHIT! MY HEART IS STILL BEATING A MILLION MILES an hour and it's been hours since everybody left. I was not expecting nor was I prepared for any of this. When Bentley stood inches away from me and touched my chin, I almost lost it. It felt so good to be touched by someone, especially him. I almost gave in. I almost admitted that I wanted to tell him but chickened out when I saw him with Sophia that day at the bar. I know it's my fault. I had my chance, but this just proves my mom's theory. One shouldn't base decisions off love. Both times I went to tell Bentley about the baby, Sophia was there and I didn't want to mess things up for Bentley. I might not be able to stand her, but I can't blame her for being pissed. She got into a relationship thinking it was just Bentley and her, only to find out it's her and Bentley plus baby and baby mama.

After I finish making my sandwich—I have now changed my mind to bananas and mayo—don't knock it until you've tried it—I go back to lying by the pool under the umbrella. I must fall asleep because I wake up to my phone ringing. The caller ID says it's Liz and I internally groan.

Might as well get this over with.

"Hello."

"Hello? That's what you have to say all nonchalantly like I didn't just find out a few hours ago that my best fucking friend is pregnant!"

"I'm sorry?" I say it like a question because I'm not sure what to say.

"Sorry?" I hear Liz's voice break and I know she's about to start crying.

"I'm sorry, Liz. I didn't know what to do, so I ran. I couldn't tell you because I couldn't ask you to keep that secret from Cooper."

"How far along are you?"

"I'm due July 22nd."

The phone goes silent and then I hear a loud squeal.

"Oh. My. God! Kayla! Our babies are going to be like a week apart. Please tell me you're coming home so we can raise them together."

"I'm home, Liz. Las Vegas isn't my home anymore. I'll be back for your wedding, though. You know I wouldn't miss that. However, I'm not moving back to Vegas."

She's quiet for a long beat and then I hear sniffling. "Kayla, your home is here with me and Bella and this new baby. Please don't do this. I need you. You really want to raise the baby around your parents? I can't imagine your mom is thrilled to be a grandmother. I remember all too well the way she acted when she found out I was pregnant. You belong here, in Las Vegas with me. Please."

Damn her and her guilt trips.

"And just so you know, Bentley is seriously pissed at Sophia. I wouldn't be surprised if they break up soon. He was totally scolding her, telling her to never call you names again. I don't even know why he's with her. I think he's just using her to get over you."

My heart warms a bit at the thought of Bentley defending me, and I won't deny that the image of him dumping her makes me a little giddy inside. He can do so much better than her bitchy ass. It sucks that he still hasn't dumped her. What the hell? Why do I even care whether he's with her or not? Oh, I know why. Because I'm a stubborn bitch who is in love with Bentley but is too afraid to give him my heart because I don't want to get hurt again.

"I'll be there for your wedding. Why in the world are you having it so close to your due date anyway?"

"It's the only weekend before the baby comes that there isn't a fight or event going on. I just have to pray this little guy stays in here until after we say, 'I do'." She giggles and it makes me smile. I love to see her happy. My heart tightens because I miss her so much and wish I could see her and be pregnant with her. Liz found out a week ago the baby is a boy, and both her and Cooper are over the moon. I have an appointment next week for an ultrasound and I'm hoping to find out the sex. I think it's a girl, though. I just hate that I'll be doing it alone even if I only have myself to blame for that.

I clear my throat to compose myself. "I'll book my flight now."

"Okay! I can't wait to see you. I love you, Kayla."

"Me, too," I say with as much energy as I can muster up.

While I'm enjoying my sandwich, my phone rings again. This time it's Caleb. While I was living with Bentley and Caleb, we became close.

"Hey there, good looking," I say, hoping to keep it light.

I hear him breathe loudly into the phone and then he says, "Damn Kayla, it hurts you couldn't tell me, but I think I always knew."

My chest constricts. Liz let me off the hook, but Caleb's response makes me realize how badly I messed up running away. My actions are hurting other people.

"I'm sorry. I got scared."

"I get it. I do. But damn, you could have told me. You made it seem like you just couldn't be around Bentley anymore."

I think back to the night I told Caleb I was going to move to Florida.

I was sitting on the couch watching television with Caleb. It was a movie about a woman who is in love with a guy. She had her chance with him but blew it. She has to return years later to attend a funeral and sees that he's married with kids. She's forced to watch him happily kiss his wife and play with his kids. It made me feel sick.

I knew it was my fault that Bentley was dating Sophia. I could have been with him but allowed my fear of being wrong about love keep me away from Bentley, which gave him the opening to move forward.

"Do you believe in love, Caleb?"

He turned to me, lifting his one brow in question.

"Well, do you?"

"I don't know, Kayla. I haven't experienced it myself, so I just don't know."

"I think I'm going to move back to Florida."

He sat up and moved closer to me, looking angry. "Why? Why would you move so far away?"

"Caleb, please don't tell anybody this, but I'm in love with Bentley."

Caleb's head flew back as he laughed loudly, shaking his head back and forth.

"Kayla, we all know you're in love with Bentley. Look, Bentley told me a little about your mom and I get where you're coming from. Bentley has an amazingly close family. We all don't have that. ."

He stopped like he was lost in thought and I wanted to ask him about his family but felt like if he wanted me to know he would tell me.

"I just can't bring myself to be with him. He deserves more than I can give him. I'm broken, while he's perfect."

"I understand being broken, Kayla. But I don't think Bentley cares that you're broken. I think he accepts you just the way you are."

I thought about this for a few minutes and knew he was right but didn't think I could handle if he ever decided he wanted someone who wasn't broken like me. I didn't think I could handle it if I had to listen to my mom tell me I told you so once again.

"I really appreciate our friendship, Caleb." I gave him a small smile as I felt the tears well up. I didn't know when I would see Caleb again.

He nodded. "I don't trust women, Kayla, but I trust you. I don't agree with you leaving, but I get it, and I'm going to miss you."

He moved his hand to mine and patted it softly. Caleb never gave hugs or got close with women, so him patting my hand was kind of a big deal and I knew it. He left his hand there while we watched the woman continue to have her heart broken over and over again. The truth is she only had herself to blame and I could completely relate. I knew I was probably making the wrong choice, but I didn't know how else to protect my heart.

"Are you mad at me, Caleb?" I ask through the phone, praying he isn't. I know he doesn't trust women, and what I did doesn't help the way he would view a woman.

"Oh, Kayla, I'm not mad. I'm hurt but I get it. You ran. You were scared. I can't judge you because me and you are a lot alike. I just don't like to see Bentley hurting. He's a damn good guy."

"I left so I wouldn't hurt him,"

"No, you didn't. You left so he couldn't hurt *you*. There's a difference. Own up to your shit, Kayla."

I can't argue with him. I told myself I was leaving so Bentley could be happy and create a life with a woman who deserves him, but the truth is, I did run. I ran because if I would have stayed he would have wanted a life with me and I didn't want to take the chance of opening my heart up and getting hurt.

Nine

BENTLEY

Me: When is your next doctor's appointment?

Kayla: In two days. Why?

Me: I'm flying out to go. I'll pick you up so we can go together. What time?

Kayla: You don't have to...2 p.m.

Me: I'll be there.

Kayla: Okay

IT'S BEEN ALMOST A WEEK SINCE I FOUND OUT KAYLA IS pregnant, and to say shit has been rocky is an understatement. Things between Sophia and I have gone from okay, to bad, to downright awful. She's currently sitting in my living room watching some stupid reality television show. I know I have to tell her I'm flying out to join Kayla for her doctor's appointment but I also know it's going to lead to an argument and I'm so sick of arguing with her. The past week, every time I text Kayla to see how she's doing, Sophia turns it into an argument.

"Bentley, who are you texting with?" Sophia asks without looking away from the show.

"Kayla. I'm flying out tomorrow to meet her for her doctor's appointment. I should be back in a few days."

She whips her head around and glares at me. "What? You don't even know if the baby is yours! And if you're going, so am I."

"Sophia, I'm not having this argument with you again. I believe Kayla when she says the baby is mine and I'm going to be in his or her life until proven otherwise. I don't think you going would be a good idea. I can't imagine stress is good for the baby."

At this moment, Caleb walks in from the gym, throwing his gear to the side next to the door.

"What's up?" He looks at me, completely ignoring Sophia.

"Nothing much. I'm flying out tomorrow to meet Kayla for an OB appointment. I think we're going to see the baby through ultrasound or some shit."

"Damn, I miss that girl. This place feels so empty without her. Give her a hug for me, please."

Caleb is one of my best friends, but one thing about Caleb is he doesn't talk much, so when he does, it has meaning, and right now I'm getting his meaning loud and clear.

Sophia crosses her arms over her chest and pouts like a child. "Kayla is a nasty slut and the best thing that could happen was her moving away. Why am I the only one who sees the real her?"

Ah, shit. She just had to go there. Caleb is loyal to a fault and he absolutely adores Kayla. This isn't going to be good.

He walks up to her and rakes his gaze up and down her like he's checking her out, but not in a good way, more of a who-the-fuck-do-you-think-you-are way.

"I get you're Bentley's girl, so I've made sure to be nice to you out of respect for him. I listen to you whine and bitch over everything every time you're here, but I ignore it. I listened to you talk shit about my friend in Florida and I let it go because I let Bentley handle it, but now you're in my home and talking shit about one of my best friends and I'm done listening to it. Kayla has made some shitty choices, but she's still a thousand times more of a woman than you'll ever be."

I can tell he's losing his patience with her, so I cut him off. The fact is I've had enough of all this. I need to focus on my baby and Kayla.

"Caleb, can you give Sophia and me some time alone?"

He simply nods and walks to his room, closing the door.

"He's such an asshole. You seriously have the worst friends, Bentley."

"I beg to disagree. Look, Sophia, this just isn't working. I need to focus on my baby and I just don't feel like we're clicking anymore."

She puts her hand on her hip and curls her lip in annoyance. "You mean you have to focus on Kayla?"

"At this point, the baby and Kayla are one in the same. It doesn't even matter. I just know that I can't focus on you."

"Whatever! You'll regret this. She doesn't even want you." She walks around the room and grabs her belongings. She doesn't have much here. I never let her leave anything nor have I offered her a drawer or storage of any kind. I think I always knew it wouldn't work out, but I was so hurt over Kayla I latched on to the closest woman.

She slams the door on her way out and I sit on the couch finally taking a deep, cleansing breath.

Caleb walks out and looks around for Sophia.

"Is she gone?"

"Yeah, she is."

"Good. Bro, how you went from a woman like Kayla to a spoiled little girl like Sophia is beyond me."

"I think that's why I did it. They're exact opposites. I love Kayla so damn much, and I think in the back of my head I knew whoever I was with wouldn't be permanent because Kayla is all I want."

He nods slowly. "Makes sense. Look, Kayla is fragile. She comes across as being tough, but she has a lot of shit going on inside her head. Just go easy on her."

I nod knowing he's right. I'm glad him and Kayla have developed a friendship.

"Have you spoken to her?"

"Yeah, she's a mess. So when do you leave?"

"Tomorrow morning. I think I'm going to hit the gym. How's the training coming along for the fight?"

"Good. I'm working with Kaden more since Cooper semi-retired. He's working me hard. I'm hoping this upcoming fight will help me make a name for myself. Every single person I've fought and beaten has been minor compared to this guy."

"You got this shit, bro." We fist bump and I take off to the gym.

Ten

KAYLA

I'M NERVOUSLY RUNNING AROUND GETTING READY FOR MY doctor's appointment. I've been to every appointment by myself and today Bentley will be joining me. We'll also be seeing the baby through ultrasound and hopefully finding out the sex. He sent me a text this morning to let me know he has arrived and is staying at the Jupiter Beach Resort right down the street from my house, which means he isn't planning to fly back tonight.

I didn't have the guts to ask him if he's still with his girlfriend and if so, if she's with him. I know if my man were flying across the country to go hang out with his baby mama I would be right there by his side. Of course that's just one more reason why I'm single.

There's a knock on the door and I'm so thankful everybody in my house is gone. When I told my mom that Bentley was coming she gave me a huge lecture on not allowing him to steer my emotions. She knows now that I'm definitely not giving the baby up for adoption, but she has made it clear how bad of an idea she thinks it would be for

Bentley and me to get together.

When I open it up, Bentley's standing there. He's dressed in a white collared polo shirt that's tight enough to see the definition of his biceps and muscles but still loose enough that you can only imagine what's underneath. Of course I'm one of the lucky ones that have gotten to see what's underneath and it is pure. Fucking. Perfection. He's wearing dark blue jeans and Nikes. He's the epitome of sex. His hair is grown out just enough that I could pull on it while his face is buried deep between my legs. What the heck am I thinking? It's got to be the pregnancy hormones. I've been turned on like crazy lately. I swear I'm going to have to buy batteries for my vibrator in bulk at this point.

I look into his beautiful dark blue eyes and see laughter. Shaking my head, I try to snap out of my mini-lust daydream but it's too late. It's like he can read my mind.

"You can have this any time you want."

Laughing at his insinuation, I play it cool. "I don't think your girlfriend will be too keen on that idea. Or are you thinking a threesome? She's got quite a temper; I bet she likes it rough in bed."

He closes the space between us and pushes me gently against the door. "One, I don't have a girlfriend. Two, the only person I want to discuss being in bed with me is you. And three, I have no desire to share you with anybody else, man or woman. Got it?"

Well, hot damn. Maybe I won't need my vibrator after all...

"Have you been with anybody since you left?"

For a second I consider lying to him. I hate that Bentley has been with another woman since me, but I go with the truth because I always tell it like it is, and I'm not going to change who I am now.

"No, unlike you, I've only been with one person in the last year and that person is you."

He sighs and shakes his head. "I can't take back being with Sophia. I was hurt by your rejection. You have to know that she'll never compare to you. Nobody will, but fuck, what am I supposed to do when you won't give us a real chance?"

Whoa! Shit is getting way too deep. Time to change the subject.

"Oh, stop. We weren't even together. You can sleep with anybody you want. Yeah, we have crazy chemistry, but it's just sex, Bentley."

He smiles when I mention our chemistry, but it quickly morphs into a frown when I add that last tidbit in, and I immediately want to take it back. I hate to see him sad. It feels like my cold, icy heart thaws just a little bit every time he's around being so sweet to me.

He wraps his arms around my waist. "We're having a baby together, Kayla. You're stuck with me for life. That means I have the rest of our lives to convince you that it's okay to love me. It's okay to have feelings. What that guy did to you was wrong. I don't know what happened, but whatever he did, he was an immature little boy who didn't deserve your heart. And what your mom said was way the fuck wrong. Parents should encourage love not discourage it. One day you'll give me your heart, baby, and it will be nothing short of amazing because love is a beautiful thing."

He gives me a soft kiss on my cheek and then moves me from the door, closing it so we can leave to my appointment. He doesn't even wait for a reply, and that's probably a good thing because what the heck would I say to that? Everything he says is true, but it doesn't stop me from still being afraid.

We arrive at the doctor's office at two on the dot. I sign in and we have a seat in the waiting room. A very pregnant woman with two little kids is sitting just to the left of us. Her kids are playing with blocks and she's rubbing her huge belly.

"Do you want more kids?" I don't know what comes over me when I blurt out this question. I swear I'm blaming all my craziness on my pregnancy hormones.

Bentley grins at me. "Damn, woman, you're still pregnant with our first kid and you're already thinking about having more?"

I smack him on his shoulder and he just laughs. "No! I was just curious how many you plan to have. You are an only child."

"Well, I guess that depends on you. How many do you want?"

I roll my eyes but answer. "I have one brother, but we aren't close. I kind of wish we were. I think it would be nice to have a couple kids. "

He nods and then leans in to me. "Once you admit that you love me, I'll give you as many kids as you want."

I chuckle at that and then smirk. "I'm pretty sure all I need to do is get you drunk and find a bathroom like the last time."

"Kayla, that shit isn't cool." His features are no longer carefree but brooding. I was only joking, but it's clear he doesn't think it's funny.

Once my name is called, we go to the ultrasound room and I get undressed below my waist, lie down on the bed, and leave my stomach bare. The ultrasound tech comes in and says hello while squirting the blue gunk on my belly to do the ultrasound.

Within seconds I hear the *Whoosh. Whoosh. Whoosh,* making me smile. Bentley looks confused, so I explain to him what he's hearing. "That's her heartbeat."

His gaze becomes mesmerized and in awe as he glances from my belly and back to the screen several times.

"So amazing." His lips curl into the biggest grin like he's already in love with her, and I feel like such a piece of shit for attempting to keep all this from him. He deserves to watch our baby grow. She's as much his as she is mine.

"You said baby girl. Did you already find out the sex?" the ultrasound tech asks.

"No, it's just a mother's intuition."

"Well, do you want to know if your intuition is correct?"

I glance at Bentley and he gives me a small smile letting me know he's okay with finding out the sex.

"Yes, please!"

She moves the doppler around my stomach, then stops and presses some buttons to zoom in and get a clearer picture.

"See those three lines right there? You're having a little girl and she's growing right on track with your due date. You were right about your mother's intuition. I'll take a couple screen shots for the doctor to look over more thoroughly and print some up for you to take home."

"Thank you."

"Um, miss," Bentley says to the tech. "Can you print some up for both of us, please? I would like to have some." Bentley looks so uncomfortable asking because it means we aren't going to the same home. I doubt she knows that, but I know that's why he's asking, and I feel horrible. But how do I change the way I feel? How do I open my heart up and risk getting hurt again? I know what happened to me was when I was younger, but the concept doesn't change once you're an adult. If I give me heart to Bentley, I risk being hurt, only this time the stakes are higher because now we have a daughter on the way.

"Sure thing," the tech says brightly.

After I get dressed and she gives us the photos, we head out. I'm thinking Bentley will take me straight home but instead he stops at an Italian restaurant down the street from the OB's office.

"Is this okay? I figured you might be hungry and it's almost dinner time."

"Yeah, sounds good." I feel so guilty I'd probably agree to anything the man wants right now.

We walk into the restaurant and my eyes go straight to the boy—well technically now he's a man—that broke my heart. What are the freaking odds of seeing him here?

Eleven

BENTLEY

THIS AFTERNOON HAS BEEN AMAZING. GETTING TO SEE our precious little girl on the ultrasound screen and hearing her heartbeat is nothing short of a miracle. When Kayla threw it in my face that it was just drunken sex that created our baby, I wanted to punch something, but I let it go. Sometimes when I look at Kayla I think she might be coming around, but then she closes up, and it feels like I have to start again from square one.

We walk into the restaurant for an early dinner at a local Italian restaurant I looked up and read good things about. Kayla is in front of me, and when she stops short before making it to the hostess stand, I run right into her, then grab her from behind to make sure she doesn't fall over.

"Kayla Peterson, is that you?"

A sleazy-looking guy walks up to us, never taking his eyes off Kayla.

"It is you! How are you? What's it been like, ten years?"

I'm still holding onto her and can feel her entire body tense when he speaks to her. I wait for her to say something and when she doesn't, I take over.

"I'm Bentley, and you are?" I hold my hand out to shake his and he shakes mine in return.

"Oh, shit! Aren't you the UFC Fighter? I watched your fight a few months back. My name is Jake."

Kayla is still standing there frozen in place so I continue talking to this guy. "Yeah, that's me. So how do you know Kayla?"

Yeah, I'm talking like she isn't even here, but I don't know what else to do. She isn't saying shit,

"We hung out for a little bit back in high school. Fun times."

"Fun times?" Kayla practically shrieks.

Okay. I guess she's found her voice and it doesn't sound like she would agree with the term fun.

"Fun times?" she repeats. "I wouldn't call you pretending to like me just so you could have sex with me and then dump me right afterward fun times! I wouldn't call you spreading it all over social media fun times, either! Or how about when I told you I loved you and in return you laughed at me and left? Was that fun for you? Because it sure as hell wasn't fun for me! Oh! And how about afterward, when I had to spend the next three years going to school with guys that just wanted me for sex since you told everybody how easy I was before you left for the summer and then ended up moving away? Nope, definitely wouldn't call any of those *fun times.*"

Suddenly it's all making sense—Kayla not believing in love, the guy who broke her heart who she refuses to speak of, her listening to her mom when she told her love doesn't belong in a relationship. The guy who helped make her who she is today is standing right in front of me, with his eyes wide open like the scared little pussy he is, and it's taking everything in me not to deck him straight in his face for everything he's done to Kayla.

"Look, Kayla…" he begins, but I've had enough, so I cut in. I'm not about to sit here and listen to his excuses.

"No, you don't have shit to say to her. I think you did enough. Take your punk ass out of this restaurant and don't even think about this woman again. As a matter of fact, if you ever even see her again you walk the other way. Got me?" I don't bother waiting for his answer. I take Kayla by the hand and lead her to the podium to request a table.

When we sit down, she's visibly shaking. I could ask her to tell me about what happened, but based on what she said to him, I can piece it together enough to know that piece of shit used her for sex and then dumped her. I do have one thing I need to say, though.

"Look, I know you probably don't want to talk about what just happened or what happened all those years ago, but I just need to say one thing."

I wait for her to agree then I continue. "It sucks that I didn't meet you before him because if I would've met you before that asshole, I would have had your heart, and my guess is, it would still be intact and perfect because I would've handled it with care. You may not admit it, but what we have is more than just sex and it didn't just start recently. It started six damn years ago and if I had had you before he tore your heart to shreds and you let your mom get under your skin, I wouldn't have taken it for granted. I'll never take you for granted.

"Every day you live a lie trying to convince yourself love isn't real, you're letting him win. I'm not going to give up on you. Until you're ready to give us a real chance I'll have enough faith for the both of us. I'm here, Kayla, and I'm not going anywhere." I give her a second to let it all sink in and then say, "Now let's eat some food. I'm starving."

She smiles and nods, and I know she gets it.

Twelve

BENTLEY

"SWEETIE, I'M SO GLAD YOU BROKE UP WITH THAT SOPHIA girl."

My mom and dad are in town for the wedding. They're staying at a hotel for the weekend, so I met them at the restaurant attached to the hotel for dinner.

"If you didn't like her why didn't you say something?"

"We just want you happy, Bentley. It isn't our place to judge. How are Kayla and the baby?"

After I found out Kayla was pregnant, I immediately called my parents to let them know. As an only child, my mom has been waiting for the day she'll get a grandchild. Since I told her Kayla is having a girl she has sent me packages of girl shit every day. I hope Kayla allows my mom to be a part of this baby's life. I can't imagine why she wouldn't, though. While Kayla and I still aren't together, we have reached a new understanding. I've flown to Florida for every doctor's appointment and we've reached a level of comfort where we actually laugh and talk and joke around. I can feel her opening up, but she just isn't quite there yet.

I've brought up our living arrangements, but she's hell-bent on living in Florida. I think the lack of affection in her childhood home makes her feel safe because she doesn't have to deal with emotions with her family. Caleb has told me I'm welcome to use the third bedroom as a nursery until I figure out what I'm going to do, so I currently have a crib, bassinet, rocking chair, and other essentials in the room that I'll need for the baby. I know it's wishful thinking that I'll convince Kayla to move here with the baby, but even if she's willing to visit, I want to have everything she needs for her here.

"I think she's good. She flew in today for the wedding as well. Her parents are busy so they won't be going. Work always comes first for them. She flew with Liz's family so at least she wasn't alone on the flight."

"Isn't that her?" I look over to see a very pregnant Kayla walking past the restaurant by herself toward the lobby. While my mom has never met Kayla in person, I've shown her numerous pictures of her.

I jump out of my seat and run over to her.

"Hey!" She looks at me for a moment, confused as to why I'm here.

"My mom and dad are staying here. We just sat down for dinner. Want to join us?"

She looks nervous, and I can tell she's about to say no when my mom walks over to introduce herself. She gives Kayla a hug like she's known her for years. At first Kayla stiffens, but then she relaxes.

"I'm sorry! You don't even know who I am and I'm over here

hugging you! I just feel like I know you already from all the pictures Bentley has shown me of you, and I swear the boy never stops talking about you or the baby. My name is Kathleen. I'm Bentley's mom. The man over there is Ryan, his dad. Do you mind?"

She looks down at Kayla's very pregnant belly wanting to touch it.

"Mom..." I begin, but Kayla cuts me off, giving me a small smile.

"No, it's okay. Go ahead. It's rock hard. She's definitely outgrowing her space in here." She giggles a little and it makes my heart beat faster. She's so damn beautiful.

"Oh, how precious! I can't wait to meet her. Have you seen all the stuff we've sent to Bentley for the baby? If there's anything you don't like, just let me know. Everything is returnable. I just couldn't help myself. Our first grandchild! This is so exciting."

Kayla looks at me with a questioning glance. I've told my mom Kayla is living in Florida, and she knows we aren't together, but I haven't told Kayla about all the stuff I have for the baby.

Kayla gives her another small smile. "Thank you. I'm sure everything is lovely."

My mom gives me a questioning look but doesn't say anything in return. Instead she says, "We are just about to eat. Please say you'll join us. I would love to get to know you better."

Leave it to my mom to ask without actually asking. Kayla obviously can't say no to my mom because she nods and we head back to the table.

My mom introduces Kayla to my dad and then we all order.

"So, Kayla. Have you thought of any names yet?" my mom asks, attempting to keep the conversation light.

"Not really. I'm hoping it will come to me once I see her."

"I'm sure it will. I wasn't sure what we were going to name Bentley until I saw him. Will your parents be there for the delivery?"

"No, I don't think so. They're really busy at work. I'm living with them and they've offered to hire a nanny to help me in the beginning. I found a job near me, but I won't be starting until six weeks after the baby is born. There was no point in starting now and then have to take off once I have her."

"I know we just met, but would it be okay if I was there? I would be honored to be a part of the delivery, and maybe we could stay for a couple weeks?"

"You would fly all the way to Florida just to see the delivery?" Kayla asks with a mixture of shock and awe in her voice.

"Of course we would! I know Bentley will be there and I don't want to intrude, but this is our first grandbaby. I want to see her as much as possible." And this is why I love my mom. She doesn't judge. She just opens her arms for anybody.

"What the hell? I should have guessed this is how it would end." We all turn our heads to see Sophia standing there with her friends. Her hands are on her hips and she looks like she just smelled something rotten. Now that I'm thinking about it, maybe that's just her permanent facial expression. Knowing this is one of Sophia's favorite places to eat, it doesn't surprise me that she's here.

I can see Kayla clam up, not wanting any issues in front of my parents.

"Hello there, Sophia," my mom says. "I'm sorry but we're having dinner. If you need to speak to Bentley, can you please do it another time? I'm getting to know Kayla and the stress isn't good for the baby." *Go Mom!*

Sophia glares at my mom and then around the table, and luckily, deciding this isn't a battle she's going to win, walks away.

"Now where were we?" She gives Kayla a wink and continues talking about the baby. Kayla visibly relaxes and actually starts to speak comfortably with everyone.

After dinner my parents not so subtly retreat back to their room, leaving Kayla and me alone at the table.

"Your parents are really nice, and I swear the entire meal they couldn't keep their hands off each other. It was so adorable" Kayla laughs and I join in. I know I should be embarrassed at my parents' public displays of affection, but I'm not.

"Yeah, I wasn't kidding when I said they still act like teenagers."

There is a short pause and I decide to just say what is on my mind. "I want us to be together."

She gasps and then quickly collects herself. "Bentley, you just got out of a relationship a few months ago, and we're getting along great as friends. Why mess with something that is working?"

"Just because it's working doesn't mean it's for the best. Sure, a Kia will get you from point A to point B but have you ever driven in a Ferrari?"

"Yeah, well I don't think either of us can afford the Ferrari. At least the Kia won't break my bank account."

I move my seat toward her and put my hand on her thigh. She shivers, and I can feel her skin goose bump. I love that I can do that to her. I know she feels what I feel, but she's just so damn stubborn.

"Is there more than what you're telling me?"

She looks a bit taken back at my question, but after a few seconds she answers softly. "Look, Bentley. My mom warned me all those years ago I would get hurt if I lived my life through my heart, and she was right. I had to listen to her tell me how right she was and what an embarrassment I was to the family. I told myself I would never put myself in that position again. Now I'm pregnant and living with my mom listening to her once again tell me how right she was. I can't handle it. You just don't get it."

So it's not just about getting hurt. It's also seeking the approval of her mom. A mom that wouldn't know what love was if it smacked her in the head. I know how it feels to want the approval of your parents. The problem is her mom is only hurting her with her negative notions about love.

"Please. Just have a little faith in us. I can afford the Ferrari and it won't break your bank account. I promise. I know you were hurt, but isn't what we could have together worth the risk? Your mom is wrong about love and you don't need her approval. We can have what my parents have. We can be happy."

She bites her bottom lip so hard it begins to turn white, so I take my thumb and pull it out from her teeth.

"Can I think about it?"

"That's what you said all those years ago on the beach before you ran for your life."

She throws her head back and laughs. "That's true. I did say that and then ran. But I'm not running this time. I promise."

"Okay, will you go to the wedding with me? I know you'll be there with Liz as her maid-of-honor, but will you be my date as well?"

"Okay."

After we finish eating dessert I walk her up to her hotel room. When we get to the door I can tell she's torn as to whether or not to invite me inside. She has her eyes nervously darting everywhere besides at me. After a few seconds, she mumbles something that I can't hear.

"What?" I ask, refusing to give her an out.

This time she speaks loud enough for me to hear but still at a whisper. "Um, do you want to come in and watch a movie or something?"

"Sure, sounds good."

We head into the living room area and have a seat while she excuses herself to go change into something more comfortable. When she comes back she's in a cute matching two-piece pajama set. The tank top rides up and shows a small piece of her belly.

She looks down at herself shyly. "I swear it fit better the other day. It feels like I'm getting bigger by the minute."

"Pregnancy suits you."

"Oh, she's kicking!" She comes over and sits right up against me then takes my hand and places it on her belly. I immediately feel the baby kick, and my heart constricts in my chest.

"Isn't that so cool? There's a baby in here."

I laugh at her comment. "I would hope so! Otherwise you would have some serious explaining to do as to why your stomach is growing outward like that."

"Shut up! You know what I mean. When Liz was pregnant we would sit for hours and feel Bella kicking. It's just so crazy to have a baby kicking in my own belly."

"She's a miracle. Our miracle."

Kayla looks at me with a soft smile. "Yeah, she is."

We spend a few more minutes with our hands on Kayla's stomach feeling our little girl move around. When my fingers touch Kayla's, a jolt of something hits my heart and when I look up I can see it affected her as well. I reluctantly move my hands off her stomach, but not before leaning down and giving my baby a kiss through her mother's belly.

"I love you, baby girl. I can't wait to meet you."

Kayla gives me a small watery smile before looking away toward the television.

We both get comfortable and I flip through the channels until I come across a movie she wants to watch. She yawns and snuggles closer to me and I know it won't be long until she's asleep.

"Thank you, Bentley," she says, sounding half asleep.

"For what?"

"For always being here."

"I'll always be here, Kayla."

I give her a kiss on her forehead and she doesn't even stir. She's already fast asleep.

Thirteen

KAYLA

THE WEDDING DÉCOR IS ABSOLUTELY BEAUTIFUL. LIZ AND Cooper decided to have a small, intimate wedding with just their friends and family and everything is perfect. Because of her being pregnant, she didn't want any type of bachelorette party and of course Cooper didn't want a bachelor party either. The wedding is being held at their house in the backyard, but you wouldn't even be able to tell it's a backyard. The entire area has been transformed into what appears to be an upscale picnic. On the outside of the aisles are bright yellow daisies and pink dahlias. In the center of the reception tables are gorgeous planters with the same flowers, but instead of just water filling each vase, there are sliced lemons, strawberries, and kiwis inside each one to look like pitchers of lemonade.

The linens are light pink and cover country style wooden picnic tables. Next to everyone's plates are designer sunglasses for the sun. There are also little umbrellas sticking out of everybody's cups. On the back of every wooden chair are cute handmade fans that have Cooper and Liz's name on them with the date of the wedding. The reception area is covered with large white tents and on the back where the food will be is the three-tier light pink cake that's filled with different colored summer flowers.

Liz got this idea from their first family outing. Cooper took Bella and her to the park where they had a family picnic. While it is stifling hot here in Las Vegas, the tents all have fans blowing from the top corners so it doesn't feel hot.

Since Bentley and I fell asleep on the couch together last night watching a movie, we decided to go by his place so he could get ready and then head over to the wedding together. After checking out all the beautiful décor, I head back inside Liz's house to find her. Instead I find Bella playing in her dress.

"Hey, pretty girl, you ready?"

"Yup!"

"Where's your mom?"

"She's in her room with Grandma and all the other ladies."

I give her a kiss on her forehead and head to Liz's room. When I walk in I'm immediately choked up. She looks absolutely stunning in her wedding dress. I spent the day with her yesterday, but I wanted to wait to see her dress until today.

She gives me a large smile and hugs me. Our bellies bump and we laugh together. Hayley, Ashley, and Liz's mom laugh at us as well.

I take her aside for a private moment.

"You ready to become Mrs. Cooper?"

"As I'll ever be. Doesn't it seem like so much has changed so quickly?"

I start tearing up and nod. "Yeah, it does, but for the better. I'll never forget all the nights we shared in that tiny apartment studying and playing with Bella. It felt like it was you and me against the world."

A tear runs down her cheek and she wipes it away. "It still is us against the world. The only difference is now we have more people on our side. You just have to let him in, Kay."

"I know. It's just hard. Between not wanting to get hurt and not wanting to hear my mom tell me *I told you so* once again...But hey! This isn't about me. Today is about you. You are about to be married with two kids!"

We both laugh through our tears and give each other one more hug.

"I love you, Liz. You are my best friend. I'm so happy for you."

"I love you, too. I'll always be your best friend. Please just let Bentley in. Stop worrying about your mom and come home. I miss you."

I don't respond because I don't think I can come back here. I've never lied to Liz and I'm not about to start now.

We fix our makeup and then head downstairs to meet the guys. Cooper is already outside at the alter waiting. Bella is the flower girl and running all over holding onto her basket with flowers. The music begins to play and Bella heads down the aisle dropping flowers on to the ground. Since I'm the maid-of-honor and Bentley is the best man, we head down the aisle next. I wrap my arm around Bentley's and let him take the lead.

"You look gorgeous."

I turn my head slightly and laugh softly. "Yeah, right. I look like a damn cow."

He chuckles but then says, "No, you don't. You're glowing. You were sexy before, but seeing you carrying my baby makes you even sexier."

I nearly choke at his honesty. Luckily we make it down the aisle quickly and have to separate so I don't have time to respond. Hayley and Caleb walk down next, and then Ashley and Kaden.

The music changes to the wedding march and Liz walks down the aisle with her father. She's walking so fast people start to chuckle. She realizes what she's doing and blushes. She's so adorable.

The priest begins the ceremony and both Liz and Cooper opt to say their own vows.

"Liz, the moment I met you I knew you were the one. Unfortunately it took us quite a few years to get here, but here we are, six years later, and I don't want to ever imagine my life without you or Bella, or the little guy in your belly waiting to come out..."

I look over at Bentley and he's staring at me with unshed tears in his eyes. I want to believe he's emotional from the words that are being spoken, but the way he's looking at me leads me to believe his emotions are for me. I get a lump in my throat as I listen to Cooper continue.

"...And I promise to always laugh with you and to never go to bed angry. I promise to be patient when you say you'll be ready in fifteen minutes and aren't ready for an hour. I promise to fight for both of us when one of us isn't strong enough to fight, and I promise to remind you every day why giving us a second chance was the best decision you ever made. But most of all, I promise to love you through the storms and the sunshine for the rest of my days. I'm the luckiest fucking guy in the world to get to grow old with you."

Everybody laughs and Cooper apologizes to the priest for his foul language.

"Coop, first of all, I would just like it on record that I never agree to be ready in fifteen minutes."

Bella yells out in agreement. "That's true, Daddy. Mommy keeps saying you're crazy!"

Everybody laughs and then Liz continues. "I promise to try to get ready quicker. Okay, probably not. I don't want to lie in my vows. But I do promise to trust you and respect you. I promise to support you and encourage you. I promise to give you at least one more baby..."

"You said two!"

Everybody laughs again and Bentley smiles at me and then glances down at my belly. Listening to their vows makes me think about my parents' vows. What they must have promised each other, if they made any promises at all. Then my mind goes to Jake and how he didn't want any promises. I was so willing to give him my heart and all he wanted was my body and to make a fool out of me. I look at Bentley and see the emotions in his eyes. Could I have what Liz and Cooper have together? Could I be with Bentley for more than just to raise a baby with? Could we love each other and make promises and keep them without destroying each other, or will we end up with divorce attorneys fighting over assets?

The priest announces Liz and Cooper husband and wife and they kiss. Everybody cheers and claps, and Bella runs up to join her parents. They walk back down the aisle together as a family and we follow after them.

The reception is lovely. Everybody eats and mingles and then the music starts as Liz and Cooper are called onto the makeshift dance floor to have their first dance. They dance closely to *All My Life* by K.C. and Jo Jo. Once their song ends another begins and other couples make their way to the dance floor to dance as well.

Finally it is time to cut the cake. Pieces are passed out and I enjoy the sugary goodness while watching everybody continue to dance.

Bentley comes over, and putting his hand out, says, "May I have this dance?"

I smile and nod and then stand as he takes my hand in his. He walks us to the middle of the dance floor and takes my arms and places them around his neck and then puts his arms around me as much as he can with my protruding belly in the way. We sway to the music without saying a word. For these few minutes it feels like we are in a bubble, just the two of us, and I think about how easy it could be if I would just give in and let this amazing man love me the way he wants to. The song ends and Bentley leans down and whispers in my ear, "Thank you for the dance."

As we're walking away from the dance floor I begin to feel lightheaded. Bentley takes my arm to hold on to me when he feels me stumble. A sudden pain hits my abdomen and I double over grabbing my stomach. Something feels wrong, very wrong. I look up at Bentley and he kneels down next to me. That's when I feel something running down the inside of my leg, and when I swipe my fingers along it, I see blood.

"The baby..." I begin to say, but suddenly everything goes black.

Fourteen

BENTLEY

I'M WALKING KAYLA AWAY FROM THE DANCE FLOOR thinking of ways to convince her to be with me. I saw the look in her eyes while Cooper and Liz were saying their vows and then again while we danced together. Whether she wants to admit it or not, she wants to be loved. She was hurt and is afraid of disappointing her mom, but nonetheless she wants it. Now I just need to convince her to have faith in us.

She begins to stumble a little and I hold onto her. When she bends over I realize something isn't right. I see her wipe blood off her inner thigh and the next thing I know she passes out in my arms.

"Fuck! Somebody call nine-one-one!" I yell while laying her down gently in the grass. As much as I want to pick her up, throw her in my vehicle, and rush her to the hospital, I'm afraid to move her.

Everybody circles around and somebody says that the ambulance is on the way.

"Kayla, wake up. Please baby, just open your eyes." I send up a prayer to the man above that he keeps her close to protect her and our baby.

"Is there a pulse?" I hear Liz ask.

I place my fingers on her neck and feel it faintly. She's sweaty and all clammy, but there's a pulse.

A few minutes later the paramedics arrive and transfer Kayla onto a gurney. I explain what happened and they tell us which hospital they're taking her to.

"I'm going with you. I'm the father." The paramedic nods and I hear my mom and Cooper telling me in the background they will meet us there.

When we get to the hospital, everything happens in fast forward. Kayla is wheeled into a room, still unconscious, and the doctor says that Kayla is experiencing placental abruption and needs a C-section immediately. Because of the blood loss, I'm not allowed in the surgical room and I'm asked to wait in the waiting room.

I walk out to the waiting room to find my parents and all of our friends there. They look at me, waiting for me to say something, and I lose it. The tears are coming down as my mom's arms wrap around me. I feel so fucking helpless.

"Bentley," Liz says. I know she's worried and the stress can't be good for her baby.

My mom lets go of me so I can tell them the little bit that I know. "I don't really know much. The doctor said the bleeding is from placental abruption and because of the loss of blood they're doing an emergency C-section. She was still unconscious when they took her into surgery.

They wouldn't let me go because of her condition. All we can do is wait to hear from the doctor."

I look around to make sure the sweet little girl can't hear all of this. "Where's Bella?"

"Ashley is watching her."

"I'm so sorry about your wedding..."

"Stop it! Our wedding was amazing. What is important right now are Kayla and the baby."

Liz gives me a hug, and I hold on to her like a lifeline, telling her it will all be okay. I keep repeating it over and over again trying to convince myself.

After about an hour, the doctor walks out. "Family of Kayla Peterson?"

We all stand and he comes over to us.

"First off, I want to say that the baby is okay. We performed an emergency cesarean on the mother and she's doing just fine. The nurses are getting her cleaned up and checking her vitals. Even though she was taken a few weeks before her due date her lungs are fully developed and she's doing well. You'll be able to go back and hold her in a few minutes.

"We didn't know what we were working with until we opened up Kayla. Not only did she suffer a placental abruption but she began to hemorrhage which caused her body to go into shock. I tried to stop the bleeding, but when her heart stopped and we had to resuscitate her, I had to make a decision. I performed a partial hysterectomy on Kayla. She's in the labor and delivery ward now in recovery and is in a medically induced coma. Because of the severe bleeding and her going into shock, I felt it was best to allow her body to heal. In the next twenty-four hours we will take her off the medication so she can slowly begin to wake up. Do you have any questions?"

"Is she going to be okay?" Thank God my mom thinks to ask the first question because I'm in shock right now.

"At this point, I believe she's going to make a complete recovery. Because of the partial hysterectomy she won't be able to carry any more children. However, I don't believe she will suffer any long term effects."

"Can we see her?" This time it's Liz who asks the question.

"Once she's situated we can allow two at a time back there to sit with her. She isn't awake and won't start waking up for at least twenty-four hours."

"Thank you, Doctor," my mom says. At least these women are on top of this because I feel lost as hell right now.

The doctor walks back through the sliding glass doors as a nurse walks out. "Father of baby Peterson."

Peterson? My baby girl is a fucking Cruz! But I let it go for now. If have my way, the baby as well as Kayla will be taking my last name sooner rather than later.

"That's me," I speak up, finally finding my voice.

"If you can follow me back, I can introduce you to your little girl, and once we get situated you can bring your family and friends back to see the baby as well."

"Umm...I don't have any idea what I'm doing. Kayla was supposed to be here. I mean, she was supposed to be awake. She said she was going to breastfeed. Can I have my mom come back with me?"

The nurse gives me a small smile. "Sure and don't worry, just because we give the baby formula now doesn't mean the mom can't nurse later."

I look at everyone and see Liz with unshed tears in her eyes. I walk over to her. "I didn't mean to leave you out. I just need my mom. As soon as we get situated, I'll have her come out and get you. I promise."

She nods in understanding and then I follow the nurse back.

When we get to the room, it's quiet. I spot the tiny portable crib and go straight for it. I've never even held a baby before. The nurse stops me before I can pick her up, though.

"Wash your hands first. Newborns have low immune systems so we try to keep germs away as much as possible."

I quickly wash my hands and then walk over to the crib and pick her up like I've held her a million times. I bring her face close to mine and inhale deeply. I can feel the tears welling up as I send a thank you to the man above. This all could have turned out differently, and not for the better.

"Oh, Bentley! She's beautiful!" my mom whispers with excitement. "Let me take a couple of pictures."

I pose with my sweet baby girl for a few pictures before she begins to stir in my arms. I should probably set her down to sleep, but I can't bring myself to let go of her. I find a recliner and sit down with her wrapped in my arms.

She has a small patch of light blonde hair like Kayla's but naturally tanned skin like me. She has Kayla's cute button nose and perfect little lips.

"Hey there sweet girl. I'm your daddy. Your mom can't be here yet but I promise you, you won't be stuck with just me." I laugh through my tears, trying to make light of this situation.

My mom comes over and puts her hand on my leg. "Hey, even if it was just you, she wouldn't be stuck. You are going to be a great dad. Thankfully, Kayla is going to be okay and you both are going to be amazing parents to...oh boy, I guess we don't have a name."

"Kayla said she would name her once she's born. She said she would just know. I can't name the baby for her."

"I understand. For now, we will just call her sweet girl."

"Can you go and get Liz? I'm sure she's going nuts not being able to see the baby."

"Sure, sweetie." She gives me a kiss on my forehead and then bends down to kiss my sweet girl on hers.

A few minutes later Liz walks in and starts to cry. "Oh my goodness, Bentley! She's beautiful and she looks just like the both of you! Can I hold her?"

I hold my daughter tighter in my arms but then give in. I know I'm going to have to share her. My mom laughs and says, "Well, I guess I should have just asked."

Liz takes my sweet girl in her arms and rocks her gently talking to her like all women talk to babies, with that weird goo-goo gaga voice. She continues to sleep soundly through it and I decide now would be a good time to go check on Kayla.

"Would you guys mind staying here with her while I go check on Kayla?"

"Absolutely!"

"Of course!"

Before I leave, I think of something. "Hey Liz, did you call Kayla's parents?"

She gives me a small frown and an eye roll. "Yeah, they said they have court and since she wasn't supposed to give birth for another few weeks they won't be able to make it until then."

I hear a growl and realize it just came from me. "They are both so selfish. I don't get why Kayla would even care about their opinion. They have no idea what love is. I'm going to show Kayla what love is, if it's the last thing I do."

I walk out of the room in search of my woman. She may not know it yet but she's mine, and I'll be damned if her stubborn ass is going back to Florida.

I get to her room, which is on the same floor as our baby's. Because she's in a medically induced coma they put her in her own room instead of her sharing one with our baby. When I walk in there's a nurse taking her vitals. "How is she doing?"

She looks up and smiles at me. "She's doing good. Her blood pressure is steady. If she continues this way, we can start weaning her from the drugs soon so she can start to wake up.

"Would it be okay if I brought our daughter in here to visit her? I know it's probably not normal protocol, but I want them to be close."

"I think we can have that arranged." She gives me a wink and then walks out.

I have a seat next to her bed, taking her hand in mine. Seeing her so quiet and still breaks my heart. Kayla isn't quiet. She's loud and the life of the party.

"Jeez, woman. You definitely gave us all a scare. You can't be doing shit like that. I haven't even convinced you that you love me yet. You can't be trying to leave me. I got to hold our baby and she's absolutely beautiful. She's a perfect mix of the two of us. We need you to get better so you can give her a name, okay? I can't do this without you, Kayla." I sit with her for a little while just watching her chest rise and fall. She's so damn strong, but lying here in this bed hooked up to these monitors she has never looked so fragile. I give her a kiss on her cheek and go to get our sweet girl.

IT'S BEEN TWENTY-FOUR HOURS SINCE OUR LITTLE GIRL was brought into this world and I'm exhausted. I've brought her in to see Kayla several times hoping Kayla knows she's here. I hate that they can't sleep in the same room.

I've spent the night feeding and changing and burping our daughter. I'm in love with this sweet little angel. I don't think I'll ever be able to leave her side. I know Kayla mentioned going back to work. I wonder if she'll mind if I stay home with the baby. I can picture it all: mornings at the park, afternoons visiting Kayla at work. I really think it can work. I just need to convince her. We're currently sitting in Kayla's room when the nurse lets me know they have reduced the medication and Kayla should begin the process of waking up.

"All right, sweet girl. Soon you'll be able to meet your mom and she can give you a name."

Our baby girl looks up at me with the most beautiful midnight blue eyes that match Kayla's. I never thought I could love somebody so quickly, but I swear the moment they set her into my arms, my heart leaped out of my chest, into her palm. There's nothing that compares to the love a parent feels when holding their baby in their arms.

Out of nowhere a loud beeping noises goes off and the monitors start going crazy. The baby is startled and starts crying. Two nurses and a doctor rush in. "Sir, you need to leave."

"What's happening?"

"Sir, we need you to leave now. Once we know more, we will let you know."

I'm removed from the room without even having a chance to put our baby in her rolling crib as the door shuts behind me. I can hear them speaking through the door and I feel so damn helpless as I hold our daughter in my arms, trying to calm her cries and praying that her mother is okay.

"Patient is coding. Grab the defibrillators."

"Clear!"

"There's no response."

"Let's go again."

"And clear!"

Silence

"Okay, we have a pulse."

I let out a breath once I hear Kayla has a heartbeat. After several minutes the door opens and I almost fall backward holding my daughter close to me. Shuffling up the best I can with her in my arms, I say, "Sorry, I didn't even realize I was sitting against the door. Is she okay?"

The nurse nods and leads me back into the room. I put our little girl in her crib and go straight to Kayla to hold her hand, needing to be close to her.

"The patient is okay for now. It seems she went into shock again once we reduced the meds. It's not common but it can happen. We had to resuscitate her once again. Because of the damage it's doing to her heart and body we're going to keep her in a medically induced coma for at least the next seventy-two hours as well as move her to the ICU. Her body needs to rest.

"Okay, thank you."

After they move her to the ICU, I have my mom watch the baby in her room. I hold on to Kayla's hand and pray once again that she's okay. I don't think I've ever prayed so much in my life. I can't do this without her. Our baby girl and I need her in our lives. I don't know how long I sit and pray, but eventually a nurse comes in and puts her hand on my shoulder to get my attention.

"Sir, can you come with us to fill out some paper work? Your daughter will be released from the hospital today."

"Yeah, no problem."

I call my mom and Liz on the way back to the labor and delivery ward and fill them in on what happened with Kayla. Liz tells me she'll come and stay with Kayla while my mom meets me to fill out the paperwork with the baby.

I'VE FINISHED FILLING OUT THE PAPERWORK AND AM waiting to see what happens next. A woman dressed in business attire comes over and introduces herself.

"Hello, I'm Darla, I'm from the data department. I was processing your paperwork but you left out the spot for the baby's name."

"Yeah, her mother is in a coma. She hasn't picked out her name yet."

"I see. Well, unfortunately we can't let the baby leave without a name. You can pick the name now and, if you decide to change it later, you can always fill out a legal name change form."

I look at my precious little girl in my mother's arms and know the name I want for her.

"Faith. Faith Lizbeth Cruz."

"Great. I'll get it filled out and bring the forms out for you to double check and sign and then you can take your little one home."

The woman walks away and I look over to my mom who has tears in her eyes.

"That's a beautiful name, Bentley. I love it."

"Yeah, now I just have to pray that Kayla will be joining us at home sooner rather than later."

"It will all work out, honey. You just have to have Faith."

Fifteen

KAYLA

EVERYTHING FEELS WEIRD. GROGGY. LIKE I'VE BEEN SLEEPING for a long time yet not long enough. There's a faint ringing noise in my ears and I have no idea where I am. My eyes are closed and I want to open them to figure it out, but they won't open. It's as if they're fastened shut. I feel drained, yet I can't remember doing anything that would cause me to feel this way.

"Kayla, baby? Can you hear me?"

I hear Bentley calling my name and want to wake up to find out why, but I'm so tired. I take a deep breath and it feels funny, like there's something in my nose. If I could just open my eyes...

"C'mon woman, please wake up. Faith wants to meet her mommy."

Mommy? Holy shit, I'm pregnant! Well, I was pregnant...Does that mean I gave birth to her? Faith? Is that her name? That's a pretty name. Okay, I just need to open my eyes. On the count of three I'm going to force my eyes to open. One...Two...Three...

I will my eyes to open and they do! Everything is blurry at first, but then it all starts to come into focus. I see Bentley next to me holding a baby. That must be our baby. Oh, thank God, she's okay. I look around and see I'm in a hospital room. Caleb is standing in the corner. Hayley is next to him. Liz is still pregnant, and she's standing next to Cooper, who has his arms wrapped around her. On the other side of me are Kathleen and Ryan, Bentley's parents.

I look back to Bentley and attempt to say something, but I end up choking and coughing. I reach up and feel something in my nostrils. It must be oxygen. I pull it out, so I can breathe the fresh air. Kathleen hands me a cup of water. I take a sip and attempt to speak again.

"What happened?"

Nobody says anything at first and I start to get nervous. The faint beeping starts to go off faster and Bentley looks worried.

"Whoa, sweetheart. Calm down. Everything is okay. You need to remain calm. The doctor should be here soon."

"Please tell me what happened. The last thing I remember is feeling a pain in my stomach at the wedding. I saw blood and then everything went black."

"You suffered from placental abruption and they had to do emergency surgery to take Faith out of you."

"Faith?"

Bentley looks at me sheepishly.

"Yeah, you've been out of it for a while. They had to keep you in a medically induced coma so your body could heal. I had to name her so I could bring her home. I named her Faith Lizbeth Cruz. If you don't like it we can change it."

Faith Lizbeth Cruz. "It's beautiful, Bentley, and you named her after Liz. Thank you. How is she?" I try to sit up, but my stomach muscles throb and I wince from the pain.

"Here, let me help you." The nurse who must have been in the corner where I couldn't see, comes over and presses a button to raise my headrest.

"Thank you." I look over at Bentley and see the beautiful little girl in his arms.

"Can I hold her?"

He smiles and nods. "Absolutely. She's been waiting patiently to meet you."

I take Faith in my arms while Bentley hovers over me. He must be nervous about whatever condition I've been in.

"Hey, sweet girl. I'm your mom." She squirms a little in my arms and I'm immediately in love. She has my blue eyes and nose with Bentley's mouth and skin tone. She's the most beautiful human being I've ever seen. I can't believe Bentley and I created this perfect little person together. She's such a miracle.

I glance up at Bentley and see tears in his eyes. "Why was I in a coma?"

I hear a throat clear and look to Liz. She gives me a sad smile and I know something is off. She walks over and sits next to me, putting my right hand into hers since my left one is holding Faith.

"Your body went into shock and you almost died a few times. You gave us quite the scare. They had to bring you back. Because of the bleeding, they had to do a partial hysterectomy. We are just so thankful you're alive. Bentley has been taking care of Faith and has been at the hospital almost every waking minute checking on you."

I take a second to process everything she just said. I had to have a partial hysterectomy. That means I'll never have another baby. I can feel the tears welling up behind my lids. I know I should feel thankful to be alive and for the fact that my baby is okay, but I also feel broken inside. A piece of me was removed and I won't be able to fix it.

I glance over at Bentley and he's assessing me closely. I go to look away and he grabs my chin. "Don't even fucking think it. You aren't broken." Holy shit! It's like he can read my mind.

"We have Faith and she's perfect, and if you ever want another baby we'll figure it out. We can find a surrogate or adopt. We'll figure it out when the time comes. Don't you even start to think of reasons to push me away."

I look down at my baby girl and he's right. She's perfect, but Bentley and I aren't together. One day he'll meet someone who can love him and give him lots of babies, unlike me, who's broken emotionally and now physically.

"There is no '*we*'."

He just glares at me and lets it go.

I bring my nose to Faith's forehead and breathe in her baby scent.

"She smells good. She doesn't smell like a hospital."

Everybody laughs and Bentley says, "Yeah, well, I gave her her first bath. I think she's like her mother. She loves the water. Every time she's fussy, I put her in the water and she calms right down."

"Yeah, our sink has been transformed into a baby bathtub," Caleb adds with a chuckle.

Kathleen comes over and gives me a kiss on my forehead. "I'm so glad you're okay. Ryan and I have decided to stay here for a while. We're renting a place close by so we can help out until you're on your feet."

"Thank you, but I'm living in Florida. I'm planning to hire a nanny for when I go back to work."

Bentley growls and everybody looks like they're nervous to say anything.

"Why don't we give Bentley and Kayla some time alone to talk?" Cooper speaks up and everybody agrees as they hurry out the door. As they are walking out it, a doctor comes walking in.

"How's my patient doing?" He takes a mini flashlight and points it into my eyes nearly blinding me.

"I'm okay, I think."

"Good." He checks my blood pressure, then pokes and prods my abdomen, while still allowing me to continue to hold my little girl. She really is the most beautiful baby I've ever seen, aside from Bella.

"Everything looks good. You might experience a headache for the next few days from the severe blood loss. That's perfectly normal. Because of the surgery, there's no lifting anything over five pounds for six weeks. If you are taking the pain medications, there's no driving. You'll follow up with your OB in six weeks as well. Also, no intercourse until your six-week checkup. You suffered severe hemorrhaging and I had no choice but to do a partial hysterectomy. I'm sorry. Not all women go into menopause, but if you do, you'll have to be placed on hormone treatments. We can cross that bridge if it comes to that. Unfortunately you won't be able to conceive in the future because I wasn't able to save a fallopian tube, but your body will heal completely. Do you have any questions for me?"

"When can I go home?"

He chuckles softly. "You should be able to get out of here tomorrow sometime. I just want you to stay the night to make sure you continue to remain stable."

"Okay, thank you."

"Congratulations on your little girl."

And with that, he shakes Bentley's hand and walks out the door.

Faith begins to fuss and Bentley reaches over to take her from me. He grabs a bottle and shakes it up, and begins to expertly feed her.

"I know you wanted to breastfeed, but I had to feed her. The doctor said if you would like to start, you can try whenever you're ready."

He seems so hesitant, like he's afraid I'm going to lose it on him, and I suddenly feel so bad for the way I've acted. I was going to have this baby and then let him know about her. Jeez, I'm such a bitch. It's only been a few days, but it's clear he's going to be an amazing dad.

"No, it's okay. It's probably for the best she's bottle-fed. I can see how much you love her and we'll have to figure out a custody agreement. It won't work if I'm breastfeeding her. You deserve to see her. You're her dad."

Bentley's jaw clenches and he glares at me for a second before he speaks. "I know you plan to go back to Florida, but it's not happening. First of all, you can't go anywhere for six weeks. Second of all, you'll be living with me. We are a family and I'm not letting Faith or you leave this state. If you want to go to Florida so damn bad, then I guess I'll have to go with you. Did you notice the people in the room? Did you notice who wasn't in the room? Your parents didn't even bother to show up."

"I wasn't supposed to give birth yet."

"What the fuck does that matter? They are your parents and they should have been here. I'm done sitting back and giving you your space. I love you and I love our daughter. Just give me a damn chance, please."

I know he's right, but it is so hard to open my heart. At least with my parents I know what I'm getting, and it doesn't include my heart broken. I look at him holding our daughter in his arms like she belongs there. She's eating and is so content with him. That's exactly how I feel when I let Bentley in. Content. But I can't let Bentley in like that because he'll eventually break my heart, and when he does, I'll be stuck in his life because of our daughter.

"Look, I'll stay in Las Vegas for the next six weeks, but that's all I can give you. We take care of Faith together as equals, but I can't do a relationship."

Bentley's jaw goes tight and he looks like he's about to explode. He closes his eyes for a few seconds and then opens them. "Okay, I'll take what I can get, but just know that I'm not going to hold my feelings back, and once you see your heart is safe with me, we *will* be a real family."

"I don't want to argue with you. Are we staying in the apartment?"

"Yeah, we are. At least for now. I already have Faith's room done and you can sleep in my room."

"You are expecting me to sleep in the bed with you? You do know I can't have sex for six weeks, right?"

He looks at me like I've just lost my mind and then says, "I don't give a shit about having sex with you. I love you, Kayla. In the next six weeks you're going to see what a real man does when a woman gives her heart over to him, and by the time the six weeks are up, you'll be begging me to make love to you."

I can't help but laugh at his cockiness. "Whatever you say, Bent. Hand me over our daughter. I need to smell her some more."

He laughs and hands her over to me so I can burp her. As I hold her close I glance from my precious little girl to Bentley and back again. Is it possible to really have it all? I guess only time will tell.

There's a knock on the door and Bentley calls whoever it is in. Liz, Cooper, and the rest of the gang all pile back in. They say congratulations and give me hugs and kisses.

Liz comes over and whispers, "Bentley really handled it all while you were out. He could be named father of the year."

I smile and glance at him talking to his parents. "He's an amazing man."

Liz's eyes open wide. "Are you two together?"

"I'm staying at least for the next six weeks and we're going to be living together to take care of Faith, but no, we aren't together. Bentley deserves to be with someone capable of love. I'm not the person for him. Maybe once we're living together and raising Faith together, he'll realize it and move on."

She gives me a big hug and kiss on my cheek. "I'm so glad you are staying and I know you two will work it out. You're meant to be together. You'll see. "

Caleb walks over and gives me a peck on my cheek. "I'm glad you're okay."

"Thanks. Are you ready for us to take over the apartment?"

"I wouldn't have it any other way. I've missed you, Kayla. I'm glad you're back."

I look over at Hayley and see her watching Caleb closely. I know she has a crush on him, but he doesn't really show any interest in her. She sees me eying her and gives me a small smile and wink. I smile back. Caleb would be lucky to snag a woman like Hayley.

Everybody stays for a while and chats while Faith is passed around and doted on. Eventually the nurse comes in and kicks everybody out saying I need rest. As much as I love the company, she's right, I do need the rest. I'm exhausted.

Bentley tells me he's going to go home for a little bit to give Faith a nap and will be back up later after I've rested. I give her a kiss and then close my eyes as I let sleep overtake me.

Sixteen

BENTLEY

IT'S FINALLY TIME TO BRING KAYLA HOME FROM THE hospital. Liz and my mom both offer to watch Faith for me, but there's no way my little girl is leaving my side yet. I'll consider it when she's a little older...Maybe. Caleb and I had all of Kayla's stuff overnighted to our place. Her parents weren't too thrilled, but I didn't really give them much choice when I told them Kayla can't fly anywhere for at least six weeks. They said to let Kayla know they will be down in a few weeks to visit, and thanked me for dealing with the situation. I wanted to yell at them and tell them Kayla almost dying isn't a fucking situation, but kept my mouth shut. They're both a waste of my time and energy.

Kayla's brother, Zach, on the other hand actually seemed genuinely concerned and said he's almost finished with a couple of his summer classes and plans to visit as soon as he takes his finals. I know they aren't close, but I have to wonder if it's more because of their parents and less because of how they feel about each other.

I finish arranging all of Kayla's stuff in my drawers and closet. The woman has a lot of damn clothes. I've just finished organizing her toiletries in our bathroom when I hear the muffled sound of Faith crying through the baby monitor. I grab a bottle from the kitchen on my way to get her. I've learned quickly that my daughter demands to be fed as soon as she wakes up, so I might as well have the bottle in hand.

"Hey there, pretty girl, you ready to go get your mom?"

She wiggles her little arms and legs and I'm pretty sure it's more of the sight of her bottle dangling in my hand and less about picking up her mom, but we can pretend. I change her diaper quickly while she fusses, wanting to be fed, and then sit on the couch to feed her. She tries to suck it all down as fast as possible and cries when I stop her from eating to burp her. She finishes her bottle and I burp her one last time and then buckle her into her car seat.

"Hey there, Mr. Mom." Caleb comes out of his room laughing.

"Ha ha, funny. I'm going to get Kayla from the hospital."

"Nice. I'll probably be at the gym when you get back, but I'll see you guys later I'm sure." He walks over to Faith and gives her a kiss on her forehead before heading out the door. The guy never shows any emotion, but since Kayla and now Faith are around, he's slowly coming out of his shell.

We get to the hospital and Kayla is ready to go. The nurse insists she has to be taken by wheelchair to the car, and once we're there, she opts to sit in the backseat with Faith. I smile as I glance in the rearview mirror at my two favorite girls in the world. They are my life.

"What are you cheesing about?" Kayla asks, when she catches me staring.

"I'm just happy. You both are healthy and okay and you're back living under the same roof as me."

She blushes and scrunches her nose up, making my heart open even more. Vulnerable Kayla doesn't show very often, but when she does, it makes my heart melt.

We get home and get situated. I have Kayla lie on the couch and put Faith in her bassinet next to her so they're close to each other. My phone goes off with texts from our friends and family, asking if we're home and if they can come by. I don't want her to feel too overwhelmed and, if I'm honest, I kind of just want my ladies to myself.

I get Kayla a glass of water and then sit on the other end of the couch, pulling her feet onto my lap. I begin to softly massage her feet as she stares at me with confusion. I ignore her and bring up something I've been thinking a lot about since Faith was born.

"So I've been thinking..."

"Oh boy, that's never good," Kayla says with a laugh. "Is that why you're giving me a foot massage? To butter me up?"

I smile wide and shake my head. "I know you want to go back to work in six weeks. I've been thinking I could stay home with Faith."

Her brows sink together in confusion. "Like a stay-at-home dad?"

"Yeah, like that. I love fighting and I plan to keep working out, but I don't have a contract with the UFC. I'm sure moms who stay home still have hobbies and such, but I want to quit training fulltime and stay home with her. Fighting would just become a hobby."

"But don't you love fighting? And can you afford that? I mean, I make a decent living, and if I decided to stay here, Cooper has already told me I have a job waiting for me, but it's not enough to live comfortably on."

I know right now I should tell her that I'm an extremely wealthy man. I come from old money passed down from generation to generation. I have more money in the bank than I'll ever spend in a lifetime, but for some reason I'm scared to tell Kayla. I don't think she's a gold-digger by any means. As a matter of fact, I think the opposite. I think me having money might scare her and make her run. She's one of the most independent women I've ever met, and if she knew the amount of money I have, and the amount of money our daughter will one day have, I honestly think she would bolt. The truth is, the only people who know about my money are Kaden, Caleb, and Cooper, and they know I don't like for it to be mentioned.

"I do love fighting, but these last few days with Faith...well, I love being home with her more. Plus, I've saved up. It will actually save money since we won't have to pay a nanny. I just can't imagine leaving her with anyone. I want to be the one to be there for her first words, steps...I just love her so damn much. I don't want to leave her with a stranger when I can be here with her."

Kayla's face falls and I think maybe I said something wrong.

"Does it make me a bad mom for wanting to go back to work?" She bites her bottom lip like she's about to cry.

I get up and move to kneel in front of her. "Hey, there is nothing wrong with you going back to work. You love your career and you'll be an amazing mom and still be able to work. We are fortunate that I'm able to stay home with our daughter. If you ever decide you don't want to work and want to stay home please know you always have that option. We can always reassess the situation. "

She laughs softly, but not in a *that's funny* way, but more of a *are you insane*? "So we'll both be without an income and stay home all day with Faith? You do realize babies need things like diapers and formula, which cost money?"

"Woman, when I tell you we are fine, I mean it. Work or don't work. I don't care. You want to move from here into a bigger house? Just pick the place. Whatever you want, I'll handle it. Faith will never want for anything."

"So are we splitting the bills down the middle or what? When I lived here before it was temporary because of the fire, so I didn't pay anything. I don't want to take advantage, especially since you won't be working."

"Kayla, you aren't paying a dime here. Caleb and I have it all covered. For the next six weeks just focus on Faith and getting better, okay?"

When her body visibly relaxes, I realize just how uncomfortable this conversation was for her. "What did you think I was going to say?"

"Well, my parents split everything down the middle, even to this day. Even when we were little, they split the nanny payment because neither of them wanted to stay home, even though they could afford for one of them to. I thought maybe you would want to do the same, and I'm not sure how much this apartment is, but I know it's not in my price range."

"Nothing about us will ever be like your parents. I know they mean well, but this isn't a business arrangement. I love you."

"Bentley..." I know what she's going to say, so I cut her off by giving her a small kiss on her lips to shut her up. Her lips are soft and gentle and they make me want so much more. She pulls away from me with a glare, but when she tries to sit up, she's quickly reminded she just had major surgery.

"Ow!" she cries out.

"Be careful."

"Well, I wouldn't have to be careful if you wouldn't attack me with your mouth!"

"Don't your parents ever kiss?"

"I'm sure they do...They do have needs, but I think right now we need to keep the line clear. I don't want it getting all blurry. Let's just focus on Faith."

I steal another kiss from her and stand, and she looks at me like I'm crazy.

"What? You can do things your way and I'll do things mine," I say as I head to the bathroom, trying discreetly to adjust the hard-on I have going on.

Seventeen

KAYLA

BENTLEY HEADS TO THE BATHROOM WHILE TRYING TO HIDE his erection...like I wouldn't notice the man's large. hard dick sticking straight out while he tries to adjust himself as he walks away. I bring my fingers up to my lips where his just were. Chemistry between Bentley and I has never been the problem. The problem is the fact that Bentley wants more and more leads to heartbreak and embarrassment.

I decide to check out the nursery while Bentley is in the bathroom. The doctor said it's important to walk around as much as possible to work the muscles that had to be cut open for the C-section. I walk past Caleb's room and then Bentley's room and into my old room. It feels like a lifetime ago, but in reality it's only been six months since I moved out.

The room has been transformed into a surfer's oasis. The entire room is painted a beautiful sky blue with a darker blue toward the bottom that makeup the waves. The trim is a tan color, which I'm assuming is to represent the sand. Faith's crib bedding is different shades of pink with multicolored surfboards all over it, and over her crib is a huge adorable umbrella-looking mobile. There's a surfboard hanging over the changing table that has her name written out across it. The rug is a large surfboard, and on the wall are pictures of surfers. When I look closer, I see they aren't just any surfers...they're of me!

"Do you like the room?"

I jump at the sound of Bentley's voice, which is insane because I'm standing in my own daughter's room. It's not like I'm sneaking through his stuff.

"How did you get these pictures of me?" I ask, pointing to them.

He smiles wide clearly proud of himself. "Google. I remembered that guy said a while back you were in various competitions and such, so I searched your name and found some photos from your surfing days."

"When did you have time to do all this? I was only out of it for like a week."

His lips tip into a frown. "Actually, most of this was all done in advance. I wanted Faith to know she always has a place here, and if we were sharing custody I wanted her to have a piece of you when she was away from you and with me."

Damn it, this man definitely does *not* fight fair.

I HAVEN'T LEFT THE HOUSE SINCE I'VE BEEN HOME FROM the hospital and I'm about to crawl out of my skin with aggravation. I need to get out of this house and off this couch! Bentley doesn't leave often, but he leaves at least once a day, usually to get groceries or go to the gym. Sometimes he'll take Faith to visit his parents. Because I can't lift, he takes Faith with him everywhere. Apparently all the guys at the gym absolutely adore her and take turns holding her. I'm not complaining because he has been the perfect partner and father. He takes care of everything and all I have to do is lie here and cuddle with our precious little girl all day, but if I don't get out of here soon I might kill somebody. Okay, yes, I'm being a bit dramatic but you get my point.

Bentley comes walking into the living room freshly showered and looking hot as hell. "My mom wants to host a Fourth of July barbecue at the place they're renting. It has a pool and big backyard, but I told her we aren't up for it..."

"Are you out of your damn mind? Call her back now! Tell her we will be there! I need to get out of this house right now! Right. Freaking. Now!"

He looks at me like I've lost my mind and puts his hands up in surrender, and in his defense I just may have.

"Okay, okay. I didn't know you were feeling this way. We can go. You sure you're up to it? You've only been out of the hospital for a short time."

"I'm definitely good to go. Get me a chair under an umbrella, a nice cold alcoholic beverage, and I'll be perfect."

He smiles and says, "Okay, done."

After we confirmed we were going, I called Liz to invite her family, and then she called everybody else to invite them.

Now I'm lounging out on the amazing back patio of a huge ass house Bentley's parents are renting, listening to music, drinking a Mike's Hard Lemonade, and holding my baby girl while I watch everyone play in the water. Cooper and Bentley are teaching Bella how to chicken fight. Cooper has Bella on his shoulders and Bentley has Ashley's son, Tristan, on his, as they explain the object of the game. The problem is Tristan is refusing to push Bella, saying it's not nice.

"You're raising him right." I say to Ashley, who's lounging in the chair next to me.

"God, I hope so. With me as his primary role model I worry every day."

"Where's his dad?"

"Kayla! Don't be so rude," Liz chirps in.

"Sorry."

"No, it's okay. Umm...Tristan's dad isn't in the picture. He left when Tristan was born. Trust me it's a good thing. It's been hard raising Tristan on my own, but it's better this way. I don't make a lot teaching, but it's enough to support us, and my parents help out when they can."

Her comment makes me think about Bentley and me. I know I could raise Faith on my own, but these last couple weeks watching Bentley with our daughter has changed the way I see things. He's so loving and protective, and after she goes to bed every night he lies on the couch and watches television with me. It feels nice to not feel so alone. I'm just so afraid that if it turns bad I'll have to call my mom to draw up the custody papers.

Nobody says anything and luckily Hayley breaks the awkward

silence. "So, I totally have a crush on Caleb and he won't give me the time of day. I think he's gay."

We all burst out laughing at her comment.

"Just because somebody doesn't want you doesn't mean he's gay!" I say through my laughter. Faith stirs in my arms but quickly goes back to sleep.

"Umm...hello? Have you seen me? I'm hot and a doctor. What's not to want?"

We all laugh harder.

"Honestly, I've never seen Caleb with anyone," Liz says. I think back to all the months I've lived here and the truth is, I don't think he has ever brought someone home.

"Just keep trying. Bentley hasn't given up yet and he's starting to wear me down, although I would never tell him that."

Laughing ensues, until Kathleen walks over.

"Am I interrupting?"

"Oh, no! Just boy talk," I say with a wink.

She sits at the end of the lounge chair and reaches out to grab Faith. I hand her over and then pull my phone out to snap a picture of her cradling her in her arms. I wish my mom were loving and supportive like this.

When I called my parents they told me it would be weeks before they could come and visit and practically blamed me because I had the baby early.

"Kayla, I don't know why you left during your third trimester to go to that wedding. Now you're stuck over there for six weeks."

"It was my best friend's wedding. I wasn't just going to miss it."

"Yeah, well, now you're shacking up with Bentley and I wouldn't be surprised if you two are back together soon, which would be a huge mistake. He's going to break your heart and then when you come crawling back home once again, I'll be the one helping you to figure out the custody arrangements of your daughter. I understood you not going to law school because, let's face it, you didn't have the drive, but to keep making these same mistakes with men is just ridiculous."

Ryan, Bentley's dad, announces the food is ready, bringing me back to the now. Everyone scurries over to the buffet they put together to grab their food. As I go to get up to get mine as well, Bentley stops me.

"I got it. Just stay here." He grabs the back of my face and, before I can stop him, he gives me a big, wet kiss soaking me...from his wet bathing suit! Get your mind out of the gutter.

Bentley's mom looks at me with a smile, not only on her face but in her eyes. "He loves you, you know."

"I know. Has he told you anything about my parents or our arrangement?"

"Yes, we're close. I hope that's okay. He's given me the shortened version I'm sure."

"I just don't know how to love like you guys do."

"Sure you do, sweetie. You just have to open your heart and let him in. He told me you were once hurt. I understand. Ever think maybe everything happens for a reason? Sure, you were hurt, but everything from that point on led you to where you are right now, with a beautiful baby girl and a man who adores you both."

"And what happens when it doesn't work out? What happens when we're just another statistic? Did you know that seventy percent of all marriages fail?"

She laughs softly and then pats my leg. "Oh, sweetie. You can't think like that. All you can do is open your heart and let the ones you love in. Nothing is ever certain, but if you don't even try you won't ever know."

Jeez! Where was she when I was a teenager and needed advice on love?

When I don't say anything, she reaches over and touches my cheek, and for some weird reason it makes me want to cry. I can't even remember the last time my parents actually showed me affection.

"Just think about it. No matter what, you have me. I'll always be here for you, even if it's just as the grandma to Faith and a friend to you."

"How long are you guys staying for?"

"We've decided to buy this place. As much as I love Colorado, I love being near you guys more."

The tears that have been threatening behind my lids, spill over, and she looks at me with concern. But before I can explain, Bentley comes over with our food and sees my tears.

"What the hell happened?" His voice carries, and Faith startles at the loudness and begins to cry.

I take her from Kathleen and put her over my shoulder patting her bottom to calm her down while glaring at Bentley.

"Sorry. I saw you crying. Is everything okay?" I think he's directing the question to me, but he's looking at his mom.

"Hey! Chill out. Your mom told me she's buying this place and it made me happy to know she'll be close by."

"And that caused you to cry?" he asks incredulously.

"Yes! Okay, I guess it's the new mom hormones but when she told me she's staying here, it made me think about the fact that my mom hasn't even made time to meet my daughter yet and your mom is moving here like it's nothing."

The tears start flowing faster and I try to wipe them off my face, but it's no use, they're falling faster than I can catch them.

Kathleen reaches over and wraps her motherly arms around Faith and me and holds me tight while whispering in my ear that it's okay, and for the first time in a long time I feel like it actually is. It also makes me realize that in my twenty-five years my mother has never held me or hugged me like this. If I had to pick a kind of mom to be like, it would definitely be a mom like Liz or Kathleen. It also makes me wonder why the hell I care what my mom thinks. Why do I keep trying to live up to her expectations? Yeah, I was hurt once, but I was young. What if this time around it works out and we live happily ever after?

Faith begins to squirm, letting us know she's ready to eat. Kathleen lets go of me and wipes my tears. I look around and see everybody staring at us and suddenly feel self-conscious. She takes the baby from me and offers to feed her while Bentley and I eat.

The rest of the day is enjoyable. It feels like I've reached a turning point and I'm seeing things in a different light. I want to be more like

Kathleen and less like my mom. I want to fall in love, and I want to be happy.

Bentley announces that it's time to go. I don't want to leave, but it's nearing dusk and Bentley is hell bent on keeping Faith on a schedule, and since he's so adorable about it, I can't say no.

We get home and I jump in the shower while Bentley gives Faith a quick bath and then lays her down in her crib. I get out to find him lying in bed watching Sports Center in nothing but his boxers over the comforter. In my towel, I walk over to the dresser to get my pajamas out of the drawers before I head into the closet to get dressed.

Up until now I've been sleeping on the couch. I've said it's because it's easier to get to the kitchen and bathroom at night, but the truth is I'm afraid to sleep with Bentley. I know his ass isn't going to play fair.

After getting dressed I lie down on the opposite side of the bed.

He rolls toward me and laughs. "Finally decided to join me in bed? Any closer to the edge and you might fall off."

"Yeah, well, my back is starting to get stiff, and since I can walk around now better, and I'm less sore, I don't need to be close to the kitchen and guest bathroom. As for sleeping on the edge...any closer to you and you might try to have your way with me."

"Kayla, I already told you this before. I don't want you for sex, and when we do have sex, it will be you begging me. Now get over here and I'll play with your hair until you fall asleep."

Well, I'm sure as hell not going to argue with that. I scoot closer to Bentley, grab a pillow to put against his hard stomach, and lay my head down on it. He runs his fingers through my hair until I pass out.

Eighteen

KAYLA

TONIGHT, BENTLEY, FAITH, AND I GOING OUT TO DINNER with our friends and family. Liz has officially reached her due date and wants to have one last dinner before they become a family of four. On top of that my parents and brother all came in this morning and are meeting us as well. While Bentley's parents have been completely hands-on and have both been a huge help, my family hasn't even met Faith yet.

I'm getting out of the shower, and about to get dressed, when I hear Bentley talking to someone, which is weird since nobody is here. I listen closer, and I can tell by the sound of his tone, he's talking to Faith. He always makes it a point to soften his tone when he talks to her. Being nosey, I sneak over to the nursery in my towel and see my man sitting in the rocking chair holding our daughter in his arms while he reads to her.

Oh shit! Did I just say *my man*? What I meant to say was that man. He's not mine! Since the first night after the barbeque when

I started to sleep in his bed he hasn't tried anything. Don't get me wrong, he sneaks in an occasional kiss here and there, but he hasn't tried anything major. He has been a complete gentleman. I'm actually starting to wonder if he wants me anymore.

I watch Bentley and Faith for a few minutes as he reads to her, and they're so precious together. She has no idea what he's reading, but she stares at him like he's hung the moon. He stops every so often and smiles at her like she's his entire world. When I watch him like this, doting on our daughter, I can't help but fall more and more for him. He was already damn near perfect, now add in doting father, and I don't stand a freaking chance.

I get dressed and then feed my precious angel while Bentley gets ready. I could hold her forever. I'm definitely going to miss her when I go back to work soon, but luckily Cooper is letting me work the hours I want so I won't have to be away from her for too long. And knowing that she'll be here with Bentley makes me feel even better.

Oh that's right, I forgot to mention I'm staying here in Vegas. Bentley and I sat down one night and talked and decided it's for the best if I stay. I haven't told him I'm seriously considering giving us a real chance yet, but I know that regardless of what happens, my home is here with Liz and Bentley and our friends. Faith deserves to see her daddy every day and I loved my job at the gym. I can't wait to watch Faith and Liz's son grow up together. I also love being close to Kathleen and Ryan. I didn't realize how unfulfilled I felt until everybody around helped fill in the emptiness.

We arrive to the restaurant and are shown to our seats. Everybody is already seated. My mom and dad stand to give me a barely-there hug and an air kiss. It brings me back to the barbeque when Kathleen held me tight and hugged me, showing me what a real mother's hug should be like. I offer to let my mom hold Faith but she declines.

"That's okay. Babies are rarely good in restaurants. We don't want to mess with her. It will be quite embarrassing if she starts crying and ruins everybody's meal. Honestly, I'm surprised you brought her. Have you not found a nanny yet?"

"Um, no, not yet."

Bentley tenses up but keeps quiet. I haven't really spoken to my mom about our plans. I just don't want to listen to her tell me how wrong I am.

I walk around the table and say hello to everyone. Liz gives me a look of sympathy and I walk over and hug her extra tight. We all have a seat and, after the waiter takes our drink orders, the conversation begins. Of course my mom is the one to start it.

"So, Bentley. Kayla tells me you have been home with her since she had the baby. Are you planning to go back to work or just apply for unemployment?" She chuckles at her joke but her tone suggests the question is one meant to be answered.

"Actually, Nancy. I'm not going back to work. At least not any time soon."

I hear her gasp as she asks, "What do you mean by that?"

Bentley clenches his jaw, so I cut in. "Bentley has decided to stay home with Faith. I'm going back to work part-time in a couple of weeks. I've decided to stay living in Las Vegas and go back to work at the gym, and instead of getting a nanny, Bentley wants to stay home with her." I smile big hoping this answer will suffice.

The entire table sits in silence, darting their eyes back and forth like one would do at a tennis match.

"So, your plan is to just live off my daughter?" She aims the question at Bentley but continues to glare at me.

Bentley's mom cuts in with an "Excuse me, but Bentley does *not* need to live off of anyone."

I'm not sure what she means by that, but Bentley shakes his head and asks her to please stay out of it. She nods once and takes a sip of her water.

Bella, in all her innocence, says, "Bentley, you can be a stay-at-home mom like my mom! Daddy said she isn't allowed to go back to work after my baby brother comes. He said he wants her in the kitchen...with no shoes on...cooking...and pregnant again."

Everybody laughs and the awkwardness has been lifted.

"Yeah, well, I might be staying home, but won't be cooking or getting pregnant again anytime soon," Liz chimes in.

I feel a lump in my throat when Liz says this. She will at least have the option. I'll never be pregnant again. Don't get me wrong, I'm not jealous of Liz, just sad I won't ever have that experience again.

Bentley puts his hand on my thigh and leans in close. "Stop thinking like that. We have a beautiful little girl, and whenever you want another baby I'll make it happen."

It's when he says shit like this I just want to go all in. My mom glares at me pointedly and I know she heard his comment.

The rest of the meal goes smoothly and soon everyone is saying goodbye. I give Liz a hug and remind her to call me when she goes into labor. She laughs and says she will. Bentley offers to take Faith home so I can spend some time with my family and I say okay.

We head to the bar and I order a Jack and Coke, knowing I'll need alcohol to get through this.

"Honey, have you thought about all this?" my dad begins.

"Thought about what?"

"Bentley seems like a great dad, but him choosing to stay home and not work doesn't bode well with me. Men don't stay home. They work. Are you on his lease? What if he loses his apartment? Please tell me you at least have your own bank account."

Then my mom jumps in. "And what is with his comment about giving you another baby? I thought you told me your relationship is strictly a mutual arrangement."

Before I can answer either of them, Zach speaks up. "Jesus Christ! Do you guys ever stop? Kayla isn't an idiot and everything in life isn't about money. Damn, this family is so fucked up. Everything isn't a business deal. Just let her be. The guy isn't going to steal her money and take off. Maybe if we were raised by parents instead of nannies Kayla and I would be able to be in an actual relationship instead of pushing everyone away."

We're all frozen in place. All this time I thought Zach felt the same way as my parents, and I'm stunned to learn he doesn't at all. It gives me the assurance I need to allow myself to be open to the possibility of being in a relationship based on feelings. I thought maybe it was just me who was having these ill feelings to toward our parents but clearly he feels the same way.

"To answer your questions, Bentley doesn't let me pay a dime for anything. My income goes to whatever I want. He won't even let me split any of the bills. We're not together in any way other than raising Faith together, but he does want more, and I'm definitely considering it."

My mom nods. "Okay, well, that's good he's somehow paying his way. Just take things slow, please. I really think you should consider writing up a custody agreement and child support arrangement in case things go awry."

I don't even bother to respond because I don't feel like arguing. We move the conversation to the weather and my parents talk about their practice and how busy they are.

We all finally say goodnight and my parents take off to their hotel. They're flying back out in the morning because they have court.

Zach and I stay sitting at the bar after they leave.

"So, were you speaking from experience?" I ask my brother who is currently nursing his Budweiser.

He shakes his head a little and then says, "Yes...No...I don't know. It's just been drilled into us for so long not to get into a relationship with feelings that I feel like I second-guess every move I make."

"Same here. After Jake fucked me up, I never let another guy in. Mom made me feel like I was so stupid and I didn't want her to throw it in my face again. Bentley wants in so badly, but I'm scared. Partly, I'm scared to get hurt..."

Zach finishes my sentence for me. "And partly you're scared that Mom and Dad will say I told you so if things don't work out."

"Yeah." We sit for a few minutes in comfortable silence drinking. It feels like something between us has changed. A wall that was between us has been dropped.

"Will you come and visit more often?" I ask.

He gets off his stool and encloses me in his arms for a bear hug. "I miss you, sis. I'll definitely visit more often. I'm sorry I stayed away. I was afraid you turned out like Mom and Dad, but I think there's still hope for us yet."

He drops me off at the apartment and comes up for a few minutes to dote on Faith before he leaves to go back to his hotel room. Since he only made plans to come for the weekend we make additional plans for him to fly out for a week soon. I can't wait to spend some real time with my brother.

Once he's gone, I lay Faith down in her crib, turn the monitor on, and snuggle up next to Bentley in bed in our usual position. I lay my head down on his chest and he plays with the strands of my hair.

"How did it go with your parents?"

"Okay. They're just all about business. But surprisingly Zach let them have it."

"Good for him."

He moves me from his chest and lies on his side facing me. He traces my shoulder and down my arm with his fingers, giving me goose bumps. His fingers continue down to my thigh and his touch causes my the apex of my thighs to clench. He sees my legs tighten and his eyes dance with laughter at what he's doing to me.

"You know I can't have sex for at least two more weeks."

His face turns serious and then to lust. "There's plenty we can do without having sex."

"I'm pretty sure anything you're talking about isn't part of our arrangement," I say jokingly. I've already made up my mind that I'm going to give Bentley and I a real chance. I just want to tell him in a more romantic way.

"I'm not asking you to marry me, Kayla, but I imagine you have needs that aren't being met. Just let me help you meet them."

He scoots closer, bridging the small gap between us, and brings his lips down to mine. He's definitely right. I do have needs and those needs haven't been met since the night I got pregnant with Faith.

I roll onto my back and Bentley climbs on top of me with his forearms on either side of my head, not letting any of his weight touch me. His lips brush against mine, first softly, but then things start to get more heated.

His tongue slides into my mouth and I suck on it, causing him to moan. I grab him by his short hair and hold his face to mine as we kiss passionately, our lips making love to each other.

Bringing my knee slightly up, I rub against his hard erection while continuing to kiss him. He stops my assault by taking one hand and separating my legs, bringing his knee down to my pussy. He begins to rub my sensitive area through my cotton shorts causing me to become wet.

God! I'm so damn turned on right now. All I want is for this man to touch me and caress me, and never fucking stop.

"Bentley, touch me please. I need you to touch me." I stop our kiss just long enough to get the words out of my mouth.

"My pleasure," he growls, and suddenly he's off my body and his face is down near my pussy. He grips my shorts and panties and pulls them off in one fell swoop while I remove my shirt and bra so I'm completely naked in front of him. I should probably feel self-conscious because I did recently have a baby, but the way he touches me and looks at me like he wants nothing more than to devour me gives me all the confidence I need to be okay with my body.

He starts at my foot, kissing the inside of my sole, and slowly works his way up, placing small, wet kisses up my calf and then my thigh before moving to my inner thigh. I think he's finally going to give me what I so badly need when he bypasses my pussy altogether and goes for my breasts. He first starts off kissing each one then takes one of my nipples in his mouth and closes his lips around it. He alternates between sucking and licking. He sucks so hard it hurts, but then he licks it to soothe away the pain. He moves to my other nipple and gives it the same attention.

My thighs are squeezing so tight, trying to release the pent up tension, I swear I'm going to combust. It doesn't do any good though because Bentley's body is between my legs, so I'm just squeezing his thighs with mine. I know he can feel me pressing into him because he chuckles softly.

"Bentley, please!" I say, fully aware I'm now begging. But holy hell, it's been over nine months. I can't be held accountable for my actions at this point.

He gives me a chaste kiss and then moves his way back down to the area that is in dire need of attention. Separating my pussy lips, he puts his tongue right onto my clit and leaves it there for a second. I'm staring at him and watch him inhale deeply. I go to close my legs, but it's pointless because he's still lying between them.

"What are you doing?" I whisper-yell. I need to make sure our daughter doesn't get woken up before I get attended to.

"I'm smelling your pussy, and woman, I've missed this smell. Fuck, I'm addicted to this smell."

He doesn't give me a chance to respond before his tongue is back on my clit, licking from bottom to top, causing me to squirm and moan. My head falls onto the pillow and I let go, enjoying his mouth pleasuring me. He lifts my butt a little bit and then shocks the hell out of me when he licks my *other* hole, causing me to jump.

"Kayla...Has anybody ever fucked you here?" Him referring to anal sex so nonchalantly has my cheeks heating up. If I barely do feelings, I definitely don't do anal. I would never let a man see me that exposed and vulnerable.

My head pops back up to look at him. "No," I say softly with a shake of my head. His face lights up, and he says, "We don't have time right now, but I'll take you here...and soon." And then he goes back to licking me. He stops at my hole and pokes his tongue in quickly. I want to say it feels like he's violating me, but the truth is it feels good. That shouldn't surprise me, though, because everything this man does to me feels so damn good.

He brings his mouth back up to my clit and focuses his attention there, bringing me close to the edge and then pulling back just enough that I'm ready to lose it. He brings his fingers near my entrance, and just when I think he's forgotten I can't have intercourse and is going to stick them in me, he gathers my juices and brings them to my tight-rimmed hole, getting it all wet.

Has he changed his mind? Is he going to take me right now in the ass? His dick remains in his pants, so I don't think he is. He takes one finger and slowly inserts it into my puckered hole. At first, it feels odd...but as he pushes it in and then slowly pulls it out, it feels like he's massaging my insides. I had no idea anal play could feel this good. While fingerfucking me in my ass, he goes back to my clit. He licks and sucks and slurps up my juices, bringing me closer and closer to the precipice. He must know I'm about to fall because he inserts his finger a little farther into me and licks faster...and I lose it. My body shakes and my pussy convulses as I come harder than I've ever come before, all over his mouth. I bite down on my lip so hard to stay quiet I can taste blood.

I glance down at him as he removes his finger and then sits up on his knees. He then proceeds to make a show of licking my juices from his lips, making it clear how much he wants me in every way.

Without needing to think about it for more than a second, I sit up and grab the button of his pants, so I can return the favor, when the baby monitor goes off with the sounds of Faith crying. Bentley laughs and shakes his head, not an ounce of angry or disappointment showing in his features. He's so selfless, it's scary.

"Go wash your face and hands and I'll grab her," I say as I get up and throw on my shorts.

I walk into her room and Caleb is already standing over the crib holding her.

"Hey there."

He turns around and smiles sheepishly. "Sorry, I heard her crying and couldn't help myself. Plus, based off the noises that were coming from the room I wasn't sure if you would be physically capable of making it out here." He laughs at his own joke, and I playfully swat at him.

"Oh, my God, I thought I was being quiet! And I didn't even know you were home." I'm so mortified that I can't even look Caleb in the eyes. I go to the kitchen and grab a bottle and he hands Faith over to me so I can feed her.

"Hey," he says, his tone now serious. "You have nothing to be embarrassed about. I'm glad you and Bentley are finally together."

"We aren't together," I say. I want to tell Caleb that I plan to change that but feel like I should tell Bentley first. "I feel bad. It's like we're taking up your whole apartment. We should probably look for a place to live so you don't have a baby cramping your style. I just don't know what we can afford with neither of us working right now."

"No way, you aren't cramping anything. You know I love you guys here," he says before he goes back to giving Faith his attention.

Nineteen

BENTLEY

I COME OUT FROM THE BATHROOM AND OVERHEAR KAYLA telling Caleb we aren't together. It's a punch to my gut that she needs to remind everyone around us that she doesn't want me for anything more than to help raise our child. Every time I think I'm making progress she reminds me that she doesn't feel the same way. Maybe it is time to take a step back. A guy can only take so much rejection.

BECAUSE LIZ IS NOW OVERDUE, THEY'RE INDUCING HER today and Kayla has offered to watch Bella for them so their parents can join them at the hospital. I'm giving Faith a bottle when Bella comes barreling into the apartment and jumps on the couch to join me.

"Hey, Uncle Bentley! I'm going to get a baby brother just like Faith but with boy parts!"

She's honestly the most adorable kid I've ever met, and every time she calls me Uncle Bentley I just want to hand over my wallet and tell her to go buy anything her little heart desires.

"I know, sweetie. Are you excited?"

"I'm so excited! And I get to stay with Auntie Kay and you while they have the baby. Will you help me train for the UFC while I'm here?"

Bella is determined to follow in her father's footsteps and one day be a part of the UFC. She's only five years old but swears one day she's going to be the next Ronda Rousey. It drives Liz nuts with worry every time Bella wants to practice her fighting moves, so she put her into mixed-martial-arts classes at the gym Cooper just started up for kids and teens. When he asked me if I would be interested in funding the program I didn't think twice. It's a great program and gets kids off the streets since they're offering it at a discounted and free rate if the family's income qualifies. I'm glad my money can go toward something to help kids.

I lift Faith over my shoulder to burp her. "I'm sure that can be arranged."

"What can be arranged?" Kayla asks, walking through the door from saying bye to Liz and Cooper, so they can head to the hospital. She takes Faith from me so she can lay her down.

"Bella wants to practice some MMA while she's with us."

Kayla smiles wide. She loves how tough Bella is. "That sounds like fun. Why don't you two go to the gym and I'll stay here with Faith. I can order a pizza for when you get back and we can watch a movie. What are you into these days?"

Bella looks like she's just been told she's going to Disney Land. "Yes! Yes! Let's go! I brought a movie with me. I'll show it to you later."

She runs to the door ready to head to the gym. I grab my gym bag and head out with her. We get to the gym and Bella tells me she's going to warm up on the punching bag before we get started. I see Caleb in the ring and join him.

"Yo, Caleb!" I call out. He turns around and nods a quick hello. I jump in the ring and ask if he wants a sparring partner.

"Bring it new daddy." He chuckles.

"Where's Kayla and Faith?" he asks as we circle each other. getting into a rhythm. I punch, he blocks; he punches, I block.

"They're home. I brought Bella here to practice her MMA. She's at the bag warming up." I nod my head toward the bags where the cute little girl is throwing kicks and punches to the bag with all her might, yet the bag doesn't even look like it's being touched.

Caleb looks over and laughs. "That girl is serious about fighting. I took over for Cooper this week, running the kids MMA program, and you should see her. The boys don't want to touch her and it's just making her even madder. I can't imagine being a little girl in a boy's world."

I throw a sweeping kick to the back of Caleb's knee hoping to knock him off balance, but he sees it coming and grapples me to the ground, pinning me down for the fake win.

"Damn, I'm so out of shape," I say through a laugh. "You're getting good, fucker."

Caleb smiles. "Damn right, I am. I'm going to win this upcoming fight. I want it so fucking bad."

He stands first and gives me a hand to pull me up.

"I'm ready!" Bella comes over all cute and sweaty.

"Okay, fighter. Who do you want to fight? Caleb or me?"

She thinks for a second, but before she answers, a boy says, "I'll fight her."

I raise one brow up wondering why the hell this kid wants to fight Bella. He looks older than her but not yet a teenager. I turn to Caleb and he answers my unspoken thoughts.

"Hey, Marco! This is Bentley. Bentley, this is Marco. He's part of the kids MMA program."

"What's up, kid? Why you wanna fight Bella?" I ask out of curiosity.

"Because she's good," Marco says with a shrug. "And she has a better chance of beating me than you two. Plus nobody else wants to fight her because she's a girl."

I look over at Bella and she nods. "If she's okay with it, I am. How old are you?"

Marco puffs out his chest, and I hold back my laughter. "I'm eleven, almost twelve.

"Where are your parents?" I ask, looking around and not seeing anyone but the usual guys working out.

"Umm...well..." Marco looks suddenly nervous and Caleb jumps in.

"Marco's mom works a lot, so Marco comes by after school to practice on days we don't have class. His mom hasn't been by to sign him up yet, but we're letting it slide for now. My only rule is he has to head home before six, so he isn't walking home in the dark. Right,

Marco?"

The kid nods, and I look him up and down with this new knowledge. He's wearing old as fuck shoes that look a size too small. His shirt is definitely old, and based on the brand, it's definitely a hand-me down. His hair looks like it hasn't been cut in a while. He's skinny, like he eats but definitely not more than necessary. This kid isn't taken care of and my heart breaks for him.

Until I had a kid of my own I never even thought about other kids. I can't imagine Faith not being taken care of. Her having to walk home by herself, or me not even knowing where she is. I need to remember to talk to Caleb later about this kid. Maybe there's something more I can do to help.

For the first time, I see how amazing Cooper and Liz are for starting this program. If it weren't for them where would Marco be right now? Out running the streets? Fuck, how many kids are out on the streets because they have nowhere else to go?

I notice a couple other kids and teenagers make their way over to watch the fight. Everybody knows Bella since she practically lives at the gym with her parents.

"All right, looks like we have ourselves a match up," I say, shaking all the thoughts from my head. I'll talk to Caleb later, but I don't want to embarrass the kid by talking about him in front of other people.

Bella puts on her headgear and Caleb gives Marco one to borrow. I stand in the middle of the ring and give them the rules.

"Okay, guys..." Bella clears her throat and glares at me. "And girls," I add, holding back from laughing.

She nods her head once, and I force my laughter down.

"No groin attacks, no knees to the head on a grounded opponent, no head butts, no eye gouging, and no biting. Keep it clean. Got it?"

Both of them say okay and I move out of the way so they can begin. Bella goes straight for Marco and throws a punch to his stomach. He's taller than her so she goes for the area where she can reach. It isn't a hard punch, but he doesn't see it coming and stumbles back with laughter in his eyes.

We all have to respect the girl. She might be the youngest and tiniest one here, but she isn't playing. She knows what she wants and she's going for it. She's determined to earn the respect.

Marco nods in a way that says, *okay, game on*, and I'm suddenly nervous. The kid isn't big, but he's bigger than Bella and could definitely hurt her if he tried.

He throws a punch straight to her face and she ducks and then kicks him. All the guys are now chanting Bella's name and it spurs her on. I pull out my phone and record her to send to her dad. I know he'll get a kick out of this.

After a few minutes of sparring, Marco gets inside and grabs Bella by her shoulders. I can see he's going to bring her down, but instead of just dropping her, he holds on to her, does a foot sweep, and almost helps her fall so she doesn't get hurt. I definitely have respect for this kid. Bella is huffing and puffing, but I know she isn't hurt. It's obvious Marco is a good kid.

Bella wrestles under him and then picks her lower body off the floor to try to push him off her. It's a damn good move, and if she was his size it would probably work, but her tiny body isn't strong enough and he closes her in, grabbing her arm to make her tap out.

They both get up and I expect Bella to cry. She's five years old. I wouldn't blame her. But she surprises me when she throws her headgear off pissed as shit.

"Damn it. I'm never going to be big enough to beat anyone." *Did my sweet innocent little Bella just curse?*

I lock eyes with Caleb and he barks out a laugh. "Clearly she's been hanging out at the gym too long," he says, shaking his head.

"Hey, bite size!" I call out. She looks over at me and glares. "Get your little behind over here and shake hands. You can be pissed, but you don't get to be a poor sport." Yeah, I know. I didn't say shit about the cursing, but c'mon...She's in a gym filled with guys. I can discuss the cursing with her later, away from everyone.

She sighs and walks over to Marco, putting her hand out. "Good fight," she says under her breath.

"You did good, Bella. Don't worry, one day you'll be bigger and you'll definitely kick ass," Marco says to her.

"Thanks," Bella says back, smiling a little.

Everybody congratulates them both on a good fight and then Bella and I gather our stuff to head out. As we're driving out of the parking lot I see Marco walking down the street. I pull up next to him and slow down.

"Need a ride, kid?"

He shakes his head. "Nah, I'm good, but thanks."

I should probably force it, but something tells me this kid is used to being on his own, and I don't want to make him uncomfortable.

"All right, see you later." I drive away and send up a small prayer that he makes it home safe, and another one saying thanks for keeping Faith and Bella safe.

Bella and I get back to the apartment, and shortly after, the pizza arrives. Bella tells Kayla all about her fight and then we all lounge out on the couches to watch a movie. Only Bella would go from trying to beat the shit out of a kid, to watching Beauty and the Beast. I hope Faith is just like her.

Twenty

KAYLA

I'M CURRENTLY SITTING IN LIZ AND COOPER'S LIVING ROOM giving baby Nathan kisses all over his face. They named him Nathan Liam Cooper. Nathan is Liz's favorite character from One Tree Hill and Liam is Cooper's real name. How she convinced him to name his child after a guy she used to crush on I'll never know. Actually, I do. Cooper is the same way with Liz as Bentley is with me. They would give us the world if they could.

Speaking of Bentley, we still aren't together. Remember when I said I wanted to tell him I want to give us a real chance in a romantic way? Well, apparently finding time for romance with an infant is easier said than done, and I still haven't told him. Also, since the night he went down on me and didn't get anything in return, he has been acting super weird. Every night when I try to return the favor he makes up some excuse as to why we can't do anything.

Hayley comes walking in the door to join us.

"I'm bored." She pouts and plops onto the couch, taking Nathan from me.

"Don't look at me," Liz says. "I just had a baby. I'm not moving from this couch."

"Kayla, come out with me, please," Hayley begs while cooing at Nathan.

"Where to?" I ask.

"We could go to the club Caleb works at," Hayley says slyly, and I know where she's going with this. I'll totally go along with this. I don't really want to go out, but I'm happy to be Hayley's wing woman.

"Okay, I'm down. Text Ashley to see if she wants to join."

"Join who, where?" Bentley asks, walking in holding a sleeping Faith in his arms.

"We're going to go to a club tonight. Want to go?"

"Are you sure you are up for that?" Cooper chimes in, looking at Liz.

"Oh no, we aren't going. Those two crazies are going. I'm staying right here in my comfy pajamas," Liz says with a laugh.

"I'll go," Bentley says. "My parents would love to watch Faith."

"Okay, Ashley is good to go and Kaden is joining as well," Hayley adds, looking up from her phone.

We spend the rest of the afternoon sipping coffee and cuddling with our babies while the guys go to the gym to work out. Once it starts getting late Hayley heads home to get changed, as do Bentley and I.

After we drop Faith off with Bentley's parents, we head to the club on the strip Caleb works at. He's actually off tonight but is still joining us. Since he works there, he's able to get us in as VIP. I have to admit that I'm looking and feeling good. For just having a baby not too long ago I'm rocking this dress. Sure, it's a couple sizes bigger than my pre-pregnancy ones, but I'm still rocking the shit out of it. Of course Ashley and Hayley look hot as hell.

Bentley invited a few of the other guys aside from our usual group so there's a bunch of women I don't know and some I don't really care to know. We're hanging out in the VIP area chatting with everyone, and every so often a woman approaches Bentley asking him to dance, but so far he has said no.

"Let's play a game!" Hayley's drunken ass shouts over the music.

"A game? What are we, five?" Kaden asks, laughing.

Ashley smacks him in the chest. I'll have to ask Ashley later if anything has happened with them yet.

"What game?" I ask.

"Hmm...Let's play truth or dare." Clearly the alcohol has gotten to her head but what the hell.

Ashley chimes in, "I want to play!"

A bunch of other people chilling with us say they're down to play as well. Give a bunch of grown adults alcohol and it's like we're teenagers all over again.

"I'll go first," I say because if you can't beat 'em you might as well join 'em.

"Caleb, truth or dare?" He glares at me and I laugh. I mean, c'mon, the guy holds his secrets in like Fort Knox.

"Dare." Dammit, I was hoping to ask him something. I look over at

Hayley and it hits me.

"I dare you to kiss Hayley." She's now glaring at me and I take a shot and crack up. I think I'm going to like this game.

"You don't have to..." she begins to say, but before she can get the sentence out, Caleb has his mouth on hers, and holy shit! The guy looks like he can kiss. There is some definite tongue action going on there while his fingers are in her hair holding her face to his. He's clearly into this kiss, and he's most definitely. Not. Gay. Everybody hoots and hollers and cheers them on.

The kiss ends and Hayley looks like she's going to pass out. I give her a small wink and she winks back. Girls have to have each other's backs.

"Okay, Caleb. Since you did the dare, it's your turn," Ashley says.

Caleb looks around and then says to one of the groupie girls I don't know, "Samantha, truth or dare?"

She giggles and says, "Truth."

"Okay. What's the craziest thing you've ever done?

She, of course, giggles as she says, "Umm...probably the time I had a threesome in the bathroom at the club."

Her friends all laugh and I throw up a little in my mouth. Please tell me I never acted like that, at least not that bad.

After they're done laughing, she looks to her friend sitting next to her and asks, "Truth or dare?"

"Dare," her ditzy friend says.

"I dare you to kiss Bentley." *Is this bitch for real?*

Hayley jumps in, "No daring couples to do sexual stuff with other people. That shit isn't cool."

The ditzy bitch says, "Yeah, but Bentley is single, right?" Fuckin' A, I'm about to cut a bitch! But I'm not about to let my anger show. I'm too mature to play these silly games.

Everybody turns to me. "Bentley can kiss whoever he wants," I say flatly. "Anyway, I'm going downstairs to dance." I walk away without looking back. I might be great at hiding my feelings, but I'm not about to watch him make out with someone else. Why did I put off telling him how I feel? Will I ever get this shit right?

I get downstairs and go to the center of the dance floor. I'm dancing for a few minutes when hands grip my waist. I swivel around to tell the person to back the fuck off when I see it's Bentley.

"Enjoy your kiss?" I sneer. Okay, I guess I'm not as mature as I thought.

"I don't know. I'll tell you in a minute." And then his mouth devours mine—tasting me, coaxing my tongue to duel with his. He tastes sweet like the liquor he was drinking mixed with something all his own. I wrap my arms around his neck and his hands move to my ass, grabbing it and pulling me closer. All too soon the kiss ends, leaving me breathless.

"I would say I enjoyed it very much." He winks and then walks off the dance floor.

Damn that man! I seriously need to tell him I want more.

We go back up to the booths where everyone is sitting and I notice the girls from earlier are all gone. When I glance over at Hayley, she laughs and walks over to me. Whispering into my ear, she says, "After you walked away, Bentley made it clear to anybody in hearing range that he's taken, and ended the game before he walked away to find you. The girls all got bored and left."

Twenty-One

BENTLEY

I'M WATCHING HAYLEY AND KAYLA WHISPER OVER IN THE booth and all I can think about is the kiss we shared. I seriously walk around with a hard-on ninety percent of the time I'm around Kayla. She looks amazing tonight in that navy blue off the shoulder dress she's wearing. You wouldn't even be able to tell she recently gave birth. Her body isn't the same as it was before she got pregnant. She definitely has curves, but every curve on this woman is sexy. Her thicker body reminds me every day that she carried our baby in her.

I can feel her giving in soon. I just need to hold out a little while longer and I'll have her.

Kaden orders a bottle of tequila and has the waitress bring over salt and limes to go with it. Before we know it, we're all downing shots.

"Remember the last time I took a shot off you?" Kayla whispers into my ear right before licking the salt off my neck she just placed there.

"Yeah, I think so," I say slowly. It's hard to concentrate with her mouth on my body.

"Mmm...it's the night we created Faith. If you want, I can give you a repeat performance." She waggles her eyebrows then tips her head back to take the shot.

I laugh at her brazen remarks. "As much as I enjoyed that night, you aren't cleared to do anything of that nature yet." I give her a kiss on the tip of her nose and wink, and then walk away once again. Damn, I love having the last word.

Twenty-Two

KAYLA

I'VE BEEN BACK TO WORK FOR A FEW DAYS AND I WOULD BE lying if I said all is well. First of all, I'm missing my little girl like crazy. I know she's safe with Bentley, but it doesn't change the fact that I'm wishing it was me home with her. I love my job, but I also love being home with Faith.

Second of all, Bentley is still totally playing hard to get. I need to get him alone so I can make sure he still wants to be with me and tell him I want more than what our current arrangement is.

I call Hayley to see if she would be willing to watch Faith. Normally I would call Liz, but after I saw Caleb kiss Hayley I think maybe forcing them into a room together might be a good idea.

I hit the Bluetooth button to call Hayley and she answers on the first ring.

"Hey, chica! How's it going?" Her voice fills my vehicle.

"What the hell are you so chipper about?"

She cracks up laughing and says, "Nothing really. Just got in and

I'm watching Caleb without a shirt on working out."

"Jeez, you have it so bad. I just left work. I must have just missed you. I have a favor to ask you."

"Okay?" she says, drawing out the word.

"Can you and Caleb watch Faith for us for the night? Bentley's birthday is coming up and I was thinking I could take him out for the night."

I hear Hayley's laughter coming through the speaker. " You mean you are going to try to seduce his ass."

"No!" I yell way too loudly.

"Oh my God, Kayla. You know he isn't going to sleep with you until you agree to really be with him." I want to tell her I'm planning to be with him but again, I want to tell Bentley first. The guy has spent months begging me to be with him. He deserves to be the first one I have this conversation with.

"Can you just watch her please? It will give you an entire night with Caleb." The line goes quiet, and I know I have her.

"Okay, I'll be there tomorrow night. But you need to let Caleb know we're babysitting together. I swear he doesn't even know I exist. Other than that one kiss from the dare he hasn't even acknowledged me."

"He does know you exist. I think he's just weird about women. I couldn't believe he even kissed you. I've never seen him kiss any woman, but damn, it was hot. Don't worry. I'll let him know. Come over tomorrow at four o'clock. Caleb doesn't work at the club on Wednesdays."

She says okay and we hang up. I call up the Mirage Las Vegas and make reservations for tomorrow night. I should tell Bentley what we're doing but decide it'll be a birthday surprise since his birthday is this week. Then I stop by *Agent Provocateur* to pick up some much needed lingerie. I want the night to be amazing.

I get home to find dinner on the table and the apartment quiet.

"Hello? Anybody home?"

Bentley walks down the hall in nothing but sweatpants, which are hanging low, showing off his sexy as hell body. My insides tighten, and if it were possible, I would totally have a lady boner. He just smirks and puts a finger to his lips to shush me.

"Faith is asleep. I made dinner. I thought you would be home sooner, but I can heat it back up real quick."

I look at the table and there are two plates of delicious-looking lasagna, two bowls filled with salad, and Italian bread.

"Did you make all this?"

"He grins and nods. "Yeah, I looked up the recipe online and made it earlier while Faith was having her morning nap. I just had to throw it in the oven once it was time to bake it. I should have asked if you were going to be late." He grabs the two plates and brings them over to the microwave to reheat them.

"I'm sorry," I tell him. "Next time I'll call when I'm going to be late. I stopped at the store to pick something up." And then I hurry and change the subject before he can ask what I bought. I don't want to give anything away. "This smells so good. Thank you."

"No problem."

We sit at the table with our plates of food and begin to eat. I look around and see the place is spotless and smells freshly cleaned. The clothes on the table are folded and ready to be put away.

"You were busy today," I comment, nodding toward the clothes.

"Yeah, it's just about finding a schedule. Faith is a really good baby. My mom also came over for a little bit and played with her while I got some stuff done."

I don't know what comes over me, but tears start pouring out of my eyes and I'm ugly crying. Bentley gets out of his seat and comes over and hugs me.

"Woman, what is the matter with you? It's just folded laundry. I promise I didn't ruin anything," he jokes.

"I-I think it's my hormones. I just feel so emotional. I miss Faith so much. I love my job, but I miss her. You get to spend all day with her and you don't even need help. My parents never did any of this themselves."

"Shh...it's okay," Bentley says, continuing to hold me. He backs away a little bit and gives me a small smile.

"You just started back to work. You're on new medications that are most likely affecting your emotions. You are a wonderful mom and there is nothing wrong with you working. Once things get situated, Faith and I will even come to visit you at work, okay? It's all good."

I sniffle loudly. "Okay, I'm sorry. It's just going to take some getting used to, I guess."

He gives me a kiss on my forehead, and I wish he were kissing my lips. Hopefully starting tomorrow night things will change between us.

"You have nothing to be sorry for. Now let's eat."

EVERYTHING IS PACKED. I HAVE THE LINGERIE, BATHING suits for the hot tub, change of clothes, and toiletries for both of us in a suitcase by the door waiting for Bentley to get home. When I spoke with Kathleen and told her my plans, we decided to do a dinner for Bentley this weekend with everyone. Since she wanted to see him on his actual birthday, he went over there with Faith this afternoon to visit and should be back anytime now.

Caleb comes out of the guest bathroom in his towel, and before I can ask why he's showering in there, he says, "Sorry, my bathroom has a small leak. Maintenance is coming to fix it, but I figured it would be best to shower in the guest bathroom until they do."

As he's explaining himself, there's a knock at the door and without thinking about it, I open it up to let Hayley in. She spots Caleb immediately and her entire face turns beet red. Caleb looks uncomfortable and hurries to his room.

"Oh my God! You get to see that fine specimen of a man like that every day? Did you see his tattoos? Holy shit!" Hayley whispers rather loudly.

"I guess his shower is broken. He doesn't usually walk around like that." I glance back to Caleb's door wondering why he's so uncomfortable around women. I really need to corner him and ask him what's up.

Caleb comes back out dressed in a Henley and jeans and sits on the couch. Hayley sits as well, on the other side of the couch. It's beyond awkward and after a few minutes I feel the need to speak up.

"Soooo...thank you guys for watching Faith tonight. I know either of you could have probably done it alone, but I just thought two people are better than one. I wrote down all the instructions and if you need anything please call me."

Caleb nods and then glances at Hayley real quick. She looks at him and he turns away. Jeez, I hope it isn't this awkward all night.

Luckily, Bentley walks in the door with Faith. Go time!

"Are we having a party over here I didn't know about?" he asks, looking around the room.

"Actually," I say as I take Faith from him, give her a big kiss, and then hand her to Caleb. "We're going out. Caleb and Hayley are going to watch Faith for us."

Bentley's lips curl into a frown as he opens his mouth to argue. I cover his lips with my fingers. "Nope. No arguing. It's your birthday and we're going to celebrate. They know what to do and Faith will be fine."

I grab the suitcase, give Faith one more kiss, and take Bentley's hand to drag him out the door.

Once we are in my SUV, he starts his complaining. "I don't want to leave her, Kayla. What if she thinks we aren't coming back? We just left her the other night to go to that club. What if they don't know what to do if there's an emergency? I don't like this. Maybe my parents should have watched her."

"Stop! You have been super dad and partner since we brought Faith home. We've only left her once for a couple hours to go out. One night away will be good for you. Plus, leaving her with your parents would mean Hayley and Caleb wouldn't be stuck in the house together all night."

"Wait! What do you mean 'one night'? Like all night? As in we aren't coming home tonight? And woman, leave my boy alone! Don't try to play matchmaker."

I let out a sigh. "Yes, all night. Just chill out. It will be fun. Trust me. And I'm not playing matchmaker. I'm just giving them a little nudge in the right direction."

He mumbles something under his breath, but I ignore it.

We pull up to the Mirage and I have the vehicle valet parked. I grab the suitcase and head to guest services to check in. Bentley is busy on his phone, probably texting Caleb to get an update on Faith.

I order room service for dinner and dessert and have a bottle of liquor sent up as well. I'm given the keys and we head up to our room.

Twenty-Three

BENTLEY

THE ENTIRE DRIVE MY THOUGHTS HAVE BEEN ON FAITH and worrying if she will be okay without us all night, but the moment the hotel comes into view my thoughts shift. It's been six months since I've gotten laid so you can't blame me for what enters my mind when I picture Kayla and me alone in a hotel.

The problem is I'm not budging on how I feel. The last time I gave in, she fucked me and left me, and while I don't regret it because it's how Faith was brought into the world, that shit isn't happening again.

I don't bother to ask her where she's going with this. I know what she's hoping for, but if she thinks I'm just going to give in, she has another thing coming. That doesn't mean I can't enjoy a night away with Kayla, though. I thoroughly enjoy and welcome her company in any way I can get it.

After Kayla checks in and orders food for us, we head to our room. She unlocks the door with the key and goes straight to the bedroom without saying a word. I sit down on the couch and wait for her to make her move. I know it's coming. While I'm waiting I text Caleb for the second...okay, maybe the fifth time to check on Faith.

Me: How is Faith?

Caleb: See above for the same damn answer I gave you three minutes ago.

Me: Send me a picture.

Caleb: (Insert picture of his ugly mug)

Me: Fucker! Send me a picture of my daughter!

Caleb: (insert picture of the most beautiful baby in the world)

While I'm staring at the picture of Faith chewing on her hand, Kayla comes out wearing a blood red string bikini. She walks past me and her bottoms are those sexy as fuck cheeky things that are barely bottoms at all. She looks fucking beautiful. Her hips are thick, her breasts are voluptuous, and her ass and thighs are perfect. Her stomach is soft from recently giving birth. Everything about Kayla post-baby turns me the fuck on.

She grabs a towel from the bathroom and throws my board shorts at me.

"Go get changed, birthday boy. There's a private Jacuzzi calling our names," she says with a wink.

I get changed and we head out to the Jacuzzi. She switches on her iPhone to some slow song I've never heard of and heads over to the Jacuzzi. I stand still, taking her in, as she enters the water slowly. Her nipples peak slightly from the change in the temperature and then are covered from the bubbles in the water. She looks absolutely exquisite without even trying.

"Are you going to stand there or join me?" she asks with a devilish grin on her face.

I get in on the other side and sink down into the water. It's warm and the jets feel good against my back. She sits across from me just staring at me with a sly smirk on her face.

"What?"

"Nothing," she says coyly.

I feel something hit my dick, springing it to life. I reach under the water and feel Kayla's foot trying to rub on me. I grab it and pull her toward me, her body hitting the water. Her hair is drenched and water is dripping down her face, but instead of being mad, she cracks up laughing. I love to hear her laughter. It's probably one of the most beautiful sounds in the world.

She stands, and with her hands on her hips, mock glares at me. I know what's coming next, so I beat her to it. Cupping both hands, I splash her with water right in her face. It's dripping all over her and she's spluttering the water out of her mouth while trying to wipe the water off her face.

I stand and walk toward her. Taking her face in my hands, I give her a soft kiss on her wet lips and tuck her wet hair behind her ear so I can see her face. "That's better," I say, admiring how beautiful she looks when she's happy.

She stands there for a moment, staring at me, and when I think she's plotting her revenge, instead she says, "I want this." There's so much she can mean by that, so I raise an eyebrow silently asking her for clarification.

She suddenly looks shy as she whispers, "Us. I mean, if you still want us that is."

Her eyes are half-lidded and she's never looked so vulnerable than she does in this moment. I grip the curves of her hips and yank her toward me as I sit back down. She lets out an audible gasp that quickly morphs into a nervous giggle. I pull her up into my lap, so she's straddling me. "Say it again."

She chews her bottom lip for a second. "I want us. I want to give us a real shot."

"You sure." I need to be sure this is what she really wants.

She nods slowly. "Woman, if you're doing this to get me to have sex with you, we're going to have major problems. Once I'm inside you, you're mine. Do you understand me? No going back."

Her eyes go wide and she nods faster.

"No, I need to hear the words."

"I'm yours. No going back. I've wanted to tell you for a while but wanted it to be romantic." That's all I need to hear. I bring my mouth to hers and my need for her consumes any other rational thoughts I might have. My tongue plunges into her mouth as she wraps herself around me. The water shifts from our bodies grinding up against each other. Her warm pussy is rubbing against my hard erection, and while I would definitely enjoy Jacuzzi sex, I need more.

I grab ahold of her ass and pick her up as I stand in the water. I step out of the Jacuzzi and lay her down on the balcony floor. I take a second to look at the beautiful woman in front of me and then kneel between her legs to remove her bikini bottoms. Her pussy is perfection. It's clean cut but not completely bald. Trimmed neatly. I spread her legs wide and slowly stick one finger into her.

She isn't quite wet enough yet, so I move up her body to her perfect tits. Moving the tiny triangles out of the way, I put my mouth around her nipple while pinching her other nipple with my thumb and forefinger.

"Oh, God, Bentley. Please," Kayla moans.

I continue to suck, lick, and pinch her nipples causing her to squirm. I move one hand back down to her pussy and stick one digit in again. It's definitely wetter. Now we're getting somewhere. One finger, then two fingers deep, and her back is arched as she continues to thrash her hips down onto my fingers so I'll go deeper inside her.

And what my woman wants, my woman gets. I remove my fingers from her, and she sighs from the absence of me. I trail kisses along her jaw down her neck as I remove my swim trunks with one hand, then I guide my hard shaft into her warm, wet pussy. Dropping my forehead on her shoulder, I stop halfway in and pray I don't blow my load before this even begins.

She buries her hands in my hair holding me close, and I begin to slowly thrust in and out. She feels so good, so tight. Her pussy is gripping my cock like a goddamn vice. I bring my mouth down to her tits and latch on to her nipple, sucking on it and pulling it the way I know she likes. I angle my cock to go a bit deeper, grinding against her clit.

"Oh...Oh...Bentley...Fuck!" she groans. Her wall tighten and she comes all over my dick.

I pump into her several more times, releasing myself completely into her. I drop my face to the dip between her tits and hold my breath, waiting for the excuses to come. Only they don't. I know she's awake because her hands are in my hair, gently massaging my scalp, but she isn't saying a word.

I finally decide to stop acting like a pussy and look up at her. "Do you still want us?"

Twenty-Four

KAYLA

I look into Bentley's beautiful blue eyes that are open like a window to his soul. He has always been this way with me. Every step along the way he's left his heart open and vulnerable, welcoming me with open arms, while I've pushed him away at every turn. I've had sex plenty of times in my life, but what we just did wasn't sex. It was making love. This man loves me. He wants me and only me, and I vow to show him every day how much he means to me.

He must take my lack of response as a no because his face morphs into anger as he shakes his head and attempts to get up. I tighten my hold on his hair and pull him down to me.

"Yes, I still want us. I'm sorry it's taken me this long to get on the same page as you, but yes, I want us. I need you, Bentley. Just please don't break my heart. I don't think my heart could take it," I plead. I don't know where the words come from, but I feel like I need him to understand that this isn't easy and I'm so damn scared.

He gets off me without saying a word and then scoops me up bridal style and heads back inside to our room. He lays me on the bed and then hovers above me. We're both still wet and naked soaking the sheets. He peppers kisses all over my bod, on my forehead, to each of my cheeks, and to the tip of my nose. He moves to my ear and sucks lightly on my lobe, then brushes his lips across my neck and moves downward to my collarbone. He lays wet kisses on each of my breasts and then descends to my belly, trailing kisses to my mound.

He doesn't stop there, though. His body moves downward, and he nips on my thigh, making me laugh.

"Bentley! That tickles! I bark out a laugh. "What are you doing?"

He looks up at me and his lips curve into a gorgeous grin. "I'm making sure you're real."

I laugh harder at his antics. He continues to kiss down my leg and when he gets to my foot, he nibbles on my toes, throwing me into a fit of laughter.

His grin widens. "Is this real? Are you really mine?"

My cheeks hurt from smiling so hard and my stomach aches from laughing. He's so adorable. I nod.

He comes back up my body, until we're face to face, and kisses me softly. His lips linger on mine, sucking my bottom lip out as he releases it and pulls back.

"I promise you, Kayla. I'll never break your heart, baby." He moves his lips down to the skin right above my left breast and kisses my chest right over my heart.

"Thank you for having faith in us. You won't ever regret it." He gives my *heart* another kiss and then comes up to lie with me.

The food arrives and, after we change the bed to dry sheets, we eat in a comfortable silence with me sitting on Bentley's lap as he feeds both of us. I have my arms around his neck and I've never felt closer to someone than I do to him right now. There's a new vibe between us and it feels good. Once we're done eating, Bentley plugs his iPhone into the speaker and says, "Dance with me."

The tears well up in my eyes at the flashbacks to the dinner in our apartment when he asked me to dance for the first time and then again at Liz and Cooper's wedding just before I gave birth to Faith. This time the song playing is faster paced. Sam Smith is singing the lyrics to *Stay With Me* through the speakers as Bentley holds me close and once again whispers the words of the song to me like he did the first time we danced together. Our bodies sway back and forth as he holds me tightly to him, almost as if he's afraid I might change my mind and leave him. What he doesn't realize is that I'm not going anywhere. I know it's going to take time to prove it to him, but I will. This man is all I want.

The song ends and he whispers into my ear, "Baby, stay with me."

"For as long as you want me," I vow.

He lets out a sigh of relief and then picks me up and carries me to the couch, where we make love for the second time tonight.

I WAKE UP TO THE SUN SHINING THROUGH THE WINDOWS and the feel of Bentley holding me close. I feel him move slightly and know he's waking up as well.

"Want to order breakfast?"

"No, baby. To be honest I just want to go home to our little girl and spend the first day of the rest of our lives together as a family."

As we drive home to our little girl, holding hands, my heart is so full of love. It feels like the switch has been turned back on, like I've been stuck in the dark alone all this time, and now I'm no longer alone. Only I didn't have to stumble and find the light myself. Bentley was here this whole time ready to switch it on for me. All I had to do was have faith in us.

Twenty-Five

BENTLEY

THE CRAZY THING ABOUT BABIES IS THAT THEY GROW LIKE damn weeds! It's the end of November, Thanksgiving just passed, and Faith is officially five months old. She's sitting up, eating solids, and when she's on the floor she does this cute rocking thing on her knees, which confirms what all the moms say is true from *Mommy and Me*—she's getting ready to crawl. Yes, that's right. I belong to a mommy and me group I found online. I still think it's ridiculous that it isn't called *Parent and Me,* but I'll pick my battles since I'm the only dad actually in the group.

Faith and I have a great schedule going on. We usually start off our morning with some oatmeal or rice with fruit, we join the other moms at the park later in the morning until it's time for Faith's nap, and then I head to the gym to visit Kayla while she's at work. Some days she'll take Faith home while I work out with the guys and other days I'll go home to make dinner for when she gets home.

Right now I'm heading to the park to meet the other moms. My phone rings over Bluetooth and Faith makes a bunch of sounds in the backseat.

"Hello?"

"Hey there, Mr. Mom! What are you up to?" It's Liz, and I would bet she's home and bored. We haven't hung out with the babies yet other than when we all hang out together as a group. She's mentioned it several times, but I figured I would let her and Kayla hang out. They can get their baby and best friend time in at once.

"I'm heading to the park with Faith. What's up?"

"Really? Would you mind if Nathan and I join you? Bella's at school until later and Cooper's at the gym."

"I'm meeting my mom's group there, but I guess you can join."

"Mom's group? Why don't I know about this? Am I not cool enough to be part of your group?"

Oh, Jeez. Here we go...

"If you want to meet us, then meet us. It's not that big of a deal."

"Okay, text me the address of the park you're going to. Be there soon! Bye!"

We get to the park and I spot Monica and Sara right away. They both have daughters that are just a little older than Faith. They wave to me and I head over to them, putting the diaper bag down on the bench along the way. There are four swings and two are empty, so I put Faith into the swing and push her lightly. Her giggles start up immediately and I snap a picture to send to Kayla.

"Hey Bentley!" both women say in unison and laugh.

"Hello, Ladies. And hello to you precious little girls," I say to their daughters, tickling each of their tummies. They both give me a baby giggle.

I go back to pushing Faith as we discuss our babies' recent milestones.

"Tori is finally crawling!" Monica announces excitedly.

"Amy is almost there, but she's standing up for a few seconds against the couch before she falls back down on her butt. Maybe she'll just go straight to walking and skip crawling," Sara chimes in.

"Nice! Faith is still doing the whole rocking on her knees thing. I've baby proofed the entire apartment though just in case."

"Just in case what?" I hear from behind me. I turn around and see Liz standing with Nathan on her hip, her eyes darting between the two women and me. Damn, she got here fast.

"Hey Liz. This is Monica and Sara." I point to the two women. "I was just telling them how Faith is almost crawling, so I baby proofed the house this weekend. Ladies, this is Liz. She's my friend Cooper's wife, and this little guy is Nathan."

"And I'm also his girlfriend's best friend," she adds with a tone that sounds off.

Both women say hello and we continue the play date. A few of the other women in the mom's group show up and soon there's almost a dozen babies crawling, walking, and running all over the park. Liz is sitting on the bench while Nathan sits in front of her as she looks intently at her phone.

I sit next to her and place Faith on the ground to play with the sand toys.

"Cooper?" I ask, nodding toward her phone. She looks up and glares at me for a second, but quickly relaxes her face into more of a grimace.

"No, actually it's Kayla. You remember your girlfriend, right?"

I ignore the dig. "Cool. Tell her I said hi."

"That's it? You said hi?"

I think about it for a second not sure what answer she's looking for here.

"Um, hi and I'll see her later at the gym?"

She huffs out a "Whatever" and goes back to texting.

A couple of the moms come over and let us know they're going to head out since it's almost nap time and invite Liz to join us the day after tomorrow at the local pool.

"I'm not sure what I have going on, but thank you for the invite."

"Okay, well, it's an open invitation, and I'll send you an invite to our online group. I'll get your email from Bentley later. Let me know if Faith starts crawling, Bentley! See you at the pool," Sara says before leaving.

Everybody else says goodbye and then it's just Liz and me left.

"Seriously?" she barks out.

"What?" I'm confused as fuck as to why this woman is acting so damn weird.

"While the girlfriend-slash-mother of your child is at work, you're hanging out at the park with a bunch of hot women who are all having Daddy Bentley fantasies?"

What in the actual fuck?

"Please don't tell me you texted that bullshit to Kayla. You already know how insecure she is about being in a relationship. Would you be saying this shit if I was a woman at the park with other women? No, you wouldn't. I can't help there are no other dads that stay home or join the mom's group."

"Whatever, Bentley. I didn't say anything to Kayla, but you should."

Faith starts to whine and I know it's time to get her home for a nap. I scoop her up and wipe the sand off her body and turn to face Liz. "I'm not doing anything wrong. Don't make this something it's not, please."

She sighs loudly but nods okay.

I get home, lay Faith down for her afternoon nap and begin to work on the laundry. I start to think about what Liz said. Does she have a point? Should I tell Kayla about the mom's group I'm in? I haven't purposely kept it from her. I tell her all about Faith's day and mine, but if I'm honest I don't include the other women I hang out with in our conversations.

Every day I hope and pray Kayla won't wake up and change her mind about us. Sometimes I feel like I walk on eggshells afraid that if I do or say the wrong thing she'll walk away from me. So maybe subconsciously I kept that tidbit of info out of our conversations to keep everything stable.

My phone rings in my pocket and I see it's my mom.

"Hey, Mom, how are you?"

"Oh, I'm good, sweetie. How are Faith and Kayla?"

"Both good. Faith is sleeping and Kayla is at work. What's up?"

"Well I was wondering if we could take Faith for the weekend. I was thinking Kayla and you can do a weekend getaway and we could watch Faith. I would love some time with my granddaughter."

I laugh at her comment. The woman spends time with her granddaughter several times a week, but I'm not going to turn down a chance to take Kayla away.

"That actually sounds really good, Mom. We haven't been away since my birthday when Kayla surprised me. Now I can surprise her. Thanks."

"No problem. Why don't you guys join us for an early dinner Friday and then take off afterward? You can pick Faith up Sunday night or Monday morning."

"Perfect. I'm going to make reservations now."

I text the guys to see if they want to make it a group thing. Cooper replies a little while later saying his mom would love to take Nathan and Bella for the weekend. Caleb says he's down, and Kaden is down as well. I tell Cooper to let Liz know I'm surprising Kayla and to invite Hayley and Ashley as well.

He texts me later letting me know Ashley's parents are good to watch her son and Hayley will be joining as well. I send out a group text letting them all know to pack warm clothes because we're flying to Breckenridge, a ski resort in Colorado. My family has a cabin up there and now seems like the perfect time to take advantage of it.

I shoot my mom a text letting her know and she replies with a smiley face. Next, I make reservations to charter a private plane from McCarran international to Eagle County Regional, which is only about an hour from the ski resort.

While I'm booking the flight I get a text from Monica confirming our play date for the pool on Thursday. I send her a *thumbs up* emoticon and continue making plans for this weekend, writing down all the shit I need to pack for us and Faith. Luckily my parents keep a lot of stuff at their house since we visit often. I also jot down to remember my favorite red bathing suit of Kayla's. We will definitely be taking advantage of the hot tub at night.

Twenty-Six

KAYLA

IT'S THURSDAY MORNING AND MY ONLY APPOINTMENT OF the day was canceled because the fighter has to go out of town for a last minute photo shoot. I decide to surprise Bentley and meet him at the pool at the local Y. Liz told me she's joining him as well. I go by the house, grab my bathing suit, and head to the swimming center.

I pay for my swimming pass and head to the locker room to change. There are a few moms changing their babies in there while conversing.

"My God, he's like sex on a stick," one woman says, fanning herself.

"Seriously, and the way he is with his daughter...If I weren't married, I would be all over that," another woman says.

"Yeah, well, I'm not married, so maybe I should be all over that," another woman says.

I hear them leave as I finish changing, and then go in search for my sex-on-a-stick. When I get to the pool I spot Bentley and Faith. Damn, he looks sexy. He's holding our daughter in the air and then brings her back down, making it look like he's plunging her into the water, but in reality he does it so gently the water barely parts. I can see her beautiful grin from here. I look for Liz and see her talking to the women I just saw in the locker room.

I walk over to join Bentley in the water, but before I can make it over, the women who were just talking to Liz join him in the pool with a baby on each of their hips.

I watch for a few minutes and it's clear he knows them. Holy shit! It hits me. *My* sex-on-a-stick is the same sex-on-a-stick they were talking about! *Oh, hell no! That shit ain't gonna fly.*

I pick up my pace and walk quickly over to the edge of the pool and walk down the steps on a mission to claim my damn man. When Bentley first sees me, he looks...shocked...or is it guilt? But then his face morphs into a huge smile.

He must tell Liz I'm here because she looks over at me and her face definitely looks guilty. One thing about my best friend is she can't hide shit from me and something tells me she knew all about this. I give her an eyebrow up silently saying *what the fuck* and her eyes bulge out knowing exactly what I mean.

I swim to Bentley and, without saying hello to anybody else around him, wrap my arms around his neck and give him a kiss that screams *mine.* He's still holding Faith and when she spots me kissing her daddy she begins to squeal in his arms wanting me to grab her.

"Surprise," I whisper to Bentley, so only he can hear.

He stares at me for a brief moment, gauging my tone, then says, "It definitely is."

He grabs the back of my neck with his available hand and kisses me once more. Faith's squeals get louder and we both separate and laugh. I take her from him and give her chubby little cheek a big wet kiss.

"I didn't know you would be joining us," Liz says nervously.

"My appointment canceled so I thought I would surprise you guys."

"Hey Bent, do you want to get out to give the babies a snack? It was my turn to bring snacks and I brought yogurts."

I look over at the woman who, not even five minutes ago, stood in the locker room and said she would be all over *that* if she wasn't married, clearly referring to my boyfriend.

"Bent?" I ask Bentley.

He at least has the decency to look sheepishly at me. "Kayla, this is Monica, Sara, and Roxy. They're in the Mommy and Me group Liz and I belong to."

I turn to glare at my best friend who has never mentioned this before.

"Um, well, actually I'm not exactly in the group. I just met them the other day. My membership is still pending upon approval from the admin."

I shoot her another death glare and she looks down at Nathan, pretending to pick imaginary lint off him. Yeah, my best friend and I will definitely be having a conversation later. But for right now, I do what any respectable woman does when she's caught off guard but can't let those catty bitches know. I fake it!

"Oh, that group! I remember you mentioning them," I first say to Liz. Then turning to the bitches that want my man, I say, "Nice to meet you. I've heard so much about you guys." I put my hand out to shake each of their hands.

Bentley looks scared as hell at this point, knowing I haven't really heard shit about the hot moms he's been chilling with.

"Sooo...yogurt?" I ask nobody in particular. Everybody nods and says yes and we all get out to get the yogurts.

Bentley tries to stop me by putting his arm on mine, but when I turn around and growl out "Not now," he stops and takes the hint.

I lay Faith on the lounge chair that Bentley has everything sprawled out on and change her wet diaper. Liz comes up to me and, like the best friends we are, apologizes with only her eyes. I nod slightly, letting her know we're good, and sit on the chair with Faith between my legs. Bentley sits on the edge of the chair and begins to feed Faith a yogurt. She gets so excited, batting at the spoon, wanting to grab it herself. This little girl is our entire world. I get choked up when I think about some other woman spending time with my daughter. Is that what Bentley needs? Does he need a woman who stays home instead of works? What if after all we've gone through to get here, I'm not the woman he needs? And then I think about the deceit. Not once has he mentioned he's hanging out with all of these hot moms during the day while I'm at work. He has to know this is wrong or else he would have mentioned it.

I close my eyes to hold back the tears that are threatening to spill over. When I open my eyes, Bentley is looking at me with a pained expression. He opens his mouth, attempting to speak, but with those women around I'm not doing this here. I shake my head, and he sighs, but nods.

We spend the rest of the afternoon at the pool, and while we have a blast as a family with our daughter, it's tainted by all the secrets that have been kept, and all the questions I want answers to. Is this where it all ends? Is this where my mom gets to say the *I told you so* I've always feared?

Twenty-Seven

BENTLEY

FUCK! I KNOW I TECHNICALLY HAVE NOTHING TO FEEL guilty over, but at the same time, I know I do. When Kayla closed her eyes, I could see it in her face, the insecurity that I might want these other moms over her. I could see the fear in her that I'm going to break her heart and that her mom was right and she was once again wrong. I wanted so badly to explain, to hold her and tell her she's all I'll ever want, but she wouldn't even let me talk.

The day comes to a close, we say our goodbyes, and since we took separate vehicles, Kayla and I part ways and agree to meet at home. Kayla takes Faith home with her, so I stop by the florist and pick up a dozen roses. I know it's totally cliché, but at this point I'll try anything.

I walk into the apartment and Kayla spots the flowers immediately. Tears start flowing down her face and I have a feeling flowers weren't the right move. I set them on the end table and go over to her. Picking her up, I carry her over to the couch. Faith is playing in her exerciser, twisting and turning, while banging the keys that make noise and light up.

I turn Kayla so her legs are straddling my thighs and let her cry into my shirt for a couple of minutes before I speak. "Baby, please stop crying. I'll throw the fucking flowers away. I'm sorry."

She looks up at me with wide, vulnerable eyes and quietly asks, "Do you still want to be with me?"

"What are you talking about, woman? Of course I still want to be with you. You are my forever." I give her a soft kiss on her lips. They taste salty from her crying, and it's officially my least favorite taste in the world.

"When I went into the locker room to change I didn't know it at the time but those women were talking about how hot you were and saying if they weren't married they would want to be with you. One woman even said she's not married and wants you! And then when I saw you with them, having fun with Faith and their kids...Is that what you want? A woman who will stay home with the baby? And why didn't you tell me about this group? Do you know how crappy it feels to be kept in the dark about what you do numerous times a week?"

Jesus...women and their big mouths. I know these women have occasionally flirted, but I've ignored it. I figured it was just innocent and since most of them are married I let it go. They have never approached me or said anything remotely inappropriate. The truth is them gossiping is the equivalent to what guys do when they see a hot woman. However, pointing that out to Kayla is not going to help the situation. I might be a guy, but I'm not a complete idiot.

"Those women can say whatever they want. You are the only

woman for me. I joined that group so Faith and I could socialize with other parents, that's it. I love being home with Faith. I love that you enjoy your job. I told you this before and I'll say it as many times as you need to hear it. I'm okay with you working. If you ever want to stay home, then you can do that. You choosing to work instead of staying home doesn't change how I feel about you. You are a great girlfriend and mother. Okay?"

She sniffles and nods. "Just promise me if you no longer want me you'll tell me. Please don't ever cheat on me, Bentley. I couldn't handle the humiliation."

"Stop! Don't say stupid shit like that. I'm not that Jackass from when you were a teenager. Nobody is cheating, leaving, or using anybody." I grab Kayla's chin and give her a quick kiss. "I love you. I love you just the way you are. I would never cheat on you. Just let me love you, baby. I'm sorry for not telling you about the mom's group. It was wrong of me. I'll never hide anything from you again."

I don't wait for a response because I know I won't get one. While she doesn't freak out when I tell her constantly that I love her, she doesn't say it back...yet. I set her down next to me on the couch, pick up Faith, and hand her to her. I reach down putting my arms on either side of Kayla's head, and give first Kayla a kiss, and then Faith one, breathing them both in. It's the best smell. I wish I could bottle it up and keep it forever. These two girls are my world. "Now, we have some packing to do!"

Kayla's eyes dart to me in confusion. "For what?"

"Surprise. My parents are taking Faith for the weekend. We leave tomorrow night after dinner with my parents. You need to pack warm clothes with plenty of layers...Oh! And that sexy-as-hell red bikini is a must. That's all I'm telling you."

"OH. MY. GOD. ARE YOU FREAKING SERIOUS?" LIZ YELLS, causing people to stop eating and look at us.

"Shh...chill the heck out," I say while feeding Faith another bite of mashed potatoes.

"This is so exciting!" Ashley chimes in.

Once I knew we were heading out to Breckenridge on an impromptu mini-vacation with all of our friends for the weekend, I decided it would be the perfect time and place to pop the question to Kayla. I already purchased the ring awhile back, now I just need to figure out the best way to do it.

I'm currently having an early lunch with Liz, Ashley, and our kids, hoping they can help me plan something romantic before we head out of town tonight.

"Do you have a ring?" Liz asks with tears in her eyes. I've never been around women as much as I have since I've started staying home with Faith, and one thing I've learned from these women is that they are full of emotions. I've always known they have emotions, but after spending so much time with all these moms, I could write a book on how crazy their emotions really are. Happy, sad, mad, I can't ever keep up. Men have one emotion. Chill.

"Of course I do, and no you aren't seeing it before Kayla does. Now help me out here. How should I propose? Alone? In front of everyone?"

Liz frowns. "Hm, I think you should do it alone. We can all celebrate afterward, but what if she says no?"

Ashley's eyebrows shoot up. "Do you think she would say no?"

"She's going to say yes. We've come a long way. We're together and we have Faith. Her biggest fear is being heartbroken. I just need to convince her that forever is the opposite of breaking her heart."

"I agree with Liz. Do it alone. That way she doesn't feel overwhelmed or pressured."

"All right. Alone it is." I attempt to give Faith another bite of potatoes, but she isn't having it. She closes her mouth tight and shakes her head. Fucking cute kid. Just as stubborn as her mother.

We continue to discuss the different ways I can propose while Bella and Tristan play with Faith and Nathan. They're making crazy faces at them, which causes them to squeal and clap in response. Faith loves all the attention.

"Has Kayla mentioned anything about not being able to have more kids?" Liz asks quietly.

"No, but if she ever wanted to, I'll make sure it happens. For now, Faith is all we need."

"You're a good guy, Bentley. Thank you for taking care of our girl."

I give Liz a wink. Nothing more needs to be said. I'll always take care of Kayla.

I pay for lunch, then we grab our kids and all head home. Everybody will be meeting at the plane tonight to fly out together.

Twenty-Eight

BENTLEY

DINNER AT MY PARENTS WENT WELL. WE SAID OUR goodbyes to Faith and thanked my parents for watching her. I decided it would be best to take a cab to the airport and leave my car at my parents so we don't have to deal with parking. Kayla's Volvo SUV has been having some issues so I need to look into getting her a new vehicle. I love my BMW so maybe I'll get her one as well.

When we get there and pull up to the private hanger, Kayla looks shocked that we aren't arriving in the regular terminal.

"Umm...Bentley? Are we flying on a private plane?" She darts her eyes from me to the plane several times making me laugh.

"Yeah, I figured it would be easier with all of us flying on such short notice."

"Who's all of us?"

We step onto the plane and her question is answered. Already on the plane are all of our friends chatting and waiting for us.

"Oh my God! Everybody is going away?" she screeches as she runs over to Liz, Hayley, and Ashley and gives them a group hug.

Cooper walks over and gives me a bro hug. "Finally using some of that dough on yourself, bro?"

I shake my head and chuckle. The truth is I couldn't spend the amount of money I have in my lifetime, especially not the way I live. Because of my father being financially savvy, I have money all over the place in various ventures, and the money I do spend is just from the interest and my earnings alone.

I walk over and bump fists with Caleb and Kaden, and then the pilot requests we fasten our seatbelts so we can take off.

Once we're seated and buckled in, Kayla asks, "Who is paying for all this?"

The guys all look at me quickly and then try to look around to not give anything away. It's not that I'm keeping my money situation from her. It's like I've said before, I don't want to scare her off. She has this crazy notion that people need to be equal in a relationship. I've finally gotten her to give us a real chance, and if she knew money-wise, it's like ninety-nine to one she might freak out on me. I'm just not ready to chance it yet.

However, I'm not going to flat out lie to her. "I did. I have money saved up and I wanted to do this for us. Please don't be upset. We're fine for money and I just want to have a good weekend with you and our friends, okay?"

She looks at me skeptically but luckily lets it go. If all goes well this weekend, we'll be one step closer to being married and then I'll tell her about my inheritance. I just need to take it one small step at a time with her.

We arrive in Colorado and have a van take us straight to the cabin to get settled in. It's cold as shit here, but I love it. We arrive at the cabin and Kaden is the first one to comment.

"Holy shit, dude! Is this your place?"

I try to look at it from their perspective. It's a large two-story cabin made of brick and stone. There's a wraparound porch on both the first and second story. There's a large chimney that goes up the entire side of the cabin, where smoke is rising out of the top. I had the housekeeper stock up and start the fire before we got here. In the background are the mountains.

To some, I guess the cabin would look over the top like something you would see in a photo, but to me it looks like home away from home. I spent my entire life coming here with my parents during many holidays including Christmas break.

"It's not my place, technically. It's my parents' place. We've been coming here every year since I was little. Actually Cooper has been here a few times with me when his parents would let him go."

Everybody walks inside and stops to take it all in. The inside is just as beautiful as the outside. All wood from floor to ceiling, comfy country chic furniture and décor my mom has decorated the place with over the years. Kayla walks up to the stone fireplace and picks up the family picture on the mantel and smiles at me.

"You look so happy in this picture. I hope one day we have pictures like this of Faith."

I wrap my arms around her waist and kiss her forehead. "We will and she'll be just as happy. She already is happy. Maybe if you like it here we can make coming here a family tradition."

"Really? I've never skied or snowboarded before. Can you teach me?" She beams with childlike excitement.

"Absolutely. And when Faith gets older, she'll learn to as well. You'll teach her to surf and I'll teach her to ski and fight," I say with a wink.

She laughs and it makes my heart pump a little faster. I love that fucking sound.

"All right, so where is everybody sleeping?" Caleb cuts in.

"Liz and I get our own room," Cooper adds.

"I can share a room with Ashley," Kaden says.

"Yeah? On the floor?" Ashley barks out with laughter.

"Shut up, crazy." Kaden laughs back.

"There are four rooms. Kayla and I are taking the master so you all can figure the rest out." I grab Kayla's hand and pull her down the hall to the bedroom. Let them figure out the sleeping arrangements. I have forty-eight hours alone with my woman. I don't have time to play camp counselor.

We get to the master bedroom, and as soon as we walk in, I close the door and push her up against it, plunging my tongue into her mouth. Her hands come up to my hair and she tugs lightly, trying to push me away. I try to ignore her and continue to swirl my tongue around when she laughs into my mouth causing me to laugh as well.

I back away and she laughs harder. "Bentley! I haven't even seen the bedroom yet!"

"It has four walls and a bed. You don't need to see anything else. Trust me. Now where were we?"

I push my erection up against her and go back to kissing her. This time she moans softly and instead of her fingers tugging my hair to push me away she pulls my face closer causing our kiss to deepen.

I reach down and grab her ass, squeezing tightly, Just as I'm about to pick her up to bring her to the bed there's a knock on the door.

I pause our kissing just long enough to yell, "Go away!" and then bring my lips back to hers to continue tasting her.

There's a knock again.

"What the fuck! Go away!" I yell again.

"Maybe they need something." Kayla laughs, while trying to give me her best glare.

I move us from the door and swing it open, about to kill whoever is on the other side.

"Umm...I'm sorry. I just wanted to see if there's any way to get to the resort. I was thinking I could maybe stay up there," Hayley says softly, clearly embarrassed to have interrupted us.

"What? Why would you do that?" Kayla says, pushing me away and walking out the door with Hayley.

"Well, there's only one room left and Caleb doesn't want to share."

I walk behind them down the hall, planning all the ways I can get even with Caleb for being the reason my dick is still hard as fuck and not balls deep inside my woman right now.

"You aren't staying anywhere else. Right, Bentley? We'll figure it out."

I nod then head to find Caleb to get this shit figured out. He's sitting on the living couch with his head hanging down.

"What's up man? Is it that big of a deal to share a room with Hayley?"

He sighs and shakes his head. All these years and I've never seen him with a woman except that night when he kissed Hayley on a dare.

"I'm sorry, man. I'm just not comfortable sharing a room with her. It's nothing against her. I just don't know her. I can stay somewhere else."

"No, man. It's fine. We'll figure it out. Can I ask you why though?

He looks at me and cringes. "I just don't trust women."

"All right, would you be okay with sleeping on the couch? I would feel like a dick if I ask her to and she's trying to leave to stay somewhere else."

Caleb sighs loudly and shakes his head. "Fuck, I know she likes me. I try to ignore it, but I see the looks and shit. I shouldn't have kissed her at the club. I don't know what the hell came over me. I don't want to be a dick. Let her sleep in the room and I'll crash on the couch as long as you're okay with that. She kept insisting I sleep in the room and she would sleep elsewhere. I didn't know what to do."

"Okay, cool. And it's only for two nights, so it's not a big deal. If you ever want to talk, I'm here."

We bump fists and head into the kitchen to let Hayley know the room is all hers.

"Are you sure, Caleb? I don't mind sharing a room with you...or I can stay on the couch." The poor girl looks so defeated. I never paid attention, but I think she really does like him.

"It's cool. Please take the room. I don't mind sleeping on the couch." He gives her a small smile and she smiles back accepting his answer.

We all decide to call it a night. It's late and we are going to get up early in the morning to go check out the skiing resort. We walk back to our room and the first thing I do is call my parents to check on Faith while Kayla gets ready for bed.

I'm finishing up the call when Kayla walks out of the bathroom in a sheer black nightgown. It shows everything yet covers it all up at the same time. Underneath is a small piece of material some would call underwear that is supposed to be covering her pussy but isn't really covering much at all. Her hair is down and it's just long enough that it covers her nipples so I can't see them, but I would bet my life they're budding out ready for me to suck on them.

She's leaning against the doorframe with a devilish grin on her face knowing exactly what she's doing to me. She looks fucking perfect. She *is* fucking perfect. And she's all mine. I don't know what the hell comes over me but all my planning flies out the window when I blurt out, "Marry me."

Her head tilts to the side unsure she heard me right. I know this isn't how it was supposed to happen, but fuck it. It's happening now.

I stand up as she walks slowly toward me waiting for me to say something. I meet her in front of the bed and turn her to sit her on the edge.

"This isn't at all how I planned this. I was going to do it tomorrow night. I reserved a private room at the restaurant at the resort, and I was going to get down on one knee after dessert. But then you come out here looking like you do, beautiful and sexy, and I couldn't wait another second to ask you to be my wife. I love you so damn much. I love our daughter and our life. I want to marry you and make you happy for the rest of our life."

I pull the ring out of the pocket of my luggage to show it to her. "Kayla Peterson, will you make me even happier than I already am and marry me?"

Twenty-Nine

KAYLA

I DON'T EVEN NEED TO LOOK AT THE RING TO KNOW MY answer. It could have been a freaking ring pop and I would still say yes to this man. He has become everything to me. He's an amazing father and partner, and has become my best friend. He's been saying *I love you* to me for so long and while I haven't once said it back, he has never commented or gotten upset. He has loved me unconditionally every step of the way. He accepts me just the way I am.

I realize that while I'm listing off every reason in my head as to why I'm going to marry Bentley, I haven't yet verbally said a word. And of course he continues to have patience, just waiting for me to sift through and process my thoughts and feelings.

When I finally speak, what comes out first is, "I love you."

His face brightens instantly and I want to freeze-frame the way he looks when he hears those words.

"I love you too, baby."

We stare at each other for a moment and then it hits me...I still didn't give him a damn answer! Jesus, I seriously suck at this. That thought makes me laugh and his smile morphs to confusion.

"Yes! Yes, I'll marry you." I jump straight into his arms and of course he catches me. My legs wrap around his back as my mouth crashes against his. We go from zero to sixty. We're all teeth and tongues. His hands are kneading my ass and my hands are gripping his hair pulling him closer to me as my pussy grinds up against his hard stomach seeking relief.

He walks us around to the side of the bed and lays me down, crawling on top of me and parting my legs with his knees. He takes my left hand and slides the ring onto my ring finger. I don't even have a chance to check it out and admire it before he growls out, "mine" and his mouth is back on mine once again.

We kiss for a long time—to the point that my lips feel numb and bruised—before Bentley moves to my neck. He licks and then bites and sucks and then licks once again. He works his way down to my breasts and after kissing each nipple over the sheer teddy, he loses his patience and rips it down the center. He kisses my nipples a second time, but this time without the material he's able to grab each one and suck on them, sending a bolt of pleasure straight to my pussy.

I buck my hips against his hardness through his pants, but it does absolutely nothing to alleviate the pent up tension my body is building from his touch. He continues to suck on each nipple and I swear I'm close to having an orgasm from this act alone.

"Bentley, please. I want you inside me."

He releases my nipple from his mouth and sits up to remove

his shirt and then removes his boxers and jeans. Every time I get a chance to see him like this, I can't believe this man is all mine. The man hasn't trained for a fight in months yet is still hard everywhere. Toned stomach and chiseled chest, and I don't even need to count anymore to know he has an eight-pack of abs. It's no wonder every mom in that stupid mom's group wants my fiancé. Holy shit! He's my fiancé! I'm engaged to Bentley Cruz. The thought suddenly has me kind of freaking out. Will I be a good wife? Will we last forever or will we become a statistic my parents always talk about?

Bentley must sense my freak out because he leans forward and whispers into my ear, "Don't overthink this, woman. You are mine and I'm yours and that ring is never coming off your finger."

My entire body visibly relaxes at his words. His ability to calm me is almost unnerving. He gives me soft kisses on my lips, my cheeks, my chin, and then works his way down. I think he's going to kiss me between my legs, but instead he grabs my waist and flips me over onto my stomach so I'm lying face down.

Before I can even question his motives, Bentley gives my ass a hard slap causing me to moan loudly as my pussy muscles clench together. I can't see what he's doing but I feel his teeth on my ass cheeks as he bites down and then licks the bite mark to soothe away the pain. Bentley is an expert at finding the perfect balance between pain and pleasure.

His one hand begins to massage the area he bit while his other hand goes under me and begins to play with my pussy, swiping up the juices that are already flowing, grazing my clit and then moving away from it.

"Bentley...Oh God...Please..."

He chuckles at my incoherent words and then I feel it. His finger, that was just in my pussy, moves into my puckered hole. He's using my juices as a lubricant, and while I should be worried, my thoughts drift back to the last time his finger was in there and how good it felt. Remembering the pleasure his finger brought me, my ass automatically raises up in an attempt to push against it seeking that same pleasure once again.

"Patience, baby," he whispers in response.

With my ass in the air, he reaches back under me and sticks his fingers back into my pussy, gathering up more of my juices, moving them to my ass. He does this a few more times, until I can feel his finger slide right in. I can't help the groan that comes out of me.

With one finger in my ass, he moves his other hand back to my pussy and begins to rub the sensitive nub.

"Play with your nipples, baby."

Leaning onto my elbows, I grab ahold of my nipples playing with them. My body is completely over stimulated and my orgasm is building at an almost alarming rate. Bentley adds another finger to my ass while simultaneously rubbing harder against my clit.

I'm just about to explode, when I feel his cock enter my pussy in one swift motion. It's all too much and I completely lose it. My pussy contracts, my clit throbs, and as if that isn't enough he pushes his fingers deeper into my ass massaging my insides. My body begins to tremble as I explode, coating him with my release.

Bentley picks up the pace going deeper and harder and then he's coming with me.

"Fuuuckkk, Kayla, you feel so fucking good." We both come down from our high and he pulls out.

"Holy shit, woman. You soaked my cock."

Neither of us makes any move to get up. Bentley drops to the side of me and rolls me to the side with him. With my back to his front, he spoons me close, and we both quickly drift to sleep.

I WAKE UP IN THE MORNING, LOOKING AROUND, AND quickly remember where we are. I glance down and laugh that we're both still naked, and then look at my left hand to see the beautiful engagement ring.

I go to get up to take a shower, but Bentley pulls me back in to his body.

"Uh-uh. Stay here."

"I need to shower and then we need to get dressed to meet everyone for breakfast."

"Only if we can shower together."

I laugh at his cuteness. "Always."

I turn the water on and let it heat up. Bentley comes in with a couple of towels and opens the door for us to go in. Grabbing the soap, I wash his body and remember back to all those years ago in the shower when he wouldn't have sex with me because he didn't have a condom.

I take the washcloth and stroke his dick, watching it get harder the more attention I give it. When it gets hard enough, I let the water rinse it off before I bend down and stick it in my mouth.

"Damn, woman," Bentley grunts.

His dick is throbbing in my mouth as I suck it root to tip. I know if I can keep going I can make him come, but that's not what I want.

I stand and Bentley looks at me confused. After pushing him lightly to sit on the bench, I turn around to face away from him and then guide my pussy right onto his hard shaft.

"Holy shit!" he growls when I'm seated all the way on his hard length.

After a few seconds of adjusting to him being inside of me, I start to move up and down, fucking him while his hand goes to my clit to help me along. Our wet bodies slap against each other as I continue to ride him. Neither of us lasts long, both of us our finding our release within minutes.

I get off of him and turn around to see a huge smile on his face. He grabs my ass and pulls me onto his lap, so I'm straddling him. He kisses me deeply, until the shower turns cold and we're forced to get out.

We're all sitting down to breakfast at a little restaurant at the base of the mountain. The closer you get the crazier the mountain looks. I've never skied before, but how much harder can it be than surfing?

We haven't even gotten comfortable when Liz is the first to notice the beautiful multi-carat princess cut ring on my finger.

"Bentley! What happened to the plan?" She lets out a frustrated huff that makes me giggle.

Yep! I freaking giggle. That's what Bentley does to me. Turns me into a giggling, lovesick, emotional, woman, and I wouldn't have it any other way.

"She happened." Bentley nods toward me like that's the answer to all of life's questions.

"We had a plan!"

"Well she walked out of the bathroom in this black see-through nightgown and the plan was shot to hell. It's not my fault. It's hers."

The guys all laugh, but the girls still look mad.

"Hey, it's okay. It was romantic and sweet," Kayla says.

Everybody congratulates us and then we order breakfast before heading to the slopes.

I WOULD LIKE IT TO BE KNOWN ON RECORD THAT SKIING and snowboarding are nothing like surfing. While the snow here is absolutely gorgeous, I've given up on trying to do anything on that damn mountain that's full of it—it's much better to look at than try to ride on. I'll stick to the water, thank you very much. After a couple hours of falling on my ass over and over again, I gave up and told Bentley to have a blast. We can still make this a family tradition, but I'll be spending my time indoors by the fireplace with a hot cup of coffee.

Which is exactly what Liz, Hayley, and I are all doing right now—sitting in the resort's lobby drinking a hot coffee by the fireplace and gossiping like the girls we are.

"I can't believe Ashley is still out there trying to snowboard. Maybe

Kaden is a better teacher," Liz says.

"I'm glad she has Kaden. They have become good friends. She needs someone like him. I don't know what her ex did to her, but she deserves to be happy."

"What about you? Are you happy?" Liz questions.

"I am." And for the first time in a long time it's the truth.

"Before Bentley, it felt like I was just going through the motions, but with him it's so much more."

"I'm so happy for you. I never imagined we would both be with amazing guys, have kids, and soon both of us will be married."

"Yeah, we've come a long way from the scared eighteen-year-old's taking care of Bella on our own."

"That's for damn sure."

I look over at Hayley and she's kind of checked out staring at the fireplace. "Hayley, what about you? Are you happy?"

She ponders the question for a few seconds before shrugging her shoulders. "I think I am. I have a nice home, a good job, parents that are loving and supportive. I just feel like I'm missing something. I want a guy to come home to, a baby to kiss and love on. I'm thirty-two years old and I'm scared it's not going to happen. I gave up all my younger years to focus on school, and then medical school. I just wonder if it was worth it."

I move closer to Hayley to give her a hug and then Liz joins in. "It's going to happen, Hayley. If it could happen for me, it can happen for you."

"Yes! Seriously! If the queen of anti-love can fall in love, it can happen for anybody!" Liz says.

We all laugh and once we end our group hug we continue our gossiping until the guys and Ashley return ready for dinner.

The rest of the weekend flies by and before I know it, we're back home and are picking up Faith from Bentley's parents. We announce our engagement and they're both overjoyed.

Kathleen gives me a hug and, through happy tears, says, "Welcome to the family...*officially*."

Bentley's dad is next, and when he hugs me, he whispers, "I've always wanted a daughter. Thank you."

I'm choked up and overwhelmed with the amount of love this small family holds within them. I'm almost positive the conversation with my parents won't be this heartfelt.

"When are you guys thinking of getting married?" Kathleen asks as we walk to the door to say our goodbyes.

"I don't know. I don't want to wait too long. I was thinking maybe a February wedding? Something small for sure."

Bentley, of course, says, "You can have any wedding you want. If you want small we can have small, but if you want a big wedding we can do that."

I'm starting to realize Bentley isn't worried about money at all. I can tell his parents have money, and based on our trip and the fact that he can stay home with Faith on his savings, shows me he's good with money, but he must realize it will run out eventually.

"We'll see. There's no reason to waste money. Especially with us only having one income."

Bentley's mom looks a bit confused but simply says, "Sweetie, you'll only get married once. Do it the way you want to."

We say goodbye and head home. If I'm honest, I don't really care about the wedding. I just want to be married to Bentley and share a last name with him and our daughter.

Thirty

KAYLA

THE NEXT COUPLE WEEKS QUICKLY PASS BY. WORK IS GOING great, Faith is almost six months old, and Christmas is right around the corner. Of course with all the good there must be bad to balance it out, which is why I'm not surprised when I get a call from my mom a few days before Christmas.

"Why did I have to hear it from your brother you're getting married?"

"I'm sorry, Mom. I've just been busy with work and Faith and Bentley."

"Well I would imagine so when you are the only person working in the family."

I let out a small sigh knowing exactly where this is going. "Mom, Bentley might not be working, but he's still paying all the bills. He also has refused to let me pay for any of the Christmas presents, and last week when my car was acting up, we went out and bought me a brand new BMW SUV. He's refusing to let me make the payment, even though it's in my name."

"Kayla, I understand you think you're in love so your blinders are on, but what happens if it doesn't work out? Can you afford the car payment to the vehicle that is in your name? Can you afford a place if he kicks you out of his apartment? You even work at the gym his best friend owns. After all the years of hearing your father and I tell you our stories you would think you'd be smarter than this. Please don't act stupid."

I want to argue with her, but my insecurity begins to creep in. *Am I putting all my metaphorical eggs into Bentley's basket and simply hoping he doesn't drop it?*

"I'm going to marry him, Mom. So what do you suggest I do?"

"Why don't I draw up a prenuptial agreement for you?"

"Mom...I don't think that's necessary."

"Just hear me out. It will detail that if your marriage doesn't work how the custody arrangement and child support will go. It will cover you so that if you split up he can't go after you for money because you've been working and he hasn't been. This is what I do for a living, Kayla."

I don't like the thought of starting a marriage with a paper stating what will happen if it ends, but it won't hurt to check it out. "Okay, mail it to me and I'll read through it. I'm not saying I'm going to use It, but I'll check it out."

"Thank you, Kayla."

"Are you and Dad coming up for Christmas?"

"No, we have some major cases to handle. Holidays are a busy time for divorce. Once the Christmas spirit has worn off and people are left with the debt their true colors shine through and, more often than not, it tends to end with divorce."

"Okay, well, I'll send you some pictures of Faith."

"Okay, Kayla."

And without even a *goodbye* or *I love you* she's gone.

Thirty-One

BENTLEY

IT'S CHRISTMAS MORNING AND EVEN THOUGH FAITH IS only six months old that didn't stop us from buying her every gift possible in her age range plus several others she won't be ready for for several months. Last night we had Christmas Eve dinner with everybody at Liz and Cooper's place. They have the large dining room, so naturally it's where we all go for each holiday—either there or my parents' place.

What nobody knows is soon we'll have one more place to go. As an engagement gift, I've purchased a home for us. What's awesome is it's right down the street from Cooper and Liz. When we were driving by it a few weeks ago, Kayla pointed out how pretty it was and I knew I had to check it out. It turned out the inside was recently completely renovated and move-in ready. I signed on the dotted lines and have the keys wrapped up as one of her gifts to surprise her.

I plan to add Kayla's name to the deed, but I have to wait because I don't want to give away the surprise.

"Babe, can you go grab my camera from my pajama drawer? I threw it in there the other day," Kayla asks while holding onto Faith as she swipes at the wrapping paper laughing at the ripping sound it makes.

"Sure." I run to our room and open the drawer that holds all her pajamas, but I don't see the camera. Maybe she meant her lingerie drawer? I open that drawer and sure enough find the camera. I'm about to close it when I see a large manila envelope addressed to her from her parents' law firm.

Opening it up, I see a contract between Kayla and me. The only thing missing are our signatures. As I skim through the attorney bullshit lingo, I see shit like custody arrangements, child support, alimony depending on the length of the marriage, and then a clause stating I give up the right to request money because I'm choosing to be unemployed. What the fuck? She had her mother draw up a fucking prenuptial agreement?

I grab the stack of papers and bring them over to the dresser, find a pen, and begin writing. Once I'm done I grab a suitcase and pack it then walk across the hall over to Faith's room to pack some stuff for her as well. I'm so fucking pissed I can't be here with this woman another fucking second.

I zip up the luggage and head to the living room. Caleb is sitting on the couch laughing as Faith crawls across the floor to get to the new toys we've already opened. He looks up and smiles at me. He doesn't smile often, but Faith tends to bring out the softie in him. I don't even have it in me to smile back.

I walk over to Faith and pick her up. She squeals from the shock of flying through the air into my arms. I hold her close and inhale her perfect baby scent. "I love you, baby girl. I'll see you soon." I give her a kiss on her cheek and set her back down.

"Hey, did you find the camera?" Kayla asks, looking back at me while picking up some of the trash. There is so much I want to say to her, but I won't do it in front of our daughter. She may be too young to understand, but I'll never put her in the middle of our fights.

"Yeah, here you go. I gotta go." I throw the camera to her and her brows dip in confusion.

"Wait, go where? It's Christmas morning." She stands to come closer to me, but I can't handle this right now.

I back up toward the door. "I'm going to stay at my parents' house for a couple days while I get my place ready. I'll let you know where to drop Faith off when you go back to work."

Caleb doesn't say a word. He just sits and watches the conversation.

Kayla looks scared, although I don't know why. She was so scared of getting her heart broken every step of the way. Meanwhile she had no problem breaking mine over and over again.

"What's going on?" she asks, her voice thick with emotion.

I glance back down at our daughter who is oblivious to what's happening. "I don't want to argue with you in front of Faith. We're done. *I'm* done."

I walk out the door and it takes everything in me not to slam it shut and then beat the shit out of everything within my reach.

As I drive over to my parents' house, my phone buzzes next to me, but I can't answer it. Not yet, anyway. Regardless of what happens,

Kayla and I'll be in each other's lives until the day we die in some way or another. We have a child together. There are going to be birthdays, holidays, graduations, hopefully Faith's wedding one day down the road (far down the road), maybe grandkids. I'm going to have to get along with Kayla, but right now I'm too fucking hurt.

What I don't get is why she didn't mention anything to me about a prenup. Doesn't she see that by drawing up a contract for if or when we divorce she's already setting us up for failure? And how ironic is it, that if anybody should be requesting a damn prenup, it should be me, yet the thought never even crossed my mind. I would give that woman anything she wants.

I arrive at my parents' house and after knocking a couple times, go in.

My mom comes out of the kitchen in her apron. "Hey, sweetie! Merry Christmas! I wasn't expecting everybody until later. This is a pleasant surprise. Where's Faith and Kayla?"

Shit! I forgot we're supposed to be coming here for dinner.

I rub the back of my neck out of stress and my mom's eyes go wide from my action.

"Bentley, what happened?"

"I think it's really over, Mom."

She bridges the gap between us and, like the mom I know and love, hugs me tight. I feel so damn defeated. There's not a single fight I've been in that makes me feel as weak and vulnerable as Kayla does without even trying.

We separate and there's a knock on the door. There's no fucking way it could be Kayla. Surely she would know not to show up here after I left.

My mom goes to the door and opens it, and sure enough Kayla is at the door holding Faith in her arms. Faith is giggling and squirming wanting my mom to take her.

They both look at me. I have no idea how to handle this. My mom must sense my frustration because she takes Faith from Kayla and walks out of the room to give us some privacy.

"Bentley, what the hell happened?" Kayla walks over to me with the intent to put her arms around me, but before she can, I back out of her reach. The look of hurt she gives me almost brings me to my knees.

"What happened? What happened was the prenup you had in your drawer, all filled out, just waiting for me to sign."

She at least has the decency to look embarrassed at the fact that I know.

"Please let me explain. My mom..."

"No, I don't need or want an explanation. The fact that you even have it is enough for me. Did you hide this to get back at me for hiding being in that stupid mom's group? You had your mom draw up papers for when we divorce one day. You never thought we would last, did you? I honestly don't even know why I ever bothered."

She cringes like she's been slapped, and I know I've probably stepped over the line.

"Wow...Okay...It's clear you have it all figured out so I'll just go."

The way she doesn't move makes it clear she's waiting for me to stop her, but it's not going to happen. When she knows this as well, she nods. I can see the tears in her eyes, but she's strong so they don't release before she heads to the kitchen to go get Faith.

I walk out back and find the closest thing to me to take my anger out on. I punch the aluminum storage cabinet over and over again until I hear my dad's voice.

"It's a good thing I was planning on replacing that thing with a new wooden one. Once you're all done we can talk."

I stop punching the storage cabinet that is now completely mutilated and grab a towel to wipe my bloodied hand on. I take a seat across from my dad at the patio table and drop my head onto the table.

"Wanna tell me why Kayla is in the kitchen with your mom bawling her eyes out?"

I look up at him and shake my head slightly out of frustration. "How do you make someone believe that love is enough?"

He gives me a sad smile. "You can't. All you can do is love that person and show her every day that you love her. Nobody said love was easy."

"It's easy for you and Mom."

He chuckles softly and shakes his head. "No, it's not. We just chose to never give up. I try to live by the five rules my dad once gave me to have a successful marriage: don't be angry with each other at the same time, never go to bed without resolving the issue, never yell at each other unless the house is on fire, never bring up the past, and most importantly, always listen to understand, don't listen to simply respond."

I can't help but laugh at the one about the house on fire.

He gets up and pats me on the shoulder, but before he goes back inside, he says, "You always knew she was a little broken. I'm not saying that's a bad thing. Nobody is perfect. Now it's up to you to love her broken or let her go so somebody else can. You have to accept people the way they are, cracks and all."

Damn him for always being right.

Thirty-Two

KAYLA

AS SOON AS BENTLEY LEFT, I GRABBED MY KEYS, THE DIAPER bag, and Faith, and chased after him. It didn't surprise me that he ended up at his mom's house. I would be damned if I was going to lose him now. I didn't know what I did wrong, but I was going to find out.

I knocked on the door and was faced with his mom and then him. After she left and he said the word prenup, I wanted to throw up. Why the hell didn't I just throw those papers away? I know why. Because I'm so messed up when it comes to relationships that I'll always end up sabotaging anything good that comes my way including having an amazing man like Bentley.

I can't blame Bentley for being mad. The papers look bad, especially since I didn't even mention them. He was completely blindsided by them, and I know I would be upset if I found something like that without being told. I know how I felt when I found out about the mom's group and that's not half as bad as finding a prenup in your fiancée's drawer. The truth is I haven't even had a chance to look at them. I threw them in the drawer and completely forgot about them.

It feels like all I ever do is hurt Bentley. He loves so hard and so deep and I'm always fucking it up.

After Bentley made it a point to hurt me with his words, I headed to the kitchen to get Faith.

I'm now sitting in the kitchen, watching Kathleen feed Faith a crumbs from a sugar cookies and suddenly feel like I just need to get out of here and be by myself. I don't belong here. I don't belong in this sweet, loving, selfless home. I'm damaged and I can't blame Bentley for no longer wanting damaged goods. He deserves perfection.

I stand up, ready to go, when Kathleen pops her head up and directs her attention away from Faith to me.

"He just needs time, sweetie. Don't overthink this. He's just hurt. He might be a fighter and look tough on the outside, but he's always had a sensitive soul."

I nod in agreement. She's right. You watch him in a fight and you would think he's nothing more than a heartless asshole, but the moment the fight is over he's back to himself. He deserves more than this shit. He deserves more than I can ever give him. I give Faith a kiss on her forehead and gather up my belongings.

"I'm going to go. I have to work tomorrow, even though it's Saturday. One of the fighters at the gym just got done with surgery on his knee and I agreed to start physical therapy with him. I'm going to leave Faith here with you guys. Bentley should be with her on Christmas."

I start to walk out the door and she stops me. "Please don't go. You shouldn't be alone on Christmas."

I choke down the sobs that are threatening and shake my head. "It's okay. It's for the best."

When I get home I find Caleb sitting on the couch watching TV.

"Everything okay?" he asks.

I shake my head and he opens his arm up and nods his head to join him. Sitting on the couch, wrapped up in Caleb's arms, I cry for everything that could have been and everything that will most likely never happen.

THE NEXT DAY AFTER WORK I GO TO LIZ'S HOUSE TO SPEND time with her and the babies. When I get there I see Faith crawling all over the ground in the living room. I immediately scoop her up and give her big kisses on her cheeks.

"Where's Bentley?" I ask, looking around.

"He and Cooper had some stuff to do so he asked me to watch her."

"He could have told me. I'm capable of watching our daughter," I snap. Liz looks at me with a frown unsure of what to say.

"I'm sorry. It's not your fault. I shouldn't have snapped at you."

She gives me a hug. "I think he just figured you would be working."

"No, he's mad and doesn't want to contact me."

"Want to talk about it?"

We sit on the couch and watch the babies play while I explain to her about the prenup and how Bentley found it before I could throw it away.

"I know I should have thrown it away, but…"

"No, you should have told your mom you didn't want it to begin with," Liz says, cutting me off.

She's right, but I just can't help but get caught in my mom's web of negativity.

"I think I was afraid that if I didn't take it, and he screwed me over, she would once again let me know how stupid I am for making the wrong choices."

"At some point, Kayla, you're going to have to realize your mom is pretty damn jaded. She isn't happy and you know it. Sure, she's successful by her standards but not by most other people's. Do you really want to live your life by her standards?"

"No, I don't. I love Bentley and my life with him."

"Just give him a few days to cool off and then go talk to him."

IT'S BEEN THREE DAYS SINCE CHRISTMAS AND I HAVEN'T heard a word from Bentley. After I left Liz's on Saturday, I went home to sulk in bed. I found the prenup on the dresser with a note.

Kayla,

I would have given you the world and you didn't need a contract to get any of this from me. Money doesn't buy happiness. I hope you find your happiness one day. I'm sorry it couldn't be with me.

—Bentley

I ripped up the stupid contract and threw it in the garbage and stayed in bed for the next twenty-four hours crying. I did what Liz suggested and gave Bentley a few days to cool down, but I've reached my breaking point. I'm off work for the next couple days since the club shuts down for New Year's, and I want to see my daughter. I decide to text him instead of calling in case he doesn't want to talk to me.

Me: Hey, I'm sorry to bother you. I just got off work and I have tomorrow off. Can I take Faith?

After a few minutes my phone dings.

Bentley: Yeah, you can pick her up at this address. It's where I'm living now.

I copy and paste the address into Google Maps and see it's in the same neighborhood as Liz and Cooper. Hmm...that's weird. How did he find a place so fast?

Me: Okay, is now good?

Bentley: Sure, see you in a few.

I'm heading out of the gym, when I see Marco and Caleb fighting in the ring. Marco practically lives at the gym these days and totally looks up to Caleb. As a mother I can't imagine my child being away from home so often, and Caleb has made several comments that Marco's mom doesn't ever drop him off or pick him up.

"Go Marco! Kick his butt!" I yell, rooting for him. They both smile and wave at me.

Caleb has been my saving grace the last few days. He has really turned out to be an amazing friend and he never judges me, which is something I really need right now. After I finished crying on his shoulder he told me I'm welcome to stay as long as I need to. It means a lot since he's Bentley's friend and could easily write me off. I know he doesn't really seem to trust many women, so it means even more to me that he trusts me.

I follow my GPS and pull up to the beautiful house I've passed a million times on my way to Liz and Cooper's place. It is two stories tall and made of mostly tan brick except the front archway, which is made of gorgeous cobblestone. It has a three-car garage and a huge U-shaped driveway. The best part is it's completely fenced in. I can see Faith riding her bike one day in the driveway or playing with chalk on there, and being completely safe. I haven't been in the house, but I know it has a fireplace because the cobblestone from the front archway also covers the outside of the chimney on the side of the house.

I pull up and there's a keypad and call button, so I press the button, and within seconds it buzzes and the electric gate opens and then closes behind me.

I park my vehicle and then knock on the front door.

Bentley opens the door with Faith in his arms and as soon as she spots me she starts making all sorts of noises putting her arms out for me to grab her. I take her and wrap her in a huge hug never wanting to let her go. I don't even realize I'm crying until I feel Bentley wipe the traitor tears that are trailing down my cheeks.

I walk into the home, and it's just how I pictured it, if not even more beautiful, and what's crazy is that it's furnished.

"Did you move in here this weekend?" I ask in shock.

"Yeah, I didn't completely furnish it yet. I just bought the basics."

"Well, it looks great. You did all that quickly. Were you planning to leave me?"

He glares at me like I've lost my mind, but what else am I supposed to think? Who buys a house and moves in completely within two days of moving out?

"No, Kayla. This house was supposed to be our engagement present. The house key is under the tree. Did you even bother to open the presents I got you?"

"I haven't touched anything under the tree since you left. You bought this house for us? This must have cost you a fortune."

He sighs and closes his eyes briefly—I think to calm himself down. Faith is squirming in my arms to get down, so I set her down on the blanket in the room and she immediately crawls over to her toys to bang on them.

"'I don't know what to do, Kayla. I've tried to show you how much you mean to me, but it's never enough. It doesn't matter how much I love you, I don't think you'll ever truly feel the same way. You'll always view love negatively. I can love you with all my heart, but I can't make you love me back. I can't make you have faith in what we have. That fact is I haven't done anything to support your bullshit negative theories about love."

His words break my heart. How can he think I don't love him? He's not done talking, though, so I let him continue.

"The truth is I'm a very wealthy man. I come from old money that's been passed down from generation to generation. On top of that, I've made quite a few good investments that have worked out in my favor. I have more money than I can ever spend, and one day Faith will have it all passed down to her."

"Why didn't you tell me?"

He brides the gap between us and it takes everything in me not to grab ahold of him and never let go. "Maybe I should have told you from the beginning, I don't know. If you had known, maybe this whole thing wouldn't have happened. I thought if you knew it would scare you off, so I kept it to myself. The only people that know are the guys. Even when I funded the youth program at Cooper's gym I kept it anonymous. I don't want my money to define me and I don't want to be judged for having it.

"I wanted you to love me for me and to be comfortable with us. And then to see a fucking prenup is a punch to my face. It sucks so bad. I wanted you forever. What's mine was supposed to be yours. I don't give a fuck about my money. All I wanted was you and Faith. I just wanted your love. One side of me is saying I need to move on, but the other side is telling me not to give up on us because I can't imagine living a life without you by my side. I just can't do this alone."

I should probably be mad that he kept his money situation from me but at the same time I can see where he's coming from. I've been hot and cold with him from day one. I can't blame him for overthinking his choices.

We're now so close I could kiss him and it's such a tease because being this close to Bentley and not being able to touch him is torture.

I open my mouth to respond, but my throat feels dry so I clear it and then begin. "I never thought love could ever be a part of me. I was just going through the motions and thought I was smart. No love meant never being hurt. But then you came along and showed me over and over again how amazing unconditional real love can feel. Please don't take that away, Bentley. Please don't give up on me. I'm sorry it's taking me so long to get on the same page as you, but I really am trying. I promise. We can sign a different prenup. One that protects you and shows you I just want you and not your money."

"Woman, you aren't getting it." He looks into my eyes and then gives me a soft kiss on my lips.

"I don't care about the money, Kayla. I don't need or want any contract that states what will happen if we divorce. When I marry you, it's forever. And if you leave me, you can take it all. A life without you and Faith isn't a life at all. It's my job to protect you and our daughter. We shouldn't need a piece of paper to protect either of us from the other."

This man could have any woman in the world, anything in the world, and all he wants is to live a life with me and our daughter. I may not deserve him, but I'm going to spend every day earning his love.

I don't know what to say, so I do the only thing I can think of and wrap my arms around his neck and kiss him with all the love I have built up inside me. His body stills in shock at first, but after a second he relaxes and kisses me back. When we separate I feel like a piece of me is missing. I want to be tied to this man in every way.

"Let's get married."

He looks at me like I'm crazy and then laughs. "Umm...I'm pretty sure that was the plan."

"No, I mean today. Well not today because it's already too late in the day, but tomorrow. Let's get married tomorrow. I don't want to wait. I don't want a wedding or any of that craziness. I just want you, me, Faith, your parents, and our friends at a Chapel on the strip."

He grins wide and it melts my heart to see him smile. I vow in that moment to make him smile like that every chance I get.

"Are you sure?"

"Yes, I'm sure. This is what I want...I mean, if you still want to marry me that is."

"Woman, stop. You want to elope that's what we'll do. The sooner I can make you officially mine the better. Let's call my parents and our friends, and then find a chapel we can reserve for tomorrow."

He wraps his hand around my neck and pulls me close to him again. "Wanna a tour of our new home?"

"Yeah, I do. But what I would really like is the special hands-on tour after Faith goes to bed."

He barks out a laugh. "Oh, that can definitely be arranged."

He grabs Faith and we go from room to room as he shows me our new home.

Epilogue

BENTLEY

"DO YOU, BENTLEY CRUZ, TAKE KAYLA PETERSON TO BE your lawfully wedded wife, to have and to hold, in sickness and in health, for richer or poorer, to love and cherish, from this day forward until death do you part?"

"I do."

It's New Year's Eve and I'm looking at the most beautiful woman in the world who is about to become my wife. I tried to get her to do it right by having the wedding at the Bellagio or even the Wynn but she wasn't having it. According to Kayla, if we're going to elope we're going to do it Vegas style. Which is why I'm currently standing in front of the ordained minister in the Little Church of The West with our family and friends, and by our family I mean Kayla's brother, Zach, and my parents. While she wanted to get married the very next day, once her brother said he would like to attend, we decided to hold off a couple days so he could fly over and give her away since her parents don't approve of the marriage and refused to be a part of it.

After I showed her around our new home, Kayla explained that her mom insisted on sending the prenup over to her in case things didn't work out. She said she planned to rip them up but felt guilty about not listening to her mom's advice. We agreed there would be no more listening to her mom's advice. When Kayla called to let her mom know we were eloping she flipped out. I took the phone from Kayla and made it clear to her mother that her negativity toward love and toward her daughter was no longer welcome.

We decided to have the ceremony at the Church and then hold the reception-slash-New Year's Eve party at our new place. There is no other way I would rather bring in the New Year than with Kayla as my wife and surrounded by the people who love us.

"Do you, Kayla Peterson, take Bentley Cruz to be your lawfully wedded husband, to have and to hold, in sickness and in health, for richer or poorer, to love and cherish, from this day forward until death do you part?"

"I do," she states excitedly with the most beautiful smile on her face.

I slide the wedding band on her finger that matches the engagement ring and then she slides my wedding band onto my finger. The ordained minister announces us husband and wife and tells me I can kiss my bride.

He doesn't have to tell me twice. I take my wife in my arms and kiss her, hoping to pass along every emotion I feel in this moment through our kiss. Everybody claps and Faith and Nathan both squeal and clap as well copying off of everybody else. We grab Faith from my mom and give her a kiss.

Liz takes a few pictures of the three of us and then some with my parents and Kayla's brother before we all head back to our house to celebrate.

We arrive at the house and a few minutes later everybody else is pulling up to join us. I notice Caleb isn't here yet. "Hey, has anybody seen Caleb?"

Nobody has heard from him since we left the church so I shoot him a text.

Me: Yo! Where are you? We're all at the house?

I wait a few minutes and, when I don't hear back from him, send him another text.

Me: Caleb! Everything okay?

I still don't hear back from him and I start to worry. I ring his cell but it goes to voicemail.

Kayla comes over and puts her arms around me from behind. "What's wrong?"

"I can't get a hold of Caleb."

"He probably just stopped off at home."

"Yeah, you're probably right."

Just as I'm about to call him again he comes walking in the door looking stressed.

"Hey, man! What happened? Did you get lost?"

"No, sorry, I had to stop at the gym on my way here. Marco didn't realize the gym was closed because of the holiday and wedding so I gave him a ride home."

Over the last several months Marco and Caleb have definitely grown closer. When he isn't attending the MMA classes, he's helping out around the gym cleaning windows and washing towels. Cooper doesn't really need the help, but if it means Marco is safe and off the streets he'll continue to find stuff for the kid to do.

"It's a good thing you do for that kid." And that's the truth. Caleb makes sure the kid is home safe every day even if it means he follows him home without the kid knowing.

"Yeah, I just wish there was more I could do."

"Like what? What are you thinking?"

"I don't know...I just don't know." He shakes his head, looking defeated, and I know the conversation is over for now.

We head to the backyard to join everyone in celebrating our wedding as well as New Year's. The radio counts down and when it hits midnight I give my wife a kiss. Everybody is cheering and hollering, but I can't stop kissing her. She moans into my mouth and I grab her by the ass and lift her into my arms, her legs wrapping around my waist.

"Bentley, stop." She giggles but continues to grind her pussy into my stomach clearly wanting me to continue.

Everybody is laughing at us and Cooper says, "We get it. We get it. You're newlyweds and need some alone time."

My parents take Faith back to their place for the night and after everybody leaves I grab my wife and bring her up to our bedroom to make love for the first time as a married couple.

KAYLA

BENTLEY AND I ARE FINALLY ALONE. WE MAKE OUR WAY UP to our bedroom and when we're near the bed he grabs my hand and pulls me to him.

"I love you, Mrs. Cruz. You have made me a very happy man today."

I can't help but laugh when he says my new name. I can't believe we're married. I really am Mrs. Bentley Cruz.

"I love you, too, Mr. Cruz. Now, are you going to make love to your wife or stare at her all night?"

"I'm definitely going to make love to you."

He turns me around and unzips my white dress I wore for our wedding. It's not a traditional wedding dress, but it flowed to my knees and hugged all the right places making me feel pretty.

Once the dress is unzipped, Bentley grabs the straps and pushes them over my shoulders, letting the dress fall to the floor.

"Damn, Mrs. Cruz, you look exquisite." Of course I'm wearing white bridal style lingerie under my dress. It's silky and sheer and barely there, just the way Bentley likes it.

Still standing behind me, he takes his hands and glides them down my arms and over my ass. He continues around to my sex, pulling my body to his. Once our bodies are flush against each other he takes my face and tilts it to the side, laying open mouth kisses along my neck and then across collarbone, heading to my shoulder.

He continues to work his way down my body, kissing every square inch of my skin until he's kneeling behind me, giving my ass cheeks kisses. He turns me around and I see that at some point he took off his clothes as well because he's only in his boxers. His face is parallel to my pussy and when I look down, he's smiling.

He reaches forward and gives my pussy a light kiss and then looks up at me giving me a sexy smirk. I back up to the bed and sit down. He spreads my legs, opens up my pussy, and begins to lick.

My head goes back in pleasure, but then he stops and says, "I want you to watch. Watch me lick your pussy, baby," and my head snaps back up.

I watch his tongue dart out to my clit and lick me up and down slowly, getting me wet with desire. He inserts a finger and then two into my core while he continues to devour me. I'm mesmerized by how erotic it is watching my husband make love to my pussy with his mouth.

When my body can't take it anymore I come all over his fingers and mouth. Before I'm even come down from my high, he's up, grabbing my legs and parting them enough so he's standing between them. He lifts one of my legs over his shoulder and my other one locks around his waist. He guides his dick into me at an angle and begins to thrust deep into me, hitting my G-spot. My already sensitive pussy begins to convulse again as he pumps into me over and over again sending my body into a complete frenzy.

Bentley picks up his speed, his eyes closed, and I know he's about to find his own release. He opens them up at the last second and stares into my eyes as he comes in me. I've never felt closer to anybody than

I feel to Bentley right now.

He bends down and gives me a kiss. "I love you, baby."

We clean up in the bathroom and then lie down in bed.

He wraps his arms around me holding me close.

"We did it," I whisper.

He chuckles and says, "Yeah, we did. Now you're mine for life, woman."

"I wouldn't have it any other way. Thank you for always having faith in us, Bentley."

"I'll always have faith in us, baby."

He gives me a kiss on my neck and we fall asleep.

BENTLEY

About four hours later

I HEAR THE PHONE RINGING AND JUMP UP TO GRAB IT. IT'S still dark out and my first thought is something must have happened to Faith.

I answer the phone without even looking at the caller ID but see the clock reads four in the morning.

"Hello?"

"Yes, hello. My name is Jillian. I'm a nurse at Sunrise Hospital. Is this Bentley Cruz?"

"Yes, it is," I say in a panic, praying my parents and Faith are okay.

"Baby, who is it?" Kayla groggily asks, barely awake.

"I have a Caleb Michaels here in the ICU. You're his emergency contact."

My body sags in relief that the call isn't pertaining to my daughter, but then immediately goes into distress learning my best friend is hurt.

"What happened?"

"He was brought in by ambulance. Somebody called nine-one-one and reported finding him. When they brought him in he was unconscious and beaten severely. I can't discuss the details over the phone, but his injuries are life threatening. Can you come down here?"

I jump up out of bed and grab whatever clothes I can find to throw on. "Yeah, I'm on my way."

Kayla is now sitting up looking scared shitless.

"It's Caleb. Somebody found him beaten almost to death. He's at the hospital in the ICU."

Kayla immediately gets out of bed and gets dressed as well. Once we are in the car, she texts our friends to let them know what we know. We ride to the hospital in silence, praying our friend will be okay.

About the Author

Reading is like breathing in, writing is like breathing out.– Pam Allyn

Nikki Ash resides in South Florida where she is an English teacher by day and a writer by night. When she's not writing, you can find her with a book in her hand. From the Boxcar Children, to Wuthering Heights, to the latest single parent romance, she has lived and breathed every type of book. While reading and writing are her passions, her two children are her entire world. You can probably find them at a Disney park before you would find them at home on the weekends!